Patricia Werner
Mistress of Blackstone Castle

ZEBRA BOOKS
KENSINGTON PUBLISHING CORP.

To Bunny

*Thanks to Dr. Craig Reese for medical advice
and to Tina Nowlin for reading the manuscript.*

ZEBRA BOOKS

are published by

Kensington Publishing Corp.
475 Park Avenue South
New York, NY 10016

First printing: October, 1991

Printed in the United States of America

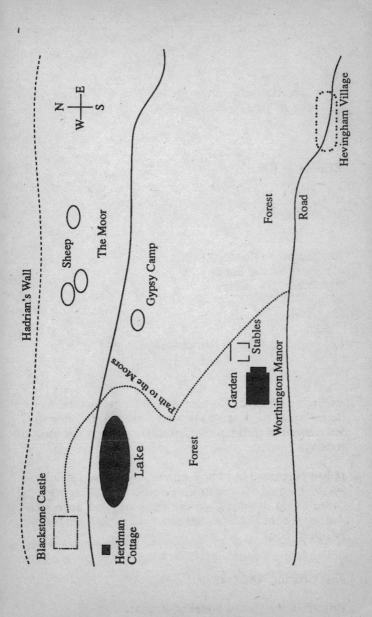

One

Nottingham, England, November, 1880

My fingers were the only part of me that still moved after ten hours at the lace factory. My back hurt from leaning over the pillow on my knees. My eyes strained from squinting at the pattern made by the threads I twisted and crossed to form the various meshes and openings.

The whistle blew, but for a moment my fingers continued to work by rote. Though I'd waited for quitting time all day, it was as if my mind had left my body, and I was little better than the machines that wove lace under this same roof. Gradually I responded to the stopping of the machines around me in the dingy factory, and my mind relayed the message to my hands to be still.

"Oh, my achin' back," said Eliza Litchfield, carefully folding the piece of Maltese pillow lace she was making next to me. "Another day gone, and I'm still alive. I'll walk with you far as Market Square. My Bill's meetin' me there if he's done with his rounds."

I took a deep breath and stood up, the muscles in my body creaking from stiffness. I hadn't stood since our brief break at midday when we were allowed to go down to the paved courtyard to get a bit of fresh air. Still, I couldn't complain too much. The workers who ran the great machines on the floors below were worse off, being on their feet most of the day.

7

"Coming, Eliza," I said, putting down my pillow and bobbins.

It took us six months to produce what the machines could produce in a day. But Mr. Biggleston got enough orders for handmade lace to warrant his hiring a half dozen of us to make the stuff. And though it was hard work, we took pride in it.

I held up my piece for Liza to see. She shook her head.

"Wonder what grand lady'll be wearin' that?"

I smiled, fingering the roses and leaves formed by my threads. "Do you ever imagine what it might be like to wear something like this someday?" I asked Eliza.

"Lord 'a mercy, Heather. That day will never come."

I pulled my woolen cape out from under the bench where I'd stuffed it and glanced toward the dirty panes of glass through which I could see a haze of gaslights from the street below.

I followed Liza across the sagging floorboards toward the stairs. In the stairwell, we joined the others whose shuffling footsteps brought them from the upper floors of the factory. Lewis Drinkhouse, a boy about my age, paused long enough for Liza and me to go ahead of him.

Down a flight, then turn, then down again to the second landing. My feet knew how many steps there were just as my fingers could make lace without my thinking anymore.

"Miss Blackstone."

My heart leapt at hearing my name called and I stopped, the boy behind me stepping on my heel.

"Sorry," he mumbled and passed by as I turned to see Henry Biggleston, owner of Biggleston & Company Lace Factory, a man I instinctively avoided when I could.

"Would you mind stepping in here, please, Miss Blackstone," he said. I could see past him into the cramped room from which he directed the affairs of his company. I had only been in that room once, four years ago, when I was fourteen and he had hired me. And I'd heard the gossip about some of the ladies he'd had in there.

Eliza stepped to the side of the flow of departing employees, her look questioning me.

"Go ahead, Liza," I said. "Bill will be waiting for you."

She gave me a grateful look, her eyes flitting up to the florid face of our employer, but I gestured with my hand that she should go on her way. In truth, my heart pounded, and I could feel perspiration on my upper lip, for Mr. Biggleston's demanding countenance underscored his order. I was wary about going there. There was no reason he would want to talk to me. This could only mean one thing—that I had lost my position.

"Are you coming, Miss Blackstone?"

His outwardly courteous manner did not hide the covert tone underlying his words. I nodded and did as I was bid, stepping hesitantly to the center of the room, which was strewn with papers and bolts of lace. I tried to swallow, so that my throat wouldn't be too dry in case it was necessary to speak.

He pressed the door shut with both his hands behind him, and I darted a glance in his direction. I was surprised to see that he no longer glowered, but even so, his heavy jowls and his protruding brow weighed down his expression.

"My dear Miss Blackstone. I was hoping for a moment alone with you." He gestured to one of the two oaken armchairs that sat before the desks. "Please sit down. Would you like some tea?"

"Tea?" I blinked. Did he offer tea to those he was going to fire. "Tea?" I said again, looking about me, for I did not see where he had the facilities to boil water.

My confusion seemed to amuse him, and he fluttered his flabby hands at me. "Sit, sit. There's a small kitchen behind that curtain with a few of the necessary conveniences."

He walked toward the curtains and parted them as I lowered myself onto the chair. My muscles responded to the warmth, for the cast iron stove radiated a cozy heat that contrasted with the damp upper floor where we worked.

Beyond the clean paned windows a light spattering of

rain had begun to fall. Below, people scurried in the dark, muffled up against the cold, their scarves trailing behind them.

Mr. Biggleston set a silver tea tray down on a desk and poured into a china cup. "Sugar?"

"Yes," I said, in a small voice. I almost never got sugar with my tea. "May I have two please?"

He set a plate of cakes in front of me, handed me the cup and poured his own. Then he took a seat in the other chair, which squeaked with his weight.

The liquid was warm, the sweetness heavy, and I closed my eyes for a moment, drinking in the comfort. But then I batted them open and stared at Mr. Biggleston, who smacked his lips. He put the cup on the desk to one side. When he looked at me again, his eyes had changed. Gone was his gentlemanly manner and in its place, something more greedy. This was the Biggleston I knew. He smiled a syrupy smile.

"Miss Blackstone, I want to commend you on your work."

I blinked, my eyes widening. I opened my mouth to speak, but I had to push out the words, "Thank you." I snatched a cake and stuffed it in my mouth, the spongy sweet taste melting on my tongue.

He picked up a length of Honiton lace that lay among the samples on the desk and fingered it. "This is your work, is it not?"

I squinted across the room. "It appears to be, though Liza Litchfield and Emmy Harris sometimes make the same."

He held the lace between thumb and forefinger of each hand. "Ah, but not quite so well, not with the same attention to the design. No, I am sure this is yours."

"If you say so." I hurriedly sipped my tea again, fearing this would be the last cup I didn't pay for myself, and I wanted to savor every drop.

"You yourself have the same naturalism as is depicted on your lace," he said, his gaze dropping over me like a net. He

10

parted his lips in a self-satisfied smile. "Oh yes, I have noticed. You are no longer the same scrawny girl that came to us from the Favorton Orphanage. How old were you then?"

"Fourteen," I managed to say. I did not like this discussion and instinctively looked toward the door.

He caught my glance and chuckled. "Don't worry. I shan't be keeping you long. In fact, you may leave now, if you wish."

I looked at him to see if he meant it, but as I started to lower my cup, he rose and crossed to me, pouring me more tea and shoving the plate of cakes in my direction.

As he gazed down at me, his right hand, brushed against the hair that fell down my back. "Such fine, dark hair," he said. He took the teacup and saucer from me and set them on the desk. Then he lifted my hand in his.

"These are the nimble fingers that work the clever patterns on the backing."

He brought his finger near my cheek, making me flinch. "And these pale cheeks. You have turned into a young woman since you've been here."

I pressed as far back in my chair as I could. Panic filled me, for he leaned closer to me now, his foul breath making me turn my face away. "What do you want?" I begged.

His hand was on my head now, and he ran it through my hair and down my shoulder. "What do I want?"

He straightened, took his hand away, and I breathed more easily.

"Simply this. I would like to make you an offer." He poured himself another cup of tea, and sipped it, staring hard at me. "You have little experience in business matters of this kind, so I will explain it to you carefully. I can elevate your station. Would you like that?"

"Elevate my station?" I glanced at him, then past him to the door, thinking I ought to move, but until he backed up a pace, I would have a very difficult time rising.

He smiled. "Would you like not to have to ruin those lovely fingers of yours on your bobbins and pins, a chance

11

to give those violet eyes a rest? Eyes like that shouldn't be wasted in a place like this."

He reached for my chin, and at his touch I flinched again. "Beauty," he said. "Beauty like this must not be wasted. It should be nourished." He squeezed my arm. "Yes, too thin. You need filling out. Nothing that a few good meals won't fix. Then there'll be something to hold on to."

Panic filled me. I should never have come in here. Why hadn't I told Eliza to wait. I tried to remain calm, trying to think my way out of the situation. Whatever he planned to do, my instinct told me I was in danger. He went on in a monotonous tone, his eyes filling with greed, his lips moistening as he continued to finger my hair.

"You should not have to wear these rags. I can clothe you in gowns of satin and silk, gowns cut to your narrow waist and your ripe bosom." He reached for a bolt of tulle. "Have you never wondered what it would be like to wear this instead of making it?"

The question echoed in my mind, for I had just asked it of Eliza upstairs.

He flexed his fingers. "Ah yes." Then he cleared his throat and stood up straight. "I can give you such things."

"May I go now?" I choked. I was afraid, and had to stifle a rising sob. "Please, may I go?"

"Not yet, my pet. Not until you've heard me out. Wouldn't you like to have pretty clothes and good things to eat? To live somewhere comfortable?"

"Please," I said in a shaking voice, "I don't know what you want, I just want to go home now."

"Home," he snapped. "Home to a garret where you cover yourself with one thin blanket. I can do better than that by you."

"H—, how?" I stammered.

"Look at me," he said. He raised my chin, since I wouldn't look at him voluntarily. His smile was that of a devil.

"You would make a man a very pretty mistress. Do you know what that is?"

"I . . . I don't know." I knew about mistresses, but I was so frightened and confused, my thoughts were not coherent.

"Come, come, I can give you time to get used to the idea. Pretty things, pretty things," he repeated. "All for providing pleasure to myself."

His hand snaked down my arm and now slid sideways to my breast.

"No," I cried, wriggling sideways, but he put his other arm around my shoulders and held me fast.

"Reluctant, are we? Need a little convincing?"

Then his mouth slobbered over my face as his hand crawled across my breast. I twisted and tried to scream, but he was so big he easily levered me against the chair. I gave a mighty kick, clawing at him at the same time. Fear gripped me, for my strength was nothing compared to his.

My squeals and kicks punctuated his grunts, but didn't stop him from pawing at my dress, using his bulk to hold me in my seat.

". . . lovely young flesh . . . can't wait . . ." he mumbled as he fumbled at my buttons, even as I tried to push his hands away.

A sudden sharp rapping on the door cut into his exertion. "Wha?" he grunted, as he half turned.

"Henry, are you in there?" came a piercing voice from behind the door.

"Damn!" He rose suddenly, and I bent over, choking.

More knocking. "Henry!"

"Cursed female," he muttered. "Supposed to be in church, she told me." Then in a sharp whisper he said, "Get up!" He grabbed me by the arm and yanked me off the chair. "Put yourself together."

"Henry!" The voice was more insistent.

"Coming, dear," he called. "Coming. I was just making some, er, ah, tea."

"In there," he hissed, shoving me behind the curtain

13

where I fell against the still-hot stove. I cried silently and held my burnt arm. Then I crouched down like a wounded animal, thankful that the assault had stopped, but unsure what new threats came with the woman who was about to invade Mr. Biggleston's office.

"Henry, what took you so long?" The door opened, and I heard the stomping of feet into the room. I cowered further behind the curtain.

"I'm sorry, dear, I was in the back. I didn't hear you. Is church over so early?"

"It's not over at all, you imbecile. I remembered the curtain lace I promised Mother. Do you have it?"

"Lace? Why, yes. Here, here it is."

"Good. Well, are you coming?"

"Coming? I was, ah, working."

"Always an excuse. Church wouldn't do you any harm you know. Mother has been asking."

"Yes, yes, all right. I'm coming."

He ushered her out and slammed the door. Only then did I realize I hadn't been breathing, and I choked on a breath, releasing my sobs as I flattened my back against the wall. I sat still, afraid they would return, but when I heard the harness jingles and the clop of hooves on the street below, I realized they must be gone.

I hopped up and threw my cape around me. Shaking, I tiptoed toward the door. Then on impulse I ran back, grabbed the bolt of Honiton and stuffed it under my cape, for I knew I was not coming back. The door wouldn't open, and I was too rattled to notice the large skeleton key protruding above the doorknob. Finally, I turned it to unlock the door. Then I fled down the stairs toward the front doors that led to the street, thankful the place had not been locked up yet.

Once on the street, my feet raced along as my arms clutched the bolt of lace under my cape, for I knew where I had to go. There were fewer people on the street now, only a group of men huddled together next to a wall. At the corner, I paused to avoid a cab that rumbled past. A woman

14

looked down at me disapprovingly from a lighted window above and then pulled a curtain over it.

I raced on, not thinking, just running. My chest hurt from the cold air, and my breath whitened before me, but I stumbled on, veering left to cross the brick street and then going on past small shops, closed now. At the end of the next street, I flung myself toward Rosa's doorway. The shop was closed, but I pounded on the door.

"It's me. Heather," I called, my voice raw and hoarse. Rosa would never hear me. I had to make a louder effort.

"Rosa," I called, rapping my knuckles hard on the door. "Let me in."

I moved to the glass window and pressed my face against it. A dim light glowed from the back, and then I saw a shadow moving.

I knocked on the glass. "Rosa. It's Heather."

The shadow became a turbaned figure with loose red silk blouse, turquoise sash and gold earrings. Then her dark face appeared at the glass, and I could see her lips form my name.

She opened the door, and I stumbled in. "Oh, Rosa, I'm glad you're here." My words came in gasps as I tried to catch my breath.

"What is it, my dear?" she said in her throaty voice. Then, seeing my distressed state, she held up a braceleted arm. "Come. You need something to warm you up first."

She beckoned for me to follow her through the fringed velvet curtains into her private back room which served as a combination sitting room, bedroom and kitchen. Then, gesturing for me to sit on her wide, lumpy sofa, she filled a tea kettle.

"Tea?" she said, then cocked her head, her black eyes narrowing. "Or perhaps something a little stronger. I have some delicious elderberry wine."

I nodded. "Yes. That is, anything."

I sank into the sofa, dropping the Honiton lace beside me, my arm throbbing with pain from the burn.

She opened a cupboard and got out two glasses. Then

15

she lifted a stopper on a carafe and poured the sweet-looking liquid. My heartbeat slowed, and when I raised the glass to my lips, the tangy taste helped soothe my trembling. But my arm still hurt dreadfully.

"Now my young friend," said Rosa. "I see trouble."

I looked with gratitude at my Gypsy fortune-teller friend. I had always been able to talk to Rosa. But somehow now the words stuck in my throat. I took another sip of wine, waiting for it to fortify me.

"At—at the factory," I managed.

She nodded, coming to sit beside me on the low, sagging sofa. Her long bejeweled fingers reached for mine. As she half-glanced at my hand, but then concentrated her gaze on my face, I surmised that she would read what was in my heart without my having to tell her.

"Now, someone has meant you harm?"

"Yes," I said, embarrassment now filling me at the recollection. I half hiccupped. "It was awful."

"Ah, yes." She clicked her tongue. "I can see. A man?"

"It was Mr. Biggleston. He tried to, to . . . take advantage of me. He did this."

I opened my woolen cape and showed her my torn dress, gingerly pushing up my sleeve to reveal the burn. She looked at it with horror and without a word went to fetch an unguent and some gauze. Seeing that my dress was already ruined, she ripped my sleeve and dressed my arm.

Anger and humiliation started my trembling again. "Oh Rosa. He wanted to—" A sob cut off my words, but I struggled on. "But his wife came back, and I hid until they were gone."

I sniffled as she finished her work and handed me a handkerchief. She nodded, patting my hand.

I blew my nose and gulped more wine. "But I can't go back there." I would never set foot in that place again.

"No, no. Of course not."

"But what shall I do?"

She pulled a small crystal ball from her pocket and fingered it, then returned it to her pocket. I gazed at her compassionate expression, that which gained the trust of her customers. But there was no greedy trickery here. I'd known Rosa long enough to know she truly had the gift. And she enjoyed helping people.

"Do you wish Rosa to help you decide what to do?" Her rhythmic voice had a relaxing effect on me.

"I suppose so. I didn't think. I just came here."

"Of course, of course. And you did the right thing. For this, I must make myself some tea."

She left me and went to lift the teakettle onto the stove, a ritual with her. She often brewed tea before telling fortunes and then never drank it. But brewing tea seemed to help her prepare. Her movements were graceful and fluid, and I took comfort in her reassuring presence. She was both mother and friend to me.

It occurred to me that I had never known Rosa's age. She always looked the same to me. Maturity was etched in her face, but it had always been there, and the years during which I had grown from a sprout to a weed had left her untouched.

She set red china cups with gold rims on a tray. Then while the tea steeped, she led me into the front room and made me take a seat at the round table with its burgundy fringed tablecloth. She moved around the table, uncovering the luminous crystal ball between us.

I sat entranced, staring at the milky globe that reflected the moonlight. I could never see what Rosa saw there, but the ball had always seemed magical to me, ever since I was a little girl. How odd it was that I was here now, awaiting what a crystal ball would say about my future.

She gazed at me. "I have told your fortune many times before, my dear, but you know that your own emotions help me see the future better."

She passed her hands over the ball, stared intensely at it and then raised her eyes to mine. I felt as if she looked into my soul.

"Yes. Your destiny is more clear now that you have come

to this crossroads. I see that you are in danger here. But I see a journey also."

She narrowed her eyes, looking into the ball again. "There is a castle somewhere in the North. Yes," she consulted the ball. "A fortune, and a gentleman who will befriend you."

My eyes widened.

"Ah yes, it is becoming even more clear. A journey to Northumberland."

I stared agape. *Northumberland.* How could she know? Then aloud, "Did you say a castle in Northumberland?"

She glanced at me and then down at the ball. "Yes, I believe so. But there is more, a warning." Her black eyes flashed with the light from the crystal globe. "Great evil, great fortune, great danger and great love."

Two

My family had not always been poor. My ancestors were known as Roundheads during the great Civil War, and my father had told me of their great castle in Northumberland. He spoke of it many times, and even though I had been young, the story had made an impression on me.

After the restoration, Blackstone Castle passed into the hands of Royalists. But my father believed that the castle rightfully belonged to our ancestors because, in fact, our ancestors were Royalist spies. There was a document, legend had it, signed by Charles the First, swearing that the Blackstones were to retain the property after the war in reward for their service to the king. But the document had disappeared or been stolen by the usurpers, who were granted the castle by Charles the Second.

I remembered the story, for I had occasionally dreamed about it, but I never spoke of it to anyone. When my parents were killed, and I was orphaned, life's realities did much to disabuse me of such tales. I suppose I didn't actually believe it anyway, accepting it as a fantasy of my father's, for every hard-working man must have a dream, and this was his.

But the coincidence was astounding. I finally found words to speak to Rosa.

"Is there anymore?"

"Hmmm. A fortune. French gold coins." Then she

shook her head. "But now the picture goes dark." She sat back, placing her hands on her hips.

"I can't believe it," I murmured, more to myself than to her. "A castle in Northumberland?"

"That is what I saw," she said in an intimate tone. Then, "Come, the tea will be cold." She replaced the tasseled velvet cover over the ball, which seemed to have actually grown dark, and we rose.

I helped her carry the cups to the low coffee table before the sofa, and she poured.

"This castle," she said. "Do you know it?"

She must have read the astonishment on my face. "It is the family legend. My father thinks it was our ancestors'."

She glanced quickly at me. I lifted the teacup and took a sip, trying to banish the thought of the tea Mr. Biggleston had served me earlier. I told Rosa the story my father had told me many times, and she listened with great interest.

"But I never knew if it was true. And what if it is? There is no proof. Fancy—my family once having been favored by the king."

I laughed giddily, the idea lightening my heart if only for a moment, for that is what fantasies will do. But then reality descended again.

"But Rosa. It's silly, is it not? So what if there is a castle that my ancestors once possessed. Did you expect me to try to reclaim it? With what?"

The idea actually made me laugh again, and I decided the wine must have gone to my head.

But she studied me over the rim of her teacup. "That depends on you, my dear." One dark eyebrow shot up as she assessed me.

I stopped laughing and stared at her. "Rosa, you sound serious."

She shrugged in that nonchalant way Gypsies have.

"I cannot go to Northumberland," I said, this time more definite. "It's too far. I have no money and I know no one there."

Rosa got up and went to a drawer in her bedside table.

20

She rummaged at the back of it, then extracted a small green silk purse, which she brought to me. "It is time I gave you this."

"What is it?"

She pressed the purse into my hand and then sat down beside me again. "You have not forgotten the penny you once gave a poor Gypsy woman at a fair."

My lips curved upward at the recollection. At the age of five I was with my mother at the annual Nottingham Goose Fair. The colorful Gypsy dancers with their bright whirling skirts and flashing eyes attracted me. After the dance, the crowd around them threw coins to express their enjoyment. I got loose from my mother and ran up to Rosa, who I thought was the most beautiful lady.

"Of course I remember. I wanted to give you a penny, and then my mother scolded me for it."

"But you gave it anyway."

I nodded. That had begun Rosa's and my friendship.

She smiled in reminiscence. "How could I forget the violet-eyed child with such a generous heart?"

"I was only five years old."

"But even at five, the heart and character are formed. I did not forget, and when I saw you again on the street all those years later, I knew you."

It was true. After my parents had been killed and I'd been turned over to the orphanage, I'd passed by this way on errands for the matron. Madame Rosa's window had intrigued me with its painted lettering, and she saw me. How she recognized my face after five years' passage of time, I do not know, but seeing me gaze at her window, she asked me in. The colorful surroundings of the Gypsy fortune-teller fascinated me as much as had their Gypsy dance, and when we mutually recalled where we had met, our friendship was sealed.

But coming back to the present, I held up the silk purse. "Even so, Rosa, I cannot possibly accept this."

Her gesture touched me, but I did not want to take money from her.

She waved a hand. "I cannot say how things will be for you, my dear. But there is enough money here for you to journey to Northumberland and return safely."

"But what would I do there?"

She smiled and leaned forward. "You must look for a Gypsy shepherd named Raoule, one of the Faa Gypsies. You will know him by the gold earring he wears in his left ear. He will help you. This time of year he brings his flock to pastures around the village of Hevingham."

I swallowed. Hevingham was the village one must travel to if one were to go to Blackstone Castle. I had looked it up on a map.

Dare I go on this journey? A picture of Mr. Biggleston mauling me flashed before my eyes, and I clutched the little purse tighter, the humiliation of the experience still with me. My only other choice was to seek employment at one of the other factories. My skill at lacemaking might assist me at finding work. But the grim prospect of working my fingers to death and straining my eyes working ten or twelve hours a day for an equally lecherous overseer made me hesitate.

Northumberland. The name of the place always filled my head with magic. What if I went, just to see the legendary castle of my forefathers? Rosa had given me enough train fare to return here.

I looked down at the purse and pulled on the strings. "There is little here in Nottingham for me now," I said slowly. "But if I take this, I'll consider it a loan. Someday I will pay it back."

Rosa smiled gently. "If you wish."

I rose and went to Rosa to embrace her in a hug. "I'll think it over," I said.

She returned my embrace. "It is nothing. I will watch over you in spirit. Do not forget this." She picked up the bolt of lace and handed it to me. "You may need it."

"But, here, you must keep some for a veil."

Delighted at the prospect, she brought a pair of scissors,

22

and we cut a length for her to keep. The rest would go with me.

She walked me to the front door, and I pulled my cape around me against the November chill outside. She shut the door behind me with a jingle, and I met her gaze through the glass. Little did I know that I would not see Rosa again.

I hurried down the deserted street, my nerves still tingling. The dark night, the money in my pocket and the late evening hour only added to my agitation. I jumped at every footfall that sounded behind me, but when I turned, no one was there.

At last, I came to my block of tenement houses, where at least I knew the faces that might peer out at me. Once in my front door, I trudged up the stairs to my small, cold room, and shut out the world. I quickly lit my kerosene lamp, then shoveled coals into the cast iron stove in the corner.

As soon as I could stop shivering, I removed my cape and sat on the small bed, considering what to do. Gazing at my meager surroundings, I felt the weight of hopelessness descend on me. I touched the purse in my hand. Then, setting it aside, I knelt and removed the loosened floorboard beneath my bed and took out the family Bible I kept there—my only cherished possession.

I took the Bible to bed with me and sat propped up against my thin, worn pillows, images swimming in my mind, as I ran my fingers over the morocco leather. For this Bible had remained with me ever since the horrible night my parents had died.

I was only six years old, and up until then life had been a pleasant routine. We lived in a cottage on the grounds of my father's employer, Lady St. Edmund, an aristocratic lady who did not seem to care for me. But on this night, twelve years ago, my mother's ghostly face roused me from my sleep. She covered my mouth, warning me not to make a sound, and then she thrust the Bible into my hands and pushed me into a closet, locking me in and shoving a heavy table against the door.

The darkness made me tremble, but I didn't make any noise. The sounds I heard that night still ring in my ears. Great thuds and then a cry, muffled voices, then a crash as the front door was torn down.

Later, when the familiar, sharp voice of Lady St. Edmund called my name, I was still afraid, but I answered in a meager cry. The table was removed from before the door, the order to "stand back" given, and the lock smashed by two bobbies.

My parents were dead, murdered, and I was alone. Lady St. Edmund gave me shelter that night. But the next day she explained to me that I could not stay there. There was not room for another child, she said, for she already had a son to look after. I would have to go to the orphanage.

Not quite understanding what was happening to me, I was marched off to Mrs. Rathbone, matron at the Favortone Orphanage, the massive gray building that housed other urchins like myself. Though orphanage life was spare, I adjusted to it, and I quickly made friends. The orphanage wasn't so bad, when we could avoid the tempers of Matron Rathbone and the two other spinsters who helped her. My mother had taught me to read and write, and at the orphanage I learned how to sew and make lace, so that at age fourteen when I was turned out of the orphanage, I could find work.

Huddled now on my narrow bed, I looked at the Bible in my hands. "This Bible is your heritage," my father had always told me. I knew that I was never to lose it.

My lamp sputtered and went out, and I crawled deeper under my coverlet. But I slept fitfully, plagued all night by dreams of Mr. Biggleston chasing me through the streets. Before dawn, I was jolted awake in fear of my life. The scene from yesterday came back to me, and I shook with humiliation and rage.

I rose, and after my simple toilet, I put on my other dress, for the first one was in ruins. Then, without allowing myself to think about what I was doing, I packed the Bible, the lace and a few belongings in an old suitcase I had carried with me ever since the night I left my parents' cottage. I shut the door and hurried downstairs.

Outside, carts and wagons rumbled through the streets as hawkers cried their wares. Workers like me had already made their way to factories where the steam from chimneys rose to mingle with the soft rain that had begun. The sun never rose, only the sky turned leaden. Now shopkeepers trudged through the cheerless morning, their faces etched with drudgery that belied their greetings to one another.

I kept my eyes downward, even though it was doubtful I should see anyone I knew. When I reached Market Street, I turned from the way that led to Biggleston & Company Lace Factory and headed for the train station.

My fears of the night before were still with me, for I still imagined that from every stoop and window, as I crossed every street, someone watched me. But when I dared to look behind, there was nothing out of the ordinary to see.

As I passed rows and rows of grimy tenements that housed others like me, I had to warn myself not to think about what I was doing, just keep walking.

I was taking a train to Hevingham in Northumberland where a Gypsy was meeting me. And what if there was no Gypsy and no castle? Already a plan had formed in the back of my mind to meet that eventuality. I could make lace by hand. I had the proof with me. Perhaps I could find employment in some big house as a seamstress. The thought that I had one skill did something for my courage, for it set me just above the unskilled who were worked to death in factories and the starving poor who would never be able to do anything for themselves but sink into the miasma of breeding and begging.

I was near the station now. Ahead loomed the massive pillars rising to an iron roof, a sea of people passing in and out of the grand entryway. I waited as a carriage rumbled past. Then I crossed the street quickly, dodging the traffic. Once safely on the opposite curbing, I paused to catch my breath.

Just then a shiny black brougham pulled up to the Victoria Hotel, next to the train station. The top-hatted coachman in tail coat hopped down and opened the carriage door for a lady to step down.

She was covered in black fur, the sapphire-blue pleated underskirt showing beneath the edge of the coat. She wore a round plush felt hat trimmed with blue ostrich plumes, and she carried a blue velvet muff with a band of fur around it. I couldn't help but stare in admiration. She smiled brilliantly and then floated up the steps to the hotel where a doorman with shiny brass buttons held the door for her.

A sharp voice jerked me out of my reverie. "Move along, miss. Yer holdin' up traffic."

"Oh, sorry." I looked up into the eyes of a tall bobby who twirled his stick behind me.

The habit of jumping when ordered to do so already had me moving along, and I couldn't help but contrast the different stations in life that the elegant lady and I had. What was it like to be born into luxury and wealth, where every task was done for you? I would never know. One accepted one's fate. There was nothing else to do about your station in life.

I almost laughed. Here I was going off on a madcap adventure just to see what my father had once talked about in his dreams. Maybe he'd been a little mad too. My own ancestors owning a castle, now that would be something, wouldn't it?

While I was daydreaming, my feet had taken me through the big arched entrance to the station, and I found myself in the waiting room. The station was a melting pot of all the classes of England. The long rows of high-backed seats were full of uniformed military officers, frock-coated businessmen and families weighted down with luggage and parcels. Humanity sprawled everywhere, some asleep as they waited for their departures. Bootblacks and hawkers of all kinds plied their wares. A man in a blacksmith's apron and a vicar sat waiting side by side, while across from them a woman suckled her child.

Bobbies strolled through the crowd, their eyes darting here and there. I could imagine that many hampers, cloaks, suitcases and hatboxes invited pilfering. Even though I knew no one would want to steal my flimsy suitcase, it was a reminder to carefully guard the money I had with which to buy a ticket and find enough sustenance to get me to Northumberland and back.

Panic seized me as I sought my place in this hive of activity, and when I glanced upward at the vaulted ceiling above me, I felt even smaller. I fought the urge to turn and depart. I did not belong here. What had Rosa done to me?

But the next moment, the thought of Biggleston's attack came back all too vividly, and my feet moved again as if of their own accord until I stood in a queue, presumably for tickets. I could not get rid of the fear that I was being watched. But when I glanced around the milling, jabbering crowd all massed under the huge roof, no one individual stood out. I told myself it was just my imagination and the fear of doing something different.

When I got to the head of the line I stated my destination and the ticket seller gave me my round-trip ticket. "Eight o'clock, track nine," he recited. "Next."

I moved with the other passengers through the great archway that led to the mammoth train shed, an arching rib cage of iron supporting a skin of grimy glass. Here, where the tracks all ended at a platform, the noise and confusion was even greater. To my left was a cluster of immigrants from some Eastern European land. They wore shabby velveteens and shared a loaf of black bread as the railway porter tried to get a list of their names with his stubby pencil. I stood for a moment listening to the names that all seemed to end with something that sounded like a sneeze.

I clutched my suitcase tightly, still wary of the thieves that I knew made their living off the pounds of luggage that passed through the station. A few beggars plied the better-dressed passengers, and I was surprised when one poor soul with a patch over his eye raised a hand toward me as I passed. I had nothing to give and so marched resolutely by.

I skirted a woman haggling with a fruitseller until the hoot announcing her train's departure forced her to pay the hawker's price. She stuffed the pale-looking fruit into a hamper and scurried along to her train.

I had never actually boarded a railway car before, and now I located track nine and pushed along the platform past the bright green engine and its ornately trimmed tinder car, the engine number painted in yellow. I approached the conductor, who was busily directing his flock, and showed him my ticket.

"Excuse me, sir?" I said. "I'm going to Hevingham. Which car, please?"

He glanced down at my ticket. "Second class ladies only car, ten cars down," he said.

The steam hissed under the wheels and around my feet as I trudged on. I passed the vermillion first class sitting carriages and then the fancy drawing room car, thinking that this train was so long it must stretch to the edge of Nottingham itself. At last I came to the second class cars. To my dismay, the ladies only car was full. I sought a porter for assistance, but after glancing at the full to bursting compartments, he simply shrugged.

"Next train's at twelve o'five."

Twelve o'five. That would put me in Nottingham well after dark, a prospect I wanted to avoid if possible. A man cleared his throat behind me, and I turned and blinked at a light-haired gentleman in a voluminous topcoat with shoulder cape.

"Perhaps I can be of assistance," he said, handing me a small white card. Stanley Symmes, solicitor, read the engraved letters. I glanced upward at the blue eyes peering at me from behind wire-rimmed spectacles, perched on a rather short, pointed nose. He had a neatly clipped beard and blond moustache.

"I could not help but overhear your dilemma. I happen to be traveling to Hevingham myself, and there is room in

28

the compartment I am at present sharing with a cleric and his mother. If you would like a seat there, you would be most welcome. That is, if your modesty permits."

I was wary of accepting the invitation, but something made me fear that if I did not take this train, I would not go to Hevingham at all. I looked for the porter, but he was nowhere to be seen.

"I . . ."

Mr. Symmes cleared his throat again, waiting for me to decide. The whistle sounded, and Mr. Symmes glanced nervously at the train. He would have to get on before it left him.

"All right," I said, and he took my elbow and whisked me down the platform and into a compartment only seconds before the conductor called all aboard.

I grabbed a leather strap to prevent myself from falling into the vicar's lap. The older lady, who I took to be his mother, smiled over the fruit basket she held on her knees.

"Just in the nick of time, dearie," she said. "We're five minutes late as it is."

"Now, mother, you know that depends on which clock you look at," said the vicar.

"Why the one in the station of course," she said, and the two of them exchanged opinions on the schedule for the next few minutes.

I took a seat on the plum-colored upholstered seat and slid over next to the window. Mr. Symmes removed his topcoat and stuffed it in the rack above our heads. He straightened the sleeves of his brown and maroon checked jacket and sat down. Then, seeing the suitcase at my feet, he turned to me once again.

"Would you like your luggage stowed above?" he asked.

He looked at me very seriously through his round wire-rimmed glasses. I looked doubtfully at the rack, unsure if it would hold the suitcase, but I nodded, and he hopped to his feet and rearranged things above us to accommodate my suitcase. It felt better to be able to move my feet around.

29

The compartment was paneled in plain varnished wood with an oil lamp hanging from a brass fixture mounted on the ceiling. Mr. Symmes sat down again, then purchased a newspaper from a boy who stuck his head in our compartment. Looking at my three traveling companions, I decided I had no reason to be nervous, though my heart rattled from the excitement of the venture.

Through my window I could see there had been no lessening of activity along the platform. The conductor repeated all aboard and the next instant the train moved. My face was pressed against the glass as we moved out of the train shed and through the train yard that I had seen so many times from the street above.

The train crawled to the outskirts of the city, and the houses dropped away until we left them altogether. As we plunged into Sherwood Forest, I peered at the glades of oaks and birches, catching glimpses of the great houses of the estates. I spared a thought for Robin Hood and his band of outlaws. It was said he robbed from the rich to aid the poor. I wondered if he really had and thought if I'd been born then I would have liked to have known him.

Then we were out of the forest and into the fields with hedgerows and low stone walls dividing them. We were coming to higher ground, a vast marshland stretching out below us, when the gentleman at my side, who I had nearly forgotten, startled me with a question.

"Have you friends in Hevingham?" he asked.

I turned, unsure if he was speaking to me, but I could see now that his gaze, fixed in a polite expression, was directed at me.

"Er, yes," I managed.

"I'm traveling there myself," he said. "Lovely place to my way of thinking. But perhaps you come from there?"

I swallowed. "Not . . . not exactly. But my family did."

"Well then, do let me know if there's anything I can do. You have my card."

I looked at the card I had crumpled in my hand. It gave a street address near Market Square in Nottingham.

"Thank you," I said, staring at him blankly. I had never met a solicitor before, but I thought they dealt with matters of the law.

He gave a benign smile and then unfolded his newspaper and buried his nose in it. I stared at the scenery, trying to recall when I had last been to the country. When I was very small my parents took me on their day off. It was on one of those occasions, hazy in memory now, that my father had first told me about Blackstone Castle.

Three

I was still keyed up, apprehensive about what I would find in Hevingham, but the fear of being watched had abated since I had boarded the train. Now I was caught up in the newness, and trying not to act like the simpleton I felt I was.

We stopped at a market town, and more passengers got off and on. Then we followed a river for some distance. The rolling hills and the clackity clack beneath us began to lull me, and I finally leaned my head against the back of the seat and dozed.

I was jarred awake by a lurch of the train and looked out to see that we were climbing through a rocky landscape, and then we plunged into a tunnel.

"Sheffield," announced my seat partner when he saw me awaken and look out the window. He consulted his thick Bradshaw and then his pocket watch, judging, I suppose, whether we were on time. Then he clicked his tongue and gave me a sideways glance.

"Railway travel," he said. "No one would travel in this manner who had time to go leisurely over hills and between fields, but we cannot stop progress, eh? It transforms a man into a parcel, being catapulted to his destination. But such is progress, is it not?"

I was surprised by his long speech, for he had seemed more taciturn when we had first met. But I suppose the miles only induced boredom for a man like him. It was then that I wondered what business took him to Hevingham, but I did not ask.

He coughed against his hand, then addressed me. "Well, now, Miss . . . ?"

"Blackstone," I supplied, remembering I had not introduced myself when he had given me his card.

"Well, Miss Blackstone. It is noontime, and you have not had your luncheon. I don't know if the jiggling of this train has left you any appetite, but I plan to visit the dining car. It would be my pleasure if you would accompany me."

I was surprised at this invitation from a perfect stranger, and though my stomach announced to me that the middle of the day had come indeed, I refused.

"Thank you sir, but I am not hungry."

In truth, I was afraid to spend any money on the train for food. Not knowing what things cost, I was afraid of going through my money too fast, and at all costs, I had to hang on to my money for emergencies.

"Please, please," he said, his expression showing no sign that he had guessed my predicament. "I insist that you be my guest."

I was still wary, and in any other circumstance would have held firm, for I was all too aware of the dangers of a young woman traveling alone. But Mr. Symmes seemed harmless enough, and we could not help but be among people on the train. And the notion of food was a strong temptation.

"Well . . ."

He was already out of the seat offering me his hand. Something else stirred in my thoughts. Rosa said I was to meet a gentleman who would befriend me. Could I have met him so soon? Then, shaking off the silly thought, I rose and followed Mr. Symmes out of the compartment.

We staggered through the side corridor until we reached the dining car that served second class. Even so, I felt I was not dressed well enough to dine in here, but my companion seemed not to notice. I stared at the heraldry carved on walnut panels, and at the elegantly laid tables covered with

33

white linen tablecloths and wondered at the deftness of the waiters who were serving hot dishes without spilling anything, given the swaying of the train.

Mr. Symmes held one of the plush red chairs for me, and my knees folded, dropping me into it as we came to a curve. A menu was placed before me, and I hardly knew what to ask for.

"Mmm," said my benefactor. "A decent menu. Order anything you choose."

"I . . . what do you suggest, sir?" I hoped he would lift the burden of choice from my shoulders, and he proved quite adept at doing so.

When the waiter came he asked for a sumptuous meal of roast shoulder of veal, puree of tomatoes and macaroon pudding. While we waited for the food, Mr. Symmes made polite conversation, and the panic knotted in my stomach. Sooner or later I would have to say something about myself, a thought most disconcerting. Then I realized I could lie.

After leaving the train, I would most likely never see Stanley Symmes again. Since I was on a fantastic journey in the first place, why not invent a fantasy to suit this self-indulgent meal I was about to eat. My guilt mocked me, but the indomitable will to survive that had gotten me this far in life quickly overcame any hesitation. One had to make the best of one's circumstances.

"Ever been this far north, Miss Blackstone?" asked Mr. Symmes, as he shook out the folded linen napkin and draped it on his lap.

I could feel the color rising in my face, but I adopted an air of certainty and said, "No, not actually. My, er, parents used to work for Lady St. Edmund. She has friends in Northumberland."

I had ventured into thin territory here, for I didn't know the name of any great family in Northumberland, but I plunged ahead. "She recommended me to the housekeeper there, and they said I might come for two weeks. If I found the situation to my liking I might stay in their employ."

"Ah," said Mr. Symmes. "And what is it you do?"

I straightened. "I am a seamstress. I can make fine dresses . . . and lace."

He raised his brows above the rims of his spectacles. "How fortunate that you are so skilled." He gave his kindly smile, but something about the expression in his eyes made me fear he had seen through my tale. I glanced at the table before my own thoughts might find a window in my eyes and give me away.

"What brings you to Northumberland?" I asked, idly looking at the passing scenery.

He cleared his throat. "Can't discuss much of it."

I looked at him curiously, and he leaned closer, lowering his voice. "If anyone knew what my clients were planning, the price of land around Hevingham would soar. Can't have that, no sir. So, my business is confidential."

Our waiter placed pewter platters in front of us, and as soon as he lifted off the lids the tempting smells overcame me. We spoke little until we'd made good work of the veal, the puree and the pudding. Then we ordered coffee. The dinner was so pleasant, I hated to leave the dining car behind. On our return to our car, I saw that there was a lavatory accommodation and made use of it.

We had come into Manchester, which seemed to be a city of industry at least as big as Nottingham, and we hurried to claim our seats before we might have to defend them from any arriving passengers.

Back in our own compartment, I was about to take my seat when my glance fell on my suitcase above, half covered by Mr. Symmes's topcoat. Someone must have turned it around, for the bottom was now sticking face out, but I supposed that the vicar might have had to rearrange things in order to get to his own luggage. My money was concealed on my person, and I had nothing else of value to worry about except the family Bible and the lace, the first being of sentimental value only, but the second I would need when I sought employment.

Leaving Manchester behind, we ran up into the heart of

the Pennines. The hills seemed wild and remote in spite of the canal sometimes visible at the bottom of the valleys. We passed stone towns and villages with tall mill buildings. Again I feasted my eyes on the rivers and mountains while at the same time the hollow feeling in my stomach told me that with each tunnel we plunged through I was farther and farther from anything familiar.

Grief welled up in my throat as I thought of Rosa, wishing she were with me. I closed my eyes again, the heaviness of the meal and the motion of the train lulling me to sleep.

When I awoke, a fog outside the window prevented me from seeing where we were. At last we broke through and I opened my mouth in a little gasp. We seemed to be on the side of a steep embankment, while ahead loomed a long stone viaduct. The land seemed more bleak and uncompromising than any we had passed through before. My traveling companion was snoring beside me, so I could not ask him where he thought we were. The Bradshaw lay on the seat between us and I carefully lifted it into my lap and then proceeded to thumb through it, finding our route in an attempt to see when we might arrive.

Indeed, he roused himself and seeing me studying the timetables, peered out the window and then at his pocket watch.

"Not far now," he pronounced. And as he stared out the window, something about his grim expression made me shiver. The high hills and moorland seemed to be closing in, and the strip of valley below narrowed all the time.

We emerged through a tunnel into bleak moorland with a dusting of snow. I could hardly imagine that anyone lived here, but in the distance I could see the cuts in the moor that led down to hollows where villages lay, the treetops being the only sign of life here.

My companion gave a grunt. He was attentive to the land now, and I remembered what he'd said about his business, though for the life of me I could not imagine how anyone could wrest a living from these desolate moors. Then I saw a few sheep grazing and remembered the Gypsy shepherd I was to meet.

In the distance some ruins took shape. As we came nearer the top of a hill that overlooked a green valley, I saw it was a ruined castle. My heart started to pound. These lands were once valuable to someone, I reminded myself, else why would castles be built to protect it?

We started our descent, and the views were of softer, greener land. As we curved around the side of a hill, I saw the two branches of a river that forked down the valley.

"Lead mining," said Symmes, indicating several tall chimneys that dotted the district. "Declined in the '60s. Now this is mostly hill farms."

We followed a wooded riverbank and then slowed as we entered the village.

"Hevingham," announced the conductor.

I felt my heart constrict. Now what? Mr. Symmes bustled about, getting down his topcoat and my suitcase. I pulled my cloak about me.

A low cloud cover had darkened the late afternoon sky, and we stepped out onto a small platform in front of a little rambling station, gabled and half-timbered. The railroad carriage had been warm and stuffy, and now the damp chill cut right through my thin cloak and penetrated my bones.

A few villagers had gathered to watch the three or four passengers who alighted. A mailbag and a few pieces of luggage were handed down to the stationmaster, and then with a chug, the train moved again.

"Well now," said Mr. Symmes. "May I give you a lift to your destination?"

I looked about me at the quickly emptying platform. "No, thank you," I said more bravely than I felt. "Someone is meeting me here."

"I see. Well then. It has been a pleasure to accompany you. I will be staying at the Black Rook while I make my surv . . . ah, that is while I am conducting my business here. If you should need anything . . ."

"Thank you."

37

I could see that he was already preoccupied with whatever his business was. He picked up his baggage and strode away.

I stood shivering alone on the platform, peering as far as I could see. There was no Gypsy. No one met me. But perhaps there would be someone inside the station.

I passed under the tall clock and into the small, empty waiting room. Here at least was shelter.

"Can I help you, miss?" The stationmaster came back in.

"I, uh, was waiting for someone to meet me."

"I see. Hope they hurry. Station closes in five minutes."

"Oh. Thank you."

I stood like a statue, watching out the door. But, of course. How could Rosa know that this Raoule would be here? Gypsies do not stay in one place for very long. And even if he were here, how would he know I was coming?

I heard the stationmaster's breath behind me and turned quickly. "I'll wait outside," I said as the clock outside gave a dull chime. It was only four o'clock, but the low clouds and the cold wind made it seem much later.

I picked up my suitcase and left the station, this time taking the steps down to the street. The little crowd that had gathered when the train came in had dispersed, and only dim shop windows in small stone buildings met my desperate gaze.

I shook now from the cold, and again I had the strange sense that I was being watched. If I stood still I knew I would freeze, and even though I had no destination I began to walk along the brick street. I felt an unnamed menace, and I heard the rattle of a door from one of the shops on my right.

I turned. A well-dressed gentleman in a top hat and greatcoat stepped out from a tea shop and turned his gaze on me. I felt a gust of wind and turned to take a step. I supposed I would have to find the inn Mr. Symmes spoke of.

But with the next step, I faltered. Dizziness overcame me and I felt myself begin to faint. I heard footsteps cross toward me. A deep voice spoke through the haze, and then I sank.

Strong arms caught me, and the voice called sharp orders. Hooves clopped on the bricks and a carriage rolled up. I tried to speak, but only mumbled incoherently, my shivering now uncontrollable, and the dizziness sending the bricks below my feet into a whirl.

The strong arms still supporting me, I smelled wool and the masculine scent of fresh starch. I blinked at a face with dark eyes and broad cheekbones, and I felt snowflakes land on my nose as I swayed. Then I was lifted into the carriage. Friend or foe, I wondered, but I could protest no longer, for I lost consciousness, my head falling to my chest.

When I came to I was in a warm four-poster bed with a fat calico cat purring on the pillow next to mine. A peat fire blazed in a stone fireplace in the toasty room, and a woman in a starched cap and white apron sat beside the fire sewing. I sniffed the odor of spiced tea and moved to sit up.

"Awake, now, miss?"

The woman got up and came toward the bed. Now I could see she was of middle age with thick, black hair laid in a snood. She had dark eyes, one of which, I saw now, was slightly crossed. Her colorless lips stretched into a thin line as she helped me adjust the pillows. She reached up to touch my cold cheek.

"Getting some color back in those cheeks. You looked half-dead when the master brought you here." She shook her head. "Master's like that, always bringing in waifs, stray cats and the like. Hadrian's one of them, though you'd never know it now to look at him. And a male calico at that, most unusual." She clucked her tongue. "Not that I approve of animals in the house."

I looked at her in puzzlement. Who was Hadrian?

She nodded toward the calico cat who got up and turned around, then resettled himself.

"Oh, I see," I said.

39

"Are you feeling better now?" she asked, standing back, her hands on her hips as she examined me. The one crossed eye gave me an odd feeling. It was hard to know where she was really looking.

"I, um, thank you. I am fine. But where am I?"

"Worthington Hall, miss. Was Sir Byron himself that scooped you up from the street." She shook her head. "Said you was about all alone. We sent word to the inn. There was a Mr. Symmes said he knew you, but no one knew your destination."

While she spoke she poured tea out of a kettle warming by the fire into a cup. She placed the cup and saucer on a tray and brought it to the bed, setting it on a night stand beside me.

"Cream?"

I nodded. The tea tasted refreshing, and I sat back, soaking in the comfort. Whoever these people were, they were most kind to offer me hospitality. My dilemma forced its way into my mind, and I knew I would have to explain. But I waited until the tea gave me some strength.

"I'll have some myself, if you don't mind," went on my cross-eyed companion. "My name is Mrs. MacDougal. I'm the housekeeper. It was my duty to look after you proper tonight, though Annie Heugh will be seein' to yer needs later."

She settled herself stiffly on a wooden chair by my bed and took up her tea.

"Thank you," I said. "I'm most grateful and sorry for the inconvenience. I . . . I thought someone was meeting me, but . . . they didn't."

She must have caught the dejection in my voice and seen the doubt on my face, for she shook her head. At the same time Hadrian got up and crossed behind my shoulders, taking a seat between Mrs. MacDougal and me. Apparently he, too, was interested in my explanation. But the housekeeper went on.

"Some man, no doubt." She shook her head and clucked her tongue. "Happens all the time. Changed his mind before getting as far as the altar, is that it? I only hope he didn't leave you in a predicament."

I blinked and then I realized what she was talking about. "Oh no, it isn't that. No, I'm not . . . I mean there isn't a man in that sense."

I colored, realizing that she was talking about my virtue and that she suspected I was here chasing a beau. Of course it was a sounder explanation than my own, and I wondered for a moment if I shouldn't invent such a story. But my capacity for making up a tale to suit had failed me. Now that I was this far, I preferred to tell the truth, at least as far as I could make it understood.

"And what is your name, miss? There was not much to identify you."

"My name's Heather. Heather Blackstone."

She frowned for a moment. Then looked at me for a further explanation.

"I . . . I . . ." But no more words came out.

She continued to eye me, then seeing that no explanation was forthcoming, she rose to take the tray.

"I'll send Annie with your supper tray," she said.

I wriggled under the heavy bedclothes. "There's really no need for that. I'm perfectly revived." I made a move to get out of bed, but she stood over me.

"And where would you be going this time of night?"

I opened my mouth and then shut it again. I had never been waited on before. If I was being offered a meal, I suppose I thought I should take it in the kitchen, but Mrs. MacDougal's disapproving eye seemed to press me back.

"Master's orders were to keep you in bed. Doctor More-battle will look at you this evening, though from the looks of you it's probably just undernourishment and nothing more. Now you stay here and Annie will bring you a tray. Time enough to be up and about tomorrow after a good night's rest. If you've a brain in yer head you'll take Sir Byron's generosity when it's offered. Blackstone, you said?"

I nodded. I felt as if her sharp eye looked right through

41

the bedclothes to my thin limbs and that she guessed I must have been in very poor circumstances. My pride made me thrust my chin forward. She was right, of course, but I would not remain a charity case. As soon as Doctor Morebattle satisfied this cross-eyed matron that I was fit, I would remove myself from her territory.

As soon as she left, I pushed Hadrian onto the trunk that sat at the foot of the bed and climbed out. I was wearing a quilted bed jacket with ruffled sleeves over a muslin negligee of delicate weave. The embroidery on the bed jacket was competent, though the stitches were large.

When the door opened again, a spritely red-haired maid in black cap and black satin apron over a white uniform entered with the supper tray. Seeing me seated in the wing chair by the fire, she smiled and came toward me.

"Your supper, miss," she said, bobbing in a quick curtsy before she set the tray down on a tea table.

I stood up to help her, but she had gotten it in place and the slide-out tray slid out before I could do anything. So I sat back down.

"Hope you're hungry, miss. Cook does a good stuffed chop."

When she lifted the lids off the steaming dishes before me, the irony struck me that I had eaten better this day than ever before in my life. I gave in to being treated like I was somebody and smiled at the maid.

"Are you Annie? Mrs. MacDougal said you'd be coming."

"Yes, miss. And you're the young lady Sir Byron rescued from the road."

Her green eyes widened and she sighed. "I know a number of girls wouldn't mind swoonin' in the likes of those arms, but ne'ers the chance o' that."

Hadrian had leapt up on the chair beside her and meowed, and she automatically reached out a hand to pet him. Hadrian purred loudly. I couldn't help but grin at her. She seemed so natural, and now that I was myself again I

42

was growing more and more curious about Sir Byron and his household.

"I'm sorry to be so much trouble," I said, twisting my hands. But I didn't feel nearly so nervous with Annie, for she was more my class than the others.

"Never mind that," she said with a ringing laugh. "It gives this house something to talk about. A stranger coming into our midst is something out of the ordinary, you know. At least this time of year. Heather Blackstone's a pretty name."

"Oh, why thank you. I like your name too."

The wind rattled the windowpane, and Annie went to make sure the latch was fast. When she returned her cheery expression had been subdued.

"Never do get used to them noises in the night," she said, more to herself than to me. Then she seemed to remember her task and bobbed another curtsy. "If there's anything else you want, just pull that rope."

She pointed to a velvet pull rope next to the bed. Then she turned to go. I wished she would stay and talk, for I liked the company. But I forgot about everything except the chops and boiled potatoes for the next quarter of an hour. Hadrian waited until I was finished and then begged some scraps, which I gave him.

"There you go, boy. So you're another waif like me."

He blinked his yellow eyes as if to say yes.

I was sitting on the bed, propped up against the pillows, Hadrian beside me, when Doctor Morebattle made his appearance. He said very little, but examined me from head to foot in a short space of time, returned his instruments to his case and then stretched to his full height, which was not great.

"You're a strong enough lass," he said. "Nothing wrong with you that some healthy country food won't fix. From your pallor I'd say you're from the city, eh?"

I nodded. "I worked in a factory."

"Ahh," he drew it out. "That explains it, I'd say. You need some nourishment. Fattening up. Exercise." He announced each as if dictating a prescription. "I'll tell Mrs. MacDougal nothing ails you so she can release you from the bedchamber."

He winked under his bushy eyebrows and I smiled. He must have been familiar with the housekeeper's regimen. What he said next confirmed it. "Rules this wing, if I'm right. I doubt Sir Byron sets foot in this part of the house without her permission."

We laughed together and I could not help feeling better.

"I've practiced in this country since I finished medical college. Could have gone to London, but I didn't have the city life in me. Came back to my roots. Known the Worthingtons a long time.

"I'll be on my way, then. You won't be needing to see me again."

I hoped I would see him again, but not as a patient. There was something reassuring about his manner.

Annie came in to braid my hair for the night, then she took me to the necessary room where she had drawn a bath in a porcelain bathtub. I remembered such a bathtub at Lady St. Edmund's, though I'd never been in one as elegant before. After my bath, Annie tucked me into bed, and the softness of the mattress and pillows soon soothed me into a deep, untroubled sleep.

A distant clanging noise awakened me, and I sat up, at first not remembering where I was. The fire had died down, but the furniture still cast huge shadows against the walls. The house seemed silent, but I could not get back to sleep.

I patted the bed beside me, but Hadrian had gone. To look for food, I wondered?

Feeling restless, I pushed back the covers, sat up and lit the candle by my bed. Finding the slippers left for me, I put them on. The window still rattled, and I, too, inspected the latch. But there didn't seem to be anything to do about it.

I paced about in the candlelight, feeling restless now. The lull that had come from so much food and warmth had worn off and I was left with a sense of uneasiness. After examining every object in the room, from the tapestry on the wall to the decorative bronze ewer on the chest, I opened the doors of the tall armoire.

Seeing several gowns inside, I surmised that this room was normally inhabited by a lady, and I wondered who that might be. I was wide awake now, and I did not think I could go back to sleep, so I searched the room for something to read. Besides my own family Bible, which I discovered had been placed with the rest of my belongings in a drawer of the chest, there was no reading material.

Hadrian appeared from a corner and gave a little squeek in his throat as he stretched.

"Oh, there you are, puss," I whispered, reaching out to him. "I wondered where you'd gone."

He came to rub at my ankles and then trotted toward the door and scratched on the lower panel and molding, looking at me expectantly.

"Want to go out?"

I went to the door and grasped the brass door handle. It turned. I opened the heavy door slowly and expected Hadrian to slide through. Instead, he sat down in the opening and looked back at me as if to ask if I was coming too? The candlelight reflected in his yellow eyes, making him look ghostly.

My room had begun to feel like a prison, and I stepped out onto a runner that covered the oak floor. At both ends of the long hallway, oil lamps in their glass globes offered a dim light. As the wind shrieked around the house the lamps flickered. I thought I heard a door shut somewhere. Seeming to know where he was going, Hadrian walked solemnly ahead of me, and I followed.

Four

All great houses have libraries, and I thought that if I could find my way to the main part of the house, surely I would come to the library, or some place where books were kept. I had always loved to read. Books were one item the orphanage had not been scarce of, though sometimes the backs had been torn off or pages missing. Since I'd gone to work at the factory I hadn't read much. There'd been no time. Even my days off had been spent washing and mending my own garments and shopping for what meager victuals I could afford to buy.

But searching for a book was perhaps only an excuse for my curiosity. I vaguely remembered the inside of Lady St. Edmund's great house, and now that I found myself inside one again, I suppose I rather hated to waste the time sleeping. My benefactors might cast me out tomorrow. Then I would have to go seek my castle, and after setting eyes on it, return . . . return where?

I had my ticket back to Nottingham, and there was Rosa, of course. But I realized as I crept along in the dark that part of me still clung to the wild hope that I would not have to return to Nottingham. There was still my notion of becoming a seamstress, though with no references I did not know how I would gain such a position.

We came to a staircase, and I slid my hand along the polished balustrade as I followed Hadrian, trying to tip-

46

toe as quietly as he, down the carpeted stairs, which turned on a landing and led down to a wide entry hall.

Flickering oil lamps in their glass covers beckoned me on. The ceiling vaulted into the darkness above me, and I felt cold. But there seemed to be a little light coming from under one of the doors and I went that way. Hadrian and I both stopped and looked at each other. I knew he was searching for food. I was looking for something else. We seemed to bid each other good night, and as I pushed on the heavy door, he turned and trotted away.

The door squeaked a bit on its hinges, so I opened it slowly. A fire had burned down, but there was still enough light for me to be able to make out the furniture in the room. A long velvet-covered sofa dominated one wall under a densely configurated tapestry. Firelight glinted off silver candlesticks and beakers on shelves set into an oval in the wall, the intricate floral molding of the plasterwork casting weird shadows.

I took a step further into the room and then froze. I was not alone.

I sensed a presence before I saw the hand hanging from the arm of the tall wing chair with its back to me. I held my breath, my heart jumping to my throat. The fear was so strong that I turned to flee, and then I heard a murmur and a yawn.

I crashed against a small marble-topped table and reached for the porcelain vase as both table and vase began to topple. My fingers missed the side handles, and the vase thudded onto the thick rug, the table following it.

"What the devil?"

The man in the wing chair flew to his feet, the belt of his dressing gown flying around him, and I gasped as I stumbled back against the door, which shut with my weight. He flew toward me, and I shrank back. Then, as he got close enough that I could see the dark, tousled hair, the shadows on the planes of his wide-set cheek-bones and the thrust of his squared jaw, I tried to stiffen.

Momentarily, the image of Biggleston attacking me flashed in front of my face, and I threw my arm up to defend myself. But no blow came forth, no violation of my person. Instead Sir Byron, for I knew this must be he, stood there, staring at me, the surprise reflected in what I could see of his face.

For a moment neither of us breathed. Then I heard him exhale a long breath.

"Scared the life out of me, miss. What the devil are you doing in here anyway?"

I swallowed, forcing words from my throat. "I'm sorry." It seemed to come out as a sort of squeak, and I tried to force more air into my lungs and speak louder. "I couldn't sleep. I thought I'd find a book."

He stared at me a moment longer, his gaze finally leaving my face and traveling over my throat where my dressing gown had loosened, down the length of me to the material of my negligee, which peeked out from beneath my hem. I was still gazing at his face and saw his lips part and his shoulders stiffen. Then he looked at my face again.

"A book?" he said slowly.

I nodded cautiously.

Humor touched his eyes. As he finally took a step backward, I saw the grace in his movement.

"A book," he said in a more normal voice, which filled the room. Then he ran a hand through his thick hair and dropped it to his side, giving a laugh.

His laughter went on for some seconds, and I wished I could shrink out of his sight. But when the sound subsided, he shook his head and walked back to me, reaching for my hand.

"Forgive me. You do not find the situation humorous."

48

"No," I said, looking seriously into his eyes. There had been nothing in my life for some time that I could call humorous.

He walked to a side table, just inches from the one I had knocked over and unstopped a crystal carafe.

"Now that we are both awake, would you join me in some refreshment?"

I blinked and managed to nod. "Thank you."

He poured wine into two small silver goblets and held one out for me.

"Please," he said, seeing I had not moved from the door. "Come sit down."

Though my heart had slowed, I still felt embarrassed. But for all the world, my host was acting like I was an expected guest in the middle of the afternoon.

My eyes had grown accustomed to the dim lighting from the fire, and I made out more details of the room. Sir Byron set his goblet down and readjusted his dressing gown over the white linen nightshirt underneath. My temples throbbed as I watched him retie the belt and walk over to poke the fire until tiny flames licked the new log he threw on.

Then he returned and eased himself onto the sofa at the other end of which I crouched, gripping my wine goblet. He tossed back his, and I took a sip from mine. Then he smiled and I felt my face warm.

"Now," he said, stretching out his long legs in front of him. "I trust you are feeling better. Or was it sleepwalking that led you here?"

His manner and the wine helped me relax enough to find my voice, and I straightened, putting down the goblet and folding my hands in my lap.

"I am perfectly fit," I said. "Though I do thank you for your hospitality."

He nodded in acknowledgement, then settled his gaze on my face, waiting for me to continue. His eyes were dark, commanding, and I was instantly fascinated by them. At the same time I tried to draw my gaze away.

"Even the doctor told me there was nothing wrong. He said I needed . . . nourishment and rest, that was all."

Again embarrassment filled me, and I knew that at any moment I would be asked to explain my presence in Northumberland.

He tilted his head at me. "I am glad to hear that. Pray excuse me. We have not been introduced. I am Byron Worthington, and you, I believe, are Miss Heather Blackstone?"

I nodded. "Yes."

The firelight danced over his face, and his eyes sparked interest. "I am pleased to offer you refuge, Heather Blackstone, but if there is anyone I should inform of your arrival . . ."

I shook my head, grasping the goblet again. He noticed I had drained it and rose to refill it.

"There is no one," I continued.

He shot me a look of curiosity. "But you arrived on the train with a gentleman who is now staying at the Black Rook."

"We were not traveling together. That is, I met him on the train." My throat felt dry, and I took another mouthful of wine. I supposed I would have to tell Sir Byron the truth.

"I come from Nottingham," I said. "But I have no real home. My parents died long ago. A . . . a friend gave me train fare to come to Hevingham, on a . . . visit. It was a whim really. My ancestors . . ."

I paused, looking into his eyes. But he only seemed to encourage me with a small nod and a smile that touched his lips.

I gathered courage. "My ancestors once lived hereabouts."

"Ah, I thought so." Understanding filled his eyes. "I

50

wondered if the name were a coincidence. But do go on, this is most fascinating."

He leaned sideways against the back of the sofa, his arm stretched along the back. I swallowed, leaning back slightly, his presence at once attractive and intimidating.

"Well," I said, "before my father died, he told me of the family legend. That there was a castle in Northumberland that once belonged to my family. He said we lost it in the Civil War."

"Oh?"

"Yes. You see the Blackstones were thought to be Roundheads. But they weren't really. They were Royalist spies, and they helped Charles the First escape from Roundhead troops when he was on his way to Scotland in 1645. He told me, my father, that is, that the Blackstones helped save the king's life. And that my ancestor promised the king he would do anything to aid him in the future, while pretending to be a Roundhead.

"For this, Charles gave him a document acknowledging his help and stating that for this reason, the Blackstones were to retain their estate when the war was over, even though they were thought to be Roundheads."

Sir Byron had not taken his eyes off me, and his brows were lifted throughout my story.

"The castle, you see, Blackstone Castle, then is . . . is rightfully ours." I said this last as if testing how it sounded.

For a moment Sir Byron did not speak. Then he boomed out, "Is that all?"

I shrugged. "Evidently our ancestor, the one who helped Charles the First, died, and his heirs had lost the document. So when Charles the Second was restored to the throne, the property was taken and assigned to his followers."

I stopped and waited to see what Sir Byron thought. Already the idea had cropped up in my mind that he might in some way be able to help me.

51

But in the next moment, that hope was dashed.

He rose, stood over me, the humor still touching his eyes. "This is quite a tale indeed. Let me guess the rest. Being in possession of the knowledge that Blackstone Castle lay in Northumberland, you, the remaining heir, traveled here to find it and repossess your property."

His words sounded formal, but in the next moment, he laughed, a rich, golden baritone. But his laughter crushed my feelings. I did not think what I had said was so funny.

"And do you have anything to prove this story?"

"No, I told you—"

"Ah, yes. I almost forgot. Said ancestor's descendents lost said document. So, no proof."

"That's right." I frowned. "But there might be something."

He stopped his pacing. "What is that?"

I stared at the dancing fire in the fireplace. "I'm not sure, really. But there is a family Bible that's come down to me. There might be something in it. My father told me never to lose it, that it was my heritage."

"Hmmm." He sounded more serious now. "Family records are often kept in such Bibles. But you say the property is not mentioned directly?"

"No. I've looked. Only marriages, births and deaths."

"I see. You say you have this Bible with you?"

I nodded.

"Then I would like to see it."

I watched him, then I lowered my gaze to my hands. "You do not believe me?"

He returned to the sofa. "I would not say it that way. But the situation is most ironic."

I stared at him.

"I will pick up your tale where you left off. When Charles the Second was restored to the throne of our fair land, he did indeed award Blackstone castle to one of his followers who had followed him into exile. The estate passed into the hands of one Cedric Worthington. He was awarded the estate and the baronetcy at that time."

In a moment I grasped what he was saying. "Your . . . ?"

He leaned closer. "Yes, my dear. My own, long-dead ancestor. For the last two hundred and twenty years this castle, its ruins that is, and the estate that goes with it, has been in my family. I am the present owner of Blackstone Castle. I have the deed."

I blinked at him, hardly knowing what to say. But he pressed on, a slight smirk now on his lips.

"I find it amusing that you have come to take it away from me."

"I did not know," I said. "I mean, that is, I . . ."

His amusement returned. "What you are saying is that you did not know what you planned. You could hardly have expected to find the present owners and simply march in and ask them to hand over the estate."

He was laughing at me, and I resented it. Anger replaced my shyness. Of course he was right. I had no definite plans. But he could have at least granted me the respect I deserved after explaining my mission. My anger was becoming twisted and confused with my awareness of Sir Byron as a man. As he talked to me, I could not stop looking at the strong features of his face and the graceful sweep of his limbs, a contrast to the weak chins and flabby paunches on some aristocrats I had seen in the past.

In this light, his eyes seemed dark and penetrating. The lips that entertained a smile or formed a thoughtful line were sensual, and I had an irrational urge to touch the rising plane of his cheek.

I realized I had not heard the last few words that he said, and that I was holding myself rigid, my chin thrust upward, perhaps in an effort to defend.

For a moment, as his eyes met mine, he seemed

lost in thought as well. Then he roused himself.

"More wine?" he offered.

"No, thank you."

"Well, then, considering the hour, perhaps we should retire . . . and discuss this in the morning."

I moved my limbs. "Very well."

He rose and offered a hand. I took it and allowed him to raise me up from the sofa. I did not move when he stood for a moment looking at me. I ought to be able to excuse my weakened knees, after all, I had never been in the presence of a baronet.

But it was more than that. My heart fluttered, sending waves of warmth throughout me, and my throat went dry. His masculinity overpowered me. It was frightening as well. I felt that if he had made any move toward me, I would simply have fled. But he did nothing. His curiosity and some of the feelings that must have stirred somewhere within him were written on his face.

Then that slight smile played around his lips and he took my arm. "Shall I escort you back to your room?" He stopped again. "How did you find your way down here in the dark?"

I gave a half-smile. "Hadrian showed me the way."

He frowned until recognition dawned. "Oh, Hadrian. Lucky feline." He laughed a hearty laugh.

We passed into the foyer, where the shadows seemed to move in league with the wind that whistled in the rafters. A window rattled behind us, and I tensed.

"Just the wind," he said, tightening his hold on my elbow.

I kept near him as he led me up the stairs and back along the hallway. We made a turn that I did not remember, but he seemed to know where we were going. When we came to the heavy oak door, he pushed it open. To my surprise the fire had been stoked.

"Who . . . ?" I did not know the time exactly, but it must be quite late. Had someone come along to check

54

on me, and not finding me, built up the fire and then searched for me?

"The fire?" he said, seeing the direction of my gaze. "Dunstan, most likely."

"Who is Dunstan?"

"Dunstan has been with the family since before I was born."

"But—" I was thinking it odd that a servant would be up so late when I heard the distant clanging again. It almost sounded like chains rattling far away, and I turned toward the window.

"What was that?"

The sound was distinct from the rattles the windows made. It was no wonder I had gotten up in the night, what with all the strange sounds in this place.

Sir Byron walked up behind me. "Just the wind. Nothing to be worried about. We seem to be having a gusty evening."

I frowned. What I had heard did not sound like the wind, though it could have been carried on the wind. I turned, but he didn't move. He raised a hand and lifted the strands of hair that had fallen in front of my shoulder. Something in me responded to the gesture. Then I remembered that if what Sir Byron said was true, my road had come to an end.

"If you own Blackstone Castle," I queried. "Why do you live here?"

"Ha," he exclaimed, dropping the hair he had wound round his fingers and gesturing to the walls within which we stood.

"My great, great grandfather built Worthington Manor as a hunting lodge in the middle of the last century. I'm afraid that after my family was deeded the estate, it became difficult to support the castle. I will show it to you. Then you will understand."

Then, in a gentler voice. "Do you think you can sleep now?"

I nodded. His face was inches from mine, and I wished the dizziness in my head would stop. This was a strange place. I was out of my depth, and it was hard to recall that I myself had been the one to so daringly adventure here after what Rosa had told me. My lids drooped. I needed to sleep. All would seem clearer in the morning. I sensed Sir Byron withdraw.

In the night my dreams were filled with trains, castles, chains rattling, thumping noises and a dark stranger. I woke up suddenly thinking someone was chasing me. When my eyes came open, I saw that it was broad daylight.

Annie poked her head in as I was sitting at the elegant dresser, letting my hair out to brush it.

"Ah, yer up, miss."

"Yes, please come in, Annie."

"Here, let me do that."

She took the silver-plated brush from me and made my hair shine with long, sweeping strokes. Then she dressed it in a chignon at the back of my head and used a curling iron, leaving soft curls around my face. Today would be the last day I would be treated like a guest. For I knew I would have to leave Worthington Manor now.

"You really oughtn't to take this much trouble, Annie," I said.

She shrugged and smiled at me in the oval mirror on the dresser before which I sat. "Why ever not? It's me job."

"I know. It's just that I'm not used to it. I was a working girl myself until just two days ago."

"That so? What'd you do?"

"I made lace."

I was sitting straighter, and the neat coif with curls accenting my face made me feel quite above myself. In the blink of an eye I saw myself as the mistress of a great castle, dressing in fine clothes every morning and ordering a great household. For an instant I felt that it was my right. It was like an image from Rosa's crystal ball. And then it was gone.

"Lace, now," said Annie as she stood back to look at her handiwork. "Very fine lace for dresses and the like?"

"Yes, that's right."

A slow smile spread across her face and lit her green eyes. Then she walked to the armoire and opened it.

"Mrs. MacDougal told me to see that you were fixed up in one of these, seein' as how your own dress was torn when you fainted last night. She'll be mendin' it."

"Oh? That's kind of her, but . . ."

My refusal faded as Annie laid two gowns on the bed, one of black and maroon-striped bengaline with velvet basque, the other of claret moire with a cashmere overskirt. I ran my hand over the material, admiring at a glance the way they had been made. These were not ready-mades.

"Whose are they?"

"Sir Byron's sister. She died."

"I'm sorry. I didn't know. It is a very kind offer."

Before I left Hevingham, I would at least see Blackstone Castle. Sir Byron had promised. I should visit the home of my ancestors in proper style.

"Very well."

I chose the bengaline, which fit me better than the other, and when Annie had finished hooking me up and I tugged the cuffs down, I looked at myself in the mirror, stunned at what I saw. My thoughts and feelings were awhirl. I felt as if I were looking at someone I knew, but it wasn't exactly me.

"Would you like breakfast now, miss? Mrs. MacDougal said there'd be something kept hot for you."

"I'd love breakfast."

"Dining room's downstairs. Dunstan'll be about. He'll show you."

So I would meet the nocturnal servant. I wondered if

he'd napped, or if he had stayed up to serve breakfast and slept later in the day.

I started out and then stopped.

"I believe I'll just get my handkerchief."

I went to the drawer where my things had been put away. I remembered bringing a good linen handkerchief that Rosa had given me last Christmas.

Pulling open the drawer, I reached into the meager pile of folded underthings. My hand froze as I grasped the handkerchief. My family Bible was gone.

Five

I rummaged in the drawer, but the Bible wasn't there. I closed that drawer and opened the one below. But that one contained only linen sheets. The rest of the drawers were empty.

"Who could've . . . ?"

I turned around, but Annie had gone. Done with her duties, she must have assumed I could find my own way to the dining room.

The loss of the Bible upset me greatly. It was my one family heirloom, the only key to my past. Sir Byron mentioned last night that he wanted to see it, but surely he would not just rifle my personal things to get it. I had said I would show it to him.

My agitation hastened my descent to the main floor. I turned in the direction opposite the drawing room I had been in last night and was wending my way through a small anteroom, filled with all manner of weapons, when a tall, thin gentleman in butler's uniform appeared from nowhere and bowed in front of me. Without saying a word, he turned and slid back a set of double doors and gestured that I should go in. I could see that ahead lay the dining room.

"Thank you," I said as I passed him.

He bowed again so that I could almost see my reflection in the shiny bald spot on the top of his head.

"Good morning, Miss Blackstone," boomed a deep and familiar voice.

My head jerked around to see Sir Byron standing at the side of a long dining table in front of one of three bay windows that ran along the wall. A door at the furthest end of the room was just sliding shut. He was wearing an earth-colored jacket and loose knee breeches with gaiters. In his hand was a soft felt hat. The cut of his coat emphasized his graceful proportions.

I stepped further into the dining room. "Good morning, sir."

"Did you sleep well?" The dark circles under his eyes made me wonder if he had slept any better than I had.

"As a matter-of-fact, not very well."

His dark gaze queried mine, and I found his just as hard to meet and yet as compelling as I had the night before. "I thought I heard noises in the night. A sort of thumping, and . . . and the rattling of chains, but very far away."

I did not miss the shadow that passed over his eyes as he quickly glanced out the windows at the sweep of garden behind the house as if to see if there was anything there now.

"Night noises, that's all," he said. And then changing his demeanor, he gestured toward the sideboard across the table from where he stood. "You'll be wanting breakfast. I ate an hour ago, but I'll join you in a cup of coffee."

Dunstan appeared at that moment and removed the silver lids from platters of eggs, browned potatoes, chops, stewed prunes and griddle cakes. I chose two griddle cakes and a little of everything else, my appetite a good match for the amount of food being offered.

Dunstan held an ornately carved chair for me, poured coffee for Sir Byron and myself and then disappeared. As soon as we were settled, I brought up the matter of the Bible. From his concern when I told him it was missing, it seemed that he himself had not taken it.

"Then you did not ask anyone to bring it to you?" I said.

"Of course not. Though I do admit a certain curiosity

60

about this Bible and its relationship, if any, to your story, I am not of the temperament to browse uninvited in the personal belongings of a guest. Nor would I expect any of the household to do so. Are you sure?"

"Quite sure." My voice took on the tremor of agitation. "It was the only thing I had left from my parents."

"Then we must find it."

The certainty in his voice helped reassure me. "Why would anyone take it?" I said and then delved into the food in front of me before it got cold.

"I will question the servants myself," he said.

When I was finished eating and had refused more food, I sat back in the high-backed chair, soaking in the comfort of such a breakfast. I remembered how Biggleston had alluded to such luxury, and when I thought of the price I might have had to pay for this, my breakfast threatened to return to my throat.

"Now," said Sir Byron, draining his coffee cup and setting it on the saucer with a clank. "I suppose you would like to see Blackstone Castle."

Though his words were polite, I thought there was a hint of mockery in his eye. Not to be put down, I sat straighter, remembering that I was a Blackstone, and there was a castle of the same name here.

"Yes, sir. I would."

His expression softened. "You look lovely in that dress, Heather. May I call you Heather?"

The way he said my name made my heart roll over. I nodded, wishing he would cease to look at me in the way that made me feel like the pudding on my supper tray last night.

"And please," he went on. "You may drop the *sir* when we are alone. Byron will do."

I had wanted to say something more about Blackstone Castle, but my words stuck in my throat. Luckily he took charge of the situation.

"It is a small distance from here. Do you ride?"

"I . . . I have ridden, but it was a long time ago, on a

very small pony." I blushed. I had also ridden the milk delivery horse when the old milkman came to the orphanage, but I refrained from saying that.

"Then I will have Robin saddle my most docile mare."

Robin, I presumed, must be the groom. How big a household did Sir Byron have? And did anyone live in it besides himself and the servants? I assumed he was not married, otherwise a wife would have appeared by now. And there seemed no evidence of children. I took his age to be at least ten or twelve years more than mine, and was suddenly curious about his life here in this isolated part of England.

I looked down at the gown I wore. "This dress is most handsome," I said, deferring any reference to my own inferior garment. "But I have nothing to ride in."

He waved away my concern. "I'm sure Mrs. MacDougal can find something. Shall we meet in, say, half an hour?"

I nodded and returned upstairs. Shortly Mrs. MacDougal returned carrying a garment wrapped in a sheet. When she laid it out on the bed I saw it was a dark green riding habit made of sturdy wool. She helped me into the stockinette breeches and high boots, covered by the long skirt. The jacket was a little large, but it would do, and the low hat made me feel very sporting, indeed.

Again I had to pinch myself to remind myself that this was really happening. I was having an adventure, and the thought of actually seeing Blackstone Castle filled me with a strange excitement.

Mrs. MacDougal was not at all talkative, seeing to her business, though she finally inquired as to where the master was taking me as she buttoned up my boots.

"To . . . to see the property," I said vaguely, not wishing to raise the issue of Blackstone Castle.

"Likes to ride up on the moors, the master does." She stopped her lacing and her good eye bored into mine. "Keep away from Hadrian's Wall if you know what's good for you. There's too many visitors go tramping up there. The spirits don't like it."

I dropped my jaw. I knew of the Roman wall built long ago to keep out the Scottish barbarians from the North. Hence, I presumed, the name of the cat that was keeping me company.

"Hadrian's Wall," I repeated. "Are we very near it?"

"Aye. The estate borders on it. Did ye not hear the soldiers tramping in the night? Still guarding the border, some of 'em are."

I said no more but watched her gather up the sheet and leave. Roman soldiers, chains clanking, the tramp of feet. I had heard such sounds in the night. A little shiver passed along my spine as I wondered if what she said could be true.

Rousing myself, I hurried out and down the stairs to meet Sir Byron in the grand foyer. By the light of day I could see the heavy beams at the top of the vaulted ceiling, the oil paintings that adorned the walls and the tasteful moldings around the doors. He was waiting for me in the parlor, and, nodding his approval at my riding costume, he led me out to the stables.

Once outside I could see that the house and stables were both stone-built. The manor was larger than it seemed when we were inside, and Sir Byron pointed out the wing his grandfather had added. The house rose to three stories, and the top was castellated, a reminder of the days when any considerable house or farm in this part of England had to be defensible. We crossed the stable yard to where a young man in stable clothes was leading out a dappled mare.

"Thank you, Robin," said Byron. Walking up to the mare, he took her harness and rubbed her nose. "Theo will take care of you," he said, motioning for me to come nearer. "Let her get your scent."

"She's been needing some exercise, sir," said the groom as he eyed me.

His eyes seemed to narrow, and his critical gaze made me feel as if he didn't quite trust me with the horse. He turned to go back into the stable.

I stood near the mare and rubbed her nose, then Byron gave me some sugar to feed her. After the horse and I had made friends, he gave me a leg up into the sidesaddle. Having only straddled the milk horse back at the orphanage, it took me a few minutes to adjust. But a dim memory came back to me of riding sidesaddle, with my father, leading a pony on his day off, around Lady St. Edmund's estate.

"Just follow me," Byron said, after he had shown me how to hold the reins. "Theo won't try to get away."

Robin returned leading a large black gelding, which Byron mounted. The horse danced sideways as Byron gathered the reins, then he tipped his hat to Robin and started toward a gate that opened onto a road. As I nodded to the groom, he squinted up at me. I could see from his expression that he did not think I could sit a horse. But I tried not to mind.

The road led along a rushing stream, which I could hear but could not see because of the thick stand of alder and birch that lined its banks. Then we came to a field, marked off by dry stone walls.

"Is this all your property?" I asked.

Sir Byron slowed his mount to let me catch up to him. "The top of that ridge marks the boundary."

Theo proved to be the gentle beast promised, and I was able to relax in the saddle and take in the broad stretch of field and hill before me. I breathed the fresh air deeply, deciding at that moment that I would not, no matter what, return to Nottingham.

We circled the field and then rode upward through sheep pastures of sweet vernal grasses, heath bedstraw, bilberry and woodruff, all of which Byron pointed out to me.

"The bracken is tall and thick here in summer," Byron said pointing to the trampled, brown remains. "It hides the sheep and the adders. You have to watch where you ride then." He gave a laugh. "There's a saying, 'under bracken's gold.' "

I started at the mention of gold, remembering Rosa's prophecy. "What do you mean?"

He shrugged. "They probably mean that where the soil depth is greater than nine inches, bracken flourishes. Better land for ploughing than the stoney upper slopes."

We came to another belt of trees, and then to the edge of a clear, frozen lake. I had seen ponds frozen to the color of frost, but nothing like these crystal depths that reflected the light of the sky.

"The lake is clear," said Byron, "because the water freezes so fast that no air gets trapped in it."

A sign posted at the edge warned of the danger of going out on the ice.

"Another month, and it's safe to walk on it. But watch for the sign."

Soon we were on the upper slopes, and here indeed was moorland with short mat grass and flowering gorse. Up here the wind threatened to push me from the saddle, and I hunched closer to Theo, grabbing handfuls of her black mane to steady myself. We drew up, and Byron pointed into the distance.

"Your castle, Miss Blackstone."

My hair whipped around my face, but I brushed it back with my hand and squinted. Growing out of a long rise was indeed the outline of a castle. Even from here I could see what looked like three turrets thrusting upward, but with deep rifts in the curtain walls between them.

My gaze was drawn to the right where a low wall snaked across the plain, dipped with the landscape, then crawled upward toward the western horizon. A huge ditch followed its line on this side with what looked like the remains of a road. This must be Hadrian's Wall.

Seeing the direction of my gaze, Byron said, "It was the castle we came to see, however, I see your interest may lie in greater antiquities. I will show you our Roman wall, if you would like."

I stared as light and shadow danced along the ruin of the wall. Even from here I could see where stones had been removed or toppled. It would certainly hold nothing back in its present condition. I sat very still, listening, but there was only the hiss of the wind as it raced across the grass toward the lands across the wall. To the north, hills rose, blue in the landscape.

Realizing I had not answered Sir Byron, I turned to him. "It is quite fascinating. Mrs. MacDougal said . . ." I hesitated. "Said there were spirits out there. Ghosts of the Roman soldiers. Is that true?"

If I had expected him to laugh and make light of my query, he surprised me. He looked toward the wall for a moment, almost with a look of pain. Then he smoothed his features and turned to me.

"You must not listen to the superstitions of the North," he said. "This was once a bloody land, and the many battles left their mark. Come, we will see the castle first."

I thought he had not answered my question and it made me wonder. I myself was convinced that if a person had had a violent death, or had left this life with something unresolved, he or she would remain in a disembodied state. Such a one might even try to communicate with the living. My hodgepodge education — between books I could find to read in the orphanage and the many nights talking to Rosa — had led me to such conclusions, and though I had never had truck with a ghost, I knew others who had.

The thought chilled me, so I tried to put it aside, reminding myself that it was broad daylight, and there was nothing here to be frightened of.

The ground sloped slightly upward until we came to a deep cut that had obviously served as a moat in former times. My heart sank as I looked at the castle. Sir Byron had been right. It was a ruin. Entire wings had fallen in, though as we got closer the masonry that remained looked solid.

We paused, looking up, before crossing a small bridge that had been built across the bottom of the dry moat.

"Often besieged and battered, as often repaired and rebuilt, like many of the other border fortresses, this one exhibits work of every century — from the twelfth to the sixteenth," said Byron.

So he was more interested in this once useful piece of architecture than he had let on, otherwise why would he have taken the trouble to study its heritage.

Some unnamed instinct rose to the defense. I did not see it as a ruin, rather as it might have been. I could squeeze my eyes almost shut and see the royal fortress rising, strong and beautiful, commanding a deep ravine and a narrow place in the river on the other side.

"If it were mine . . ."

I glanced sideways at the man beside me. I could not express my thoughts for fear he would laugh at me, but I was filled with a compelling sense of belonging that was most astounding.

"Come," I said, urging Theo forward, not even waiting for Byron. I was filled with an indescribable urge to see what I could of the inside. The horses scrambled up the slope, and we got down.

Excitement rushed over me as I turned to Byron. "Please show me inside."

He eyed me curiously and gestured to part of a wall that jutted out from what looked like the keep. "That was the great hall. The state chamber was apparently on the other side."

"How do we get in?"

"This way."

We had to pick our way over some rubble where steps had fallen in. Byron climbed over a piece of a wall and then half lifted me in. The wooden floor had rotted through in places, and he advised me to walk near the walls. I followed him to a passage that led to a round tower with stairs circling upward. There I stopped and tilted my head back looking up at two landings above and then at open sky, where there once had been a roof.

Suddenly a picture slid into place in my mind. Torches blazed from the walls. A lady in a deep blue and gold velvet gown that extended about her descended the stairs, while from the room I had just left behind, lutes, psaltery and viola da gamba played sharply accented court music.

I blinked, shook myself, then turned to stare at Byron. He seemed to be paying little attention to me, but was running his hand over the rough stone of the wall.

"The keep was much sturdier built than the east and west wing," I said.

He stopped and looked at me, and I felt as if I rose out of my body. I knew I had been here before. I could not explain how or when, but the certainty came from within the very marrow of my bones.

"The kitchen," I said, pointing past Byron. "It must be this way."

He gave a little bow and followed me down a passageway that was still mostly intact. I paused once to glance out an embrasure to the courtyard below. Grass grew between the smooth stones, and I could see now that we had come in the back way, for across the courtyard was the gatehouse and rusted machinery for a drawbridge. Suddenly remembering the sounds I had heard in the night, I looked about for chains, but I saw none.

I turned and smiled at Byron, who was watching me inquisitively.

"It's wonderful."

His dark brow arched further. "You call a moldering pile of rock wonderful?"

"Well, of course it is. It's grand. I mean it used to be. Surely you can see that."

He shrugged and grasped my arm as we made our way through a fallen-down door into the kitchens. Here, broken pots lay on an abandoned work table. The baking oven was a home for birds. But it had been functional not so many years ago. It could be made functional again.

"I'm afraid I do not share your enthusiasm. More castles dot the landscape of Northumberland than any other county in England. Most have fallen into disrepair like this one. They aren't practical to live in anymore."

Then if you don't want it, why don't you give it to me? I succeeded in keeping the thought to myself. My attachment to the place was irrational, born of Rosa's crystal ball. Yet there was something I could not put my finger on. The sense that it was mine, that I belonged here was strong. There must have been truth in the Blackstone legend. I thanked my stars that I had taken Rosa's advice and come to see it.

But now what? So what if my ancestors did once own this castle and this land. So what if now I had seen it. It wasn't mine. Sir Byron had a deed. At least he said he had.

"You say there's a deed," I said tentatively, resting my hand on the chopping block.

He gave a wry sideways smile. "Oh yes, we are forgetting the deed. I will show it to you at once."

He gave a flourish and bowed, and I resented his mockery.

"It would be interesting to see it," I clipped off my words. "And after that if you would be so kind as to put me on a train, I will trouble you no more. I have . . ." I began to falter, "seen what I came to see.

As I drew myself up proudly, I heard a splinter tear my skirt from behind.

"Now, now, let's not be hasty. I have myself given the matter some thought. It is my pleasure to have you as my guest, for . . ." he hesitated, "for as long as you wish."

I nodded stiffly. "Thank you. I appreciate your hospitality, and I will return these clothes to you as soon as Mrs. MacDougal has finished mending my dress. But I would not want to impose further."

He circled the kitchen, laying out a plan that he seemed to have thought through very thoroughly.

"I assure you it is no burden. But I can see that you are not the sort to loll around doing nothing, the occupation far too many houseguests indulge in. However, it happens, I am in a position to offer you employment."

He stopped circling long enough to glance at me for a reaction.

"Employment?" I asked. "What kind?"

"Ah. I was right. I can see I have sparked your interest."

I shrugged. "I have always worked. I do not intend to

69

return to my former place of employment. Rather, I thought I would seek a position elsewhere."

"Hmmhmm. Good. And what sort of employment did you have, if I may ask?"

"I make lace, by hand."

This brought him up. Then a smile curved his lips. "Lace. What kind?"

"Any kind you want. French lace, Spanish lace, tatting. I brought a bolt of Honiton with me if you'd like to see it."

My tone was formal and my hands were folded in front of me as if this were a proper interview instead of merely a conversation taking place in a fallen-down ruin of a castle. Sir Byron, too, kept a businesslike demeanor, which helped calm the rushing feeling I still had.

"Well then. I am aware of the fact that you read."

Humor touched the corner of his mouth, and I knew he was referring to my late night search for the library in his house. "Do you write a passable hand?"

"I believe so," I answered. "I practiced a good deal when I was at the orphanage after my parents died. I helped Matron with her letters."

"Aha." He flicked his riding crop against his boot. "Then you see, I cannot let you go. I am in dire need of a secretary to help me with my correspondence. And someone clever with her fingers to boot. Certain cravats and cuffs of mine need a bit of lace."

"I see."

As we stood there I was all too aware of what else was happening between us. It had started the night he sat beside me on the sofa. He was an attractive man, gentry, and he wore his aristocracy like a well-fitted glove, with no self-consciousness about it. Being rooted in my legend, I could almost feel an equal to him. But it was more than that. His presence set off a tingling sensation in me that began with the beating of my heart.

The very fact that he was a man and I a woman made me keep myself guarded from him. Though I knew he was nothing like the coarse Mr. Biggleston whom I had fled, I found myself stiffening whenever Byron took my arm. I was rather like a wolf pup that hungered for a piece of roasting meat, yet was afraid to go too near the fire.

What did I know of baronets? Men who flattered and, I was sure, dallied where they pleased. The men I knew had no such fancy manners, they simply took what they wanted, or tried to. I winced, thinking how close I'd come to being one such victim.

Byron must have seen the pain in my eyes, for he reached slowly for my hand and covered it with his.

"You are most welcome here," he said in a warm, gentle voice.

As we stood there, discussing my future in the shadows of the ancient stone walls, I could not help but notice his sensual mouth, the way ironic laughter and seriousness vied for expression there, the directness of his eyes, the grace of his long fingers. I forced my gaze away from him, fearing to be drawn in. But my attempt was useless, for he approached me slowly, and since I was leaning on the work table, I could not move away without looking foolish.

He stood so near I could feel his breath on my hair. When I glanced up I noticed the darkness of his eyelashes, the set line of his jaw. He spoke in almost a whisper.

"Stay a while, Heather. Surely you don't want to return to that factory. You've no family. My household is isolated, that is true. But it is comfortable. Since my sister died, it's been a lonely place . . ." His words drifted off.

I wanted to speak, but nothing came out. My lips were half parted as I saw my own reflection in the dark pools of his eyes. Then he straightened, and gave me a teasing half-smile.

"Besides, I would be remiss not to offer refuge to a damsel in distress."

"I am not—," I stopped. I thought he was having a joke again at my expense. I was so used to defending myself, to fighting for everything I got, that I bristled at anyone who laughed at me.

He lifted a dark brow. "In distress?" I believe he sensed

something of my thoughts, for he took a more formal attitude, dropping my hand. "But of course. You must decide
for yourself."

I felt better then. It was the speech he might have taken
with a lady of quality, and I responded to it, standing a
little straighter. If I were wearing the clothes of a lady of
quality, I might as well learn how to act like one.

I looked him in the eye and saw the flicker in those brown
depths. Our gazes held. But I was wrong not to speak. For
what our words did not convey, our bodies did. I was again
aware of the trembling his presence caused me, and I saw
him shift his position slightly as if moved by the same instinct that he must control.

I moistened my dry lips. His eyes flickered to my mouth
and his own lips parted slightly. Then he took a deep breath
and his face filled with emotion. I looked away, embarrassed. I had never felt such a response to a man before, but
I attributed it to the newness of everything around me, and
the fact that most of the men I'd known hadn't had the
luxury of fine living to make them look and smell so enticing.

Then he regained control of himself, and the moment
was broken. He began circling the kitchen again. Something occurred to me then, even through the fever that had
seized my body. What better way to search for the truth
about my family legend than in the house of my ancestors'
enemy?

"All right," I finally said. "I don't mind staying if I can
pay my way by working."

"Good, then it is agreed." He cleared his throat. "Of
course you may leave at any time if you feel the situation
does not suit you. You should not feel a prisoner here."

"A prisoner?"

He shook his head. "Some feel the North to be a prison,
though you cannot see the walls. Some feel trapped here.
My sister did. She always said she would leave. And then it
was too late."

I wanted to ask how she died, but felt like I would be

prying. When he wanted to tell me more about her, he would. "What was her name?"

"Erlinda."

"Erlinda. A pretty name."

We said no more, but returned the way we'd come. We mounted the horses, then I turned once more to gaze at the weather-beaten fortress before we crossed the little bridge for home. Glancing up, I thought I saw something move across the embrasure in the northmost tower, and at that moment a stone came loose and fell, bouncing off the wall and rolling down the embankment to the moat. Probably an animal had gotten up there.

So I would stay in Northumberland and try to learn more about what had happened to the Blackstones who had befriended Charles the First on his flight to Scotland so many years ago.

Six

I quickly took my place in the household. Mrs. Mac-Dougal got several of Erlinda's dresses out of a cedar chest for me to wear. I still heard sounds in the night, but I gave up trying to sort out whether they were spirits, the wind off the moors or merely some part of my dreams. I wrote Rosa as often as I could, though I kept my letters short. Rosa could not read, but I thought she could get someone to read them to her. I did not expect her to reply.

I also wrote to Eliza at home, telling her not to worry about me, but not to tell Biggleston where I'd gone.

I soon met the rest of the staff. The kitchens were run by a plump, efficient woman whom everyone addressed as Cook. She was assisted by a French kitchen maid named Louisa, whose English was mixed with French. She spoke so fast in answer to Cook, who talked in thick Northumbrian dialect to herself while she worked, that whenever I had occasion to go into the kitchen, my ears were assaulted by the rattling of utensils accompanied by the continual staccato of words, most of which I did not understand.

The downstairs was kept up by Sophie, another maid of all work. She was most often engaged in polishing brass and silver and in cleaning the oil lamps and trimming the wicks.

There was also a deaf gardener named Effram, who could most often be found clipping hedges or shoveling dirt into a wheelbarrow.

The day after it was lost, my Bible reappeared in the same drawer it had been in. I told Byron, and I could see the doubt in his eyes that it had ever been misplaced. He probably thought I had stacked some clothing on top of it. But I knew he was wrong.

As we worked each morning in his study, he showed me the papers and ledgers I would have to deal with. Some of the compartments in the big rolltop desk were locked. I was given keys only to those I would need.

Doing figures was easy for me, and Byron seemed to appreciate the fact that I might be a great help to him in keeping track of the rents he collected and the many expenses for the farming. It was agreed that I would work in the study in the mornings and use my afternoons as I pleased. In the evening I found occupation sewing.

I altered some of the dresses Mrs. MacDougal brought me to wear from Erlinda's wardrobe. And I embroidered and hemmed some linens for the household. Though I threw myself into my work most heartily, there was still time for me to do as I chose, a novelty I was not used to.

Being very anxious to acquaint myself with the village buried in the vale, I took myself off on foot one sunny afternoon, thinking there would be time to enjoy a walk.

The road was a bit muddy in spots, but I was well-wrapped in a wool coat trimmed with a border of silver beaver. The sturdy walking boots I wore seemed to give energy to my legs as I breathed deeply of the crisp November air. Erlinda's feet had been a size larger than mine, but by stuffing the toes with strips of cloth, I managed to make them fit. Byron ordered me to the cobbler in the village, so that I could have some made that fit me. I didn't want any charity, so he promised to deduct the cost from my wages. I was beginning to appreciate the comfort of well-made clothes, finding their sturdiness and warmth a blessing.

As I left the long drive that led up to the house and stepped into the road to the village, I saw a figure walking toward me from where the road curved. I thought at first it might be Robin, but as he drew nearer I saw that this young man was taller and thinner. He held himself straight and walked with a nimble, bandy-legged roll. In his hand was a shepherd's crook, and at his throat a red scarf.

We were still some distance from each other, but I could make out a face with sharp features, honey-colored skin and black eyes. When I saw the sun glance off a gold earring in his left ear, I stopped, but he kept coming toward me. When he was only a yard distant, he stopped, smiled broadly and bowed.

"You must be Heather Blackstone," he said, tossing his dark hair back from his forehead.

"How did you know?" I asked.

"Gypsies have ways of knowing," he said with a wink.

I gasped. It couldn't be. "You couldn't be Raoule, the shepherd." My eyes were round.

He twirled his shepherd's crook. "The very same." Then with a more serious glance, he said, "I regret that I was not here to find you earlier. I was, alas, driving my flock down from the highlands. Since you were taken in at the great house, I bided my time until I thought you might have need of me."

I was absolutely astonished at this speech. So Rosa had not been lying. There really was a Gypsy shepherd, Raoule, and he had in some way found out where I was. He turned, and now we walked along the road together.

"Then you really are a friend of Rosa's?"

"Ah yes, Rosa. It has been a while. In June, we gather in the Eden Valley for the New Fair."

I knew that Gypsies loved fairs, and that sometimes with no notice whatsoever, Rosa would disappear, the closed sign on her door the only indication that she was gone.

I wondered how much Raoule knew of my reason for being here. "It is because of Rosa that I am here," I said. "She saw it in her crystal ball."

He smiled and his dark eyes danced. *"Dukkeripen. That's Romany for 'saying the future.'"*

His lightheartedness rubbed off on me, something I found refreshing after the strange events that had crossed my path and the adjustments I was making to a new situation. I found that even with luxury and comfort came a certain responsibility and behavior.

Mrs. MacDougal was my strictest taskmaster, making sure I had all the proper changes of clothes and keeping an eye on my decorum. She had chided me for speaking too familiarly with Robin, the groom. My position was above that of all the servants except the housekeeper, and it would not do to forget my place. I had also seen her expression of disapproval when she caught me laughing with Byron over some small joke. I was above the servants, but beneath the master of the house, so I could not relax with anyone but Mrs. MacDougal herself, and beyond a certain point we had run out of things to say. She would probably go red with indignation, her crossed eye flashing, to see me laughing and talking with a gypsy.

I told Raoule something of my family legend, to which he listened with great fascination. "And so you have come to claim your heritage," he said as we reached the outskirts of the village.

I smiled ruefully. "There doesn't seem to be much to claim. In any case the property is safely in the possession of Sir Byron. He showed me the deed." I shrugged. "And so, I don't even know if the story is true."

We stopped at the stone bridge over the little stream that finally converged with the road. He looked serious for a moment.

"You know in your heart if the story is true."

I met his dark gaze, recalling the sensations I had experienced at the castle. Most would not set much store by them, but he was right. There was something instinctual about my feelings for the place.

"Yes," I mumbled, looking away from him at the whirling eddies below us. "I suppose you are right."

He swung his stick. "I must leave you here. But I shall keep watch over you. Send for me if you need me. My flock grazes above Fallow Burn." He gave me a wink. "You must visit our camp."

I agreed that I would ride up to the hills at the first opportunity. There was something about Raoule's sensitive countenance and fairy-like disposition that appealed to me. I was glad of the friendship, for it was a link with Rosa.

He set off along the road in a swinging stride, and as he walked, he sang in a melodious, ringing voice:

> The Gypsies they came to my Lord Cassilis' yet
> And O! but they sang bonnie;
> They sang sae sweet and sae complete,
> That down came our fair Ladie.

I listened for a moment to the song and thought that with so sweet a song, it was no wonder that the lady went off with the Gypsy laddie. Then I turned and entered the village.

Now I had time to examine the thatched cottages that stood hard by the old stone bridge that I had crossed. Though the gardens were barren now, come spring, well-laid plots would be well-tended. The lane twisted downward until I came to an old stone-built church with a tall spire and a weedy graveyard.

The brook forked just behind the churchyard, and one branch babbled by, a soothing lullaby for the sleeping gravestone owners. I was admiring the scene when a pudgy little vicar emerged from the side door and walked briskly toward the lane. Then, spying me, he paused, removed his spectacles and squinted.

"Good morning," I said.

"Morning to you, miss," he said and stepped closer. "Now let me see. I don't believe you are one of my flock, or if we have met. You'll have to forgive my poor memory."

I held out my hand to him. "I have not had the pleasure," I said. "My name is Heather Blackstone and I am newly employed at Worthington Manor."

He took my hand and pumped it up and down. "Ah,

then that explains it. And what is your position at the manor house, miss?"

"I am acting as Sir Byron's secretary."

"Well then, welcome to our village. I hope to see you in church on Sunday. I am the Reverend Carstairs Brown. I'm pleased to meet you." He smiled benevolently and rocked on his heels.

"Thank you," I said.

Then he scratched his balding head and wrinkled his brow. "Blackstone, you say. Blackstones lived in these parts long ago."

"Yes." My heart beat quicker as I took another step toward him. "Do you know of them?"

He screwed up his face. "Indeed, indeed. Gentry in the old days, masters of Blackstone castle."

"Yes, exactly. That's what I've come to find out about. Do you," I glanced at the church, "have parish records that go back before Cromwell's time?"

He shook his head sadly. "Alas, the church was gutted in a fire fifty years ago, most of the records too. A shame."

Fifty years too late, I thought with chagrin. At least it would have been something to see the name Blackstone recorded.

Then he set his finger beside his nose, and his eyes twinkled. "No parish records, but gravestones, if you'd like to see them."

"Gravestones belonging to my ancestors?"

"Why indeed so, if it is the same branch of the family. Come right this way."

He held the gate for me, and I followed him along a slightly overgrown flagstone path into the little cemetery. We passed the more recent burial plots and came to some weathered headstones, some leaning backward in the soil as if they were very tired of standing up.

He pointed to a simple white marble monument and I read the inscription: Charles Blackstone 1728–1782. Another smaller plot held a marker indicating that Charles's beloved wife, Mary Blackstone, rested here, having been buried in 1784. Moving on to what was evidently a child's plot, I bent over to read the script. Then I froze. There had been a child, all right. Heather Blackstone, died age fourteen-and-a-half.

Again the wind seemed to whisper through the trees, and dizziness threatened me. I stood, my mouth dry, feeling as if I were looking at my own grave. I could hardly speak, but looked into the small blue eyes of the vicar.

"The last of the Blackstones that were buried here," he said. "There was a younger brother, I believe, who left Northumberland in his youth."

My heart felt as if a hand squeezed it, and I pressed my hand against my chest. "Are there any others?" I asked.

"Yes, a few, over here."

I took deep gulps of air as I followed him to another plot where more Blackstones rested. But the earliest grave was marked 1674, well after the family had been dispossessed of their property.

I turned away from the shady spot, walking back toward the church, my mind spinning. I pressed the vicar with more questions.

"My family legend has it that our ancestors helped Charles the First, and were promised a reward for it. Do you know anything of that?"

"Why, no. Blackstones hereabouts were Roundheads. Reason the property passed into Worthington's hands. The estates have been owned by Worthingtons for the last two hundred years." He patted my shoulder. "If it's your family you've come to find out about, I'm afraid there's nothing left but these markers. Have you asked Sir Byron himself?"

"Yes. He showed me the deed to the castle." I shook my head. "Not much left of it now, is there?"

"A remnant of the past, that's all."

At that moment the wind ruffled the leaves and I was filled with the curious feeling that the past was somehow not so distant. Seeing the vicar reminded me of my other curious loss, and I repeated the story of how my Bible had disappeared for two days and then reappeared.

He folded and unfolded his pudgy hands, a worried look flitting across his otherwise complacent face. "Perhaps someone in the house had a need for spiritual comfort. Worthington Manor has not been a happy house."

"I didn't know."

"I've done my best to aid many of its members, but I feel I've not succeeded."

He looked over his shoulder as if making sure no one was listening, but there was no one in sight, only the empty graveyard.

"All who inherited the title died by violent means, bless their souls."

My head came up in surprise. "What sort of violent means?"

He shook his head. "Some by the knife, some from falling off a horse. The late Sir Douglas, that was Sir Byron's father, was shot in the back. Robbery it was, supposedly."

The thought was not pleasing. I wondered for a moment how Sir Byron felt about the grisly deaths. He had not mentioned them to me. However, I did not see what all this had to do with my missing Bible. I had hoped that Reverend Brown might be able to tell me exactly who in the Worthington household might have such a "spiritual" curiosity, but he was not forthcoming.

Before he bid me good day, he invited me to come to the rectory for tea any afternoon. Mrs. Brown did so enjoy company. Then I went on to the village, for I had several errands. Thoughts of my ancestry were swimming in my mind, but I decided it would do me good to put my mind on more mundane tasks. There was much to think about and to sort out, but it couldn't all be done in one day.

I passed several stone cottages and then came to the shops across from the railroad station. Sparks flew deep inside the blacksmith's accompanied by the ringing of the anvil. A gaunt-looking farmer in knee breeches, high boots, shabby coat and a black hat with a down-turned brim, sat on a bench outside the stable, watching the street, his hand resting on a carved walking stick. I nodded as I passed, and he thumped his stick as he bid me a good day.

My first stop was at the small drygoods shop where I purchased some thread. The shopkeeper, a round-faced woman with a rather snub nose and very ruddy cheeks, who introduced herself as Mrs. Goodson, showed me some fine silk thread she had up from London. I bought some, as well as some cotton thread, for Byron had asked me to work on my lacemaking. He was of the mind to decorate some of the rooms of the manor, and he thought I could help. I was flattered that he had asked me.

Out of a catalogue I ordered needles and pillows to which to attach the paper pattern in order to work the lace. I thought that if Annie was interested, I might also teach her. She seemed quick with her hands, and if she had keen eyesight as well, she might take to it.

When I told Mrs. Goodson that I worked for Sir Byron, she gave me a more thorough looking over, as if the clothes I wore represented the house I came from. An expression of doubt passed over her eyes.

"You've no family hereabouts, then?" she asked.

I was surprised at the question. "No," I said. Then I added, "Not anymore."

"Pity," she said.

"What do you mean?"

She gave me a sidelong glance as she wrapped my parcel in brown paper. "None of my business, of course. But you must have heard of the bad luck of the manor house."

"Well," I hedged. "Reverend Brown did mention something about it."

She handed me the package. "It's the reason why none o' the servants've been there very long. Some say it's a curse."

"A curse?"

"Indeed. Why else would the hand of God strike down the Worthington heirs in their prime? And that house is too near the Wall for me. Too many restless spirits up there, walking the Wall at night."

I tried to think of something to say in defense of my working for Sir Byron, but I could think of nothing. A curse? On a family who had usurped the property from the rightful owners? The idea was compelling, even though I did not really believe that God bothered himself with doling out such violent punishments. I rather thought He preferred man to sort out his own squabbles. Of course Byron had not mentioned a curse, for he must have known it would only add fuel to the fire of my imagination. Still, I wondered if he believed it himself.

I had emerged from the drygoods shop and was deciding where to go next, when I saw a familiar figure step down from a doorway and come my way. I recognized Stanley Symmes, though today he wore a double-breasted jacket, fine-checked trousers and a bowler hat. His blond moustache seemed longer than when I had last seen it, and it was waxed into an upward curl.

He seemed preoccupied, and I noticed the sign swinging above the door he had just departed. County Registry it said. He was nearly upon me before he raised his eyes, and he stopped suddenly to avoid a collision.

"Good morning, Mr. Symmes," I said.

He quickly removed his hat. "Oh, my dear Miss Blackstone. How good to see you. I'm afraid I wasn't paying any attention. How do things fare with you?"

"Very well, thank you. And you?"

"Business is moving along. Slowly, but one expects that." He glanced about. "I could do with a spot of tea. Would you care to join me?"

A combination bakery and tea shop advertised its wares with a painted sign displaying hot buns coming out of an oven. I was hungry after my walk and readily agreed.

Inside the bright, clean shop, we seated ourselves at a small, round table next to the windows. We asked for tea and hot buns with fresh butter and homemade jelly. I removed my coat, which Mr. Symmes hung on a peg by the door. As he returned to the table, he gazed appreciatively at the walking dress of striped wool I wore. I'm sure it contrasted greatly with the worn traveling costume he had seen on the train.

"Well now. You must tell me everything. What have you been doing to occupy yourself since you arrived here?"

I told him about my new post, and he expressed a great deal of interest in the Worthington household. At least he, not being from the area, did not allude to the ominous fortune of which I had learned this day. Neither did I mention my interest in Blackstone castle. I did not know Mr. Symmes very well, and for some reason I felt like keeping that matter private.

"I shall most likely call on Sir Byron soon. I may have business to discuss with him."

I was by now very curious about Mr. Symmes' mysterious business, and I formed some questions that would help me guess what he was doing. Having just come from the registry office, I guessed it might have something to do with land.

"Sir Byron seems to have a great deal of property," I said. "Indeed he does."

I did not miss the light in his translucent eyes. I recognized greed when I saw it. I'd had enough of my own greed born of scarcity. Mr. Symmes must be going to purchase land, but for what?

We chatted amiably, and I ate so many buns I thought I would pop. Then I thought I should be on my way. I bought some fresh bread and rolls to take back to the manor. Cook had asked for them.

By the time I left the village it was later than I thought. I remembered that the clouds had a way of coming up over the valley at dusk, darkening the skies earlier than one might have thought. As I crossed the stone bridge I peered ahead, almost hoping that Raoule would reappear from where he had left me and see me home.

The wind rushing through the trees, the dampness in the air, and the long shadows cast by the woods that hid the stream made the lane that had seemed sunny and inviting earlier in the day seem lonely and frightening by contrast. Now the low branches caught at my hat, while roots that had grown over rocky soil twisted toward my feet. I thought of a warm fire blazing at the manor and hurried as fast as my legs would carry me, my parcels growing heavier by the moment.

It was nearly dark by the time I reached the iron gate, and then I had to make my way up the long, winding drive. But now I could see the house, which looked dark and cold except for a light in a window on the top floor. Why weren't any fires lit downstairs, I wondered? Where was Byron? I would have thought him to be in his study at this hour. It was still two hours until dinner, and he had told me it was his habit to sip sherry and answer correspondence or read until darkness fell.

When I at last made my way to the front door, and Dunstan wordlessly opened the door, I heaved myself in, almost dropping the packages. Dunstan relieved me of the larger ones.

"Thank you, Dunstan. The bakery goods are for Cook."

I straightened my hat with one hand, took the dry goods parcels and climbed to my room. Thank heavens someone had laid a fire. I turned up the lamps. I had just got out of my coat and hat when there was a knock on the door. Mrs. MacDougal stood there, prim as usual.

"The master wishes you to dine with him this evening, if it be yer pleasure," she said with almost a trace of resentment in her voice. "Eight o'clock."

I nodded, trying not to let her jealousy affect me. For what else could her stiff manners and subtle reprimands mean? I decided she must not like having an employee of her equal station about the house. I sent her away with a message for him that I would be ready at eight.

Then I hurried out of my clothes. I had time to bathe and prepare myself. In the time I had been here, I often took my meals on a tray in my room — when I dined with the servants in the kitchen I found the atmosphere to be as strained as if I were eating with gentry every night of the week, so rigid was the hierarchy that reined. Only when I was alone with any one of them did the various employees of the household relax enough to exchange a friendly word with me. I hoped when they got to know me this would change.

I hurried along to draw myself a bath, luxuriating in the warm suds as long as I dared. Then I let Annie use the curling iron on my hair; her deft fingers twisted it up in intricate loops and swirls, leaving springy curls at the nape of my neck, my temples and behind my ears.

I had found in the back of the armoire a crimson satin gown that I dared try on. I had dined with Byron on a few other occasions, and our conversations ranged from the stiff and formal to the more relaxed and casual. There were times when he began to talk about himself and his interests so that I entirely forgot my self-appointed mission in being here and indulged in the pleasure of his company.

Perhaps it was with full knowledge that I donned the red satin gown that night, for from the way his eyes sometimes drank me in, I must have known that he, too, wanted more. Was I being a traitor to the long dead Blackstones to indulge in flirtation with their old enemy? For if he was their enemy, so must he be mine. I knew that what was happening between us was dangerous. And if what the villagers had said was true, then he, too, walked a path of danger.

I had come here on a flight of fancy. With every step I took a new question was asked. Perhaps Byron Worthington held more answers than he was telling me or that he himself knew.

Oh, sweetest enemy.

Seven

I met Byron in the now familiar parlor, which I discovered was used only for informal occasions, the formal parlor being on the other side of the parqueted entry hall. He was dressed in a dinner jacket and trousers that perfectly fit his form. He turned when I entered and paused to admire my appearance.

"Stunning," he said. "I would not have thought when I picked you up out of the street that you would add such elegance to these poor old rooms."

I felt the blush creep up my neck. "Thank you. But do these clothes not remind you of your sister?"

He came toward me and took my hand, bowing in a formal gesture. "It is not the dress that lights up the person, rather the other way around. It is you who does honor to the dress." He gave me a sly wink. "What wonders the rest and nourishment prescribed by the doctor have done."

This was at least true. Having rich food to eat every day had certainly filled out my figure. I would have to keep up my walks and rides so as not to get too fat.

I allowed him to pour me a glass of sherry, but I sipped it slowly, fearing that the drink would go to my head. I was not experienced in flirtation, and I had many questions to ask him tonight. Therefore, I needed to keep a clear head. I launched into an account of my walk to the village, selecting certain details to be discussed later.

"The Reverend Brown was quite friendly. He invited me to church."

"Then you must go, if you are so inclined."

"Do you not attend?"

He lifted his glass and twirled it absently. "I have read a great deal of church history. Much more than the Reverend Brown would suspect. While many Christian ideals are admirable, I am left with the sense that there is something missing from orthodox Christianity. I have developed my own peculiar set of beliefs. In answer to your question, no, I do not attend the village church except on holidays."

"I see."

I was honored that he would discuss so personal a thing as religion with me, and I wondered what else he might feel free to speak about this evening.

"Reverend Brown showed me the markers belonging to the Blackstones," I said.

"Ah, then you have found out something more about your family?"

"A little." I shrugged. "All the markers date from 1674. The parish records were lost in a fire fifty years ago."

"A pity." The coolness in his voice told me he did not care that I had found no earlier records.

I pressed on. "Actually, I found the reverend quite full of local lore."

"Was he now?"

Byron's tense tone of voice made me hesitate to mention the alleged curse on the Worthingtons, but I had to know if it was true.

I tried to laugh. "Probably no more than village gossip."

He tilted his head slightly. "And what gossip might that be?" His words were clipped.

My hand started to shake, and I put my glass down. "He mentioned some sort of curse. Just superstition, I suppose."

Byron walked to the windows and looked out into the darkness. There was enough moonlight to outline the treetops at the edge of the park and the dim glimmer of a lamp at the gates.

"Ah yes, the curse."

"Is it true?"

He turned slowly and gave me a mysterious smile. Then he drained his glass, set it on the mantle and held out a hand for me.

"Come," he said. "See for yourself."

Greatly curious I followed him out of the parlor and along the entry hall to a corridor that led behind the stairs. Turning left, we came to a salon with French doors opening on one side to a terrace beyond. Byron turned up the lamps in their sconces so that I could see that this was a portrait gallery.

"My illustrious ancestors," he said. Even when he spoke of his own flesh and blood the trace of irony in his tone remained.

He motioned for me to cross the room and gaze at the largest painting. From its great height it dominated the room.

"Sir Cedric," he said. I glanced at the copper plate beneath the painting. It read 1661. I turned to Byron.

"So this was . . ."

He nodded. "The man who followed Charles the Second into exile and was rewarded with the property and the baronetcy."

I stepped back to get a better look. He was a broad-shouldered man, with a bone structure similar to Byron's. This was the man who took the estate from my family. I shut my eyes, wishing I could travel back in time to know what had really happened. But I had none of the sensations or images that had assailed me the day I visited Blackstone Castle.

"He was killed in a duel in 1680," said Byron.

He moved on, pointing to a portrait that was slightly smaller but still took up a large portion of the wall.

"Cedric's son, Alfred, the second baronet."

Alfred was fairer, with greenish-hazel eyes. One wondered how true the likeness might be. I suspected portrait painters tried to flatter subjects who were paying generous fees to be immortalized in oils. I glanced questioningly at Byron.

"Died in battle, 1698."

At least that was an honorable way to go, I thought. We continued around the room. There were Lady Worthingtons, too, mostly beautiful, some fair, some dark, one with Spanish looks and dress. But it was the litany of the fate of the heirs that burned into my mind.

Sir Robert had been strangled with a sheet in 1742. His heir, a nephew who inherited the title, fell off his horse, a foot caught in the stirrup and was dragged to death. The later heirs had met similarly gruesome fates. Died at sea, died of a knife wound, died by the sword, murdered in bed. We reached the end and stood before a painting of Byron's father. I swallowed.

"Reverend Brown said Sir Douglas was shot in the back." I hugged myself, feeling cold.

Byron nodded. "While stepping down from a coach, ten years ago, at the age of forty-nine."

"Was it robbery?"

He shrugged. "At least it was made to look that way. His money and gold ring were taken by the bandits."

I looked up at Byron, whose eyes held mine, and a sudden empathy overcame me.

"How awful," I said. "I am sorry."

He chuckled. "Thank you."

It occurred to me then that the irony Byron Worthington seemed to wear like a piece of outer clothing might be born of living under this curse, or at least, if not a curse, a series of incredibly ironic circumstances governing each ancestor's death. Was that how he dealt with it? By laughing at it?

He must have followed my train of thought, for he took my arm and guided me nearer the French doors to a love seat where we sat down, the velvet seats positioned so that we faced opposite directions. By turning our bodies slightly, we faced each other directly.

"This then is the Worthington curse," he said, watching

my face to see how I would react.

"Do you not live in fear of your own fate, then?"

He lifted the corner of his mouth. The moonlight highlighted his cheekbones, but left the hollows of his cheeks in shadow.

"I do not believe in being a victim. To live in fear would be giving the devil his due. The only way to face life is head-on. Our earthly sojourn is brief. Everyone passes to the grave, possibly beyond. To fear it would be to have one foot in the grave already. My answer to your question, then, must be a resounding no. When the ferryman comes to row me across the River Styx, I'll go willingly enough. But not before I have accomplished my destiny and tasted life to the fullest."

My heart was beating quickly, so filled was I with the fascination of the tale he had laid out about his ancestors. And now his own revelations and the certainty with which he pronounced his philosophy drew me in. His gaze dropped to my lips, and the lashes on his half-closed eyelids formed shadows on his cheekbones.

He moved nearer, and I gasped as the tingling sensation shot from my toes to my head. I thought surely he could see my heart leaping toward the low neckline of my gown, for he glanced at the shadow of my decolletage. And then I felt the warmth of his sleeve on my bare shoulders as he gathered me close.

"Heather, you are a minx, an irresistible one."

I closed my eyes as his lips met mine and melted into the sweetness of his embrace. I grasped his shoulders and his kiss deepened, my mouth molding itself to his. Such intense pleasure was new to me. Seeing that I did not resist, he grasped me harder, his hand sliding down the smooth material of my back while his lips left mine to press against my jaw, my throat and then the cool skin above the lace edging of my gown.

I groaned with pleasure, running my hands through his dark hair. I knew what he wanted. It was something that I had heretofore thought ugly, the demeaning result of a man's animal natures. Hadn't I seen evidence of that myself? But these soft caresses did nothing to repel me. For his hands sizzled on my body. His mouth nourished my skin. I wanted more.

Had I not seen this coming from the first moment I'd met him? Was not part of the reason I stayed on at Worthington Manor the fact that Byron had thrown a net of fascination around me. Was this not part of Rosa's prophecy? But I gave up wasting thought on reason and returned Byron's urgent kisses, my hands wandering along his arms, exploring within his jacket, enjoying the firm torso.

His breathing was harder now, and he rose, impatient with the obstacle created by the arm of the love seat between us. He lifted me up and held me tightly so that I felt his firm length against me. I thought my eardrums would burst with the blood flowing through me.

"I want to bed you, Heather," he whispered into my ear. "Desperately."

I tried to say something, but all I could do was moan between his kisses.

The moonlight reflected the passion in his dark eyes, and my own certainly must have offered no resistance. But he gripped my arms and pulled his head back.

"My dear, you are proving too tempting for me, and I consider myself a strong and principled man where matters of the flesh are concerned. Lucky for both of us that Cook has prepared an undoubtedly sumptuous meal with which we must be satisfied for now."

"Of course."

I struggled to regain control of my runaway feelings, grateful that he held my arms for a moment until I could stand upright on my own two feet.

I forgot for the moment why we ever went to the painting gallery as we made our way back along the corridors and finally passed through the weapons room and entered the dining room. Candelabras lit the table, creating pools of light where we sat, but leaving the outer edges of the room in dark shadow. We spoke very little as we dined, commenting on trivialities between the courses served by the solemn Dunstan, who never met my eyes, as was, I suppose, his training.

The mock turtle soup, stuffed chops, roast fowl, spinach soufflé and meringue pie all passed my palate with less appreciation than they might have, so disturbed was I about what had happened between Byron and me. I tried to think of intelligent conversation to make, not to notice the way his eyes fastened on me as he leaned back in his high-backed chair and watched me as I talked.

I tried to lure him into conversation about the village, about the manor, about anything. He gave polite answers, but then settled back into watching me again, his long fingers twirling his wine glass. I asked him if he had met the solicitor Stanley Symmes and told of how I'd met him. He had not heard of the man, but when I spoke of Mr. Symmes's mysterious business in the neighborhood, Byron sat up straighter.

"I believe it has something to do with land," I said. "He must be representing someone who is planning to buy up some of the land nearby."

Byron frowned. "There have been land speculators in these parts before, and that means only one thing."

"What is that?"

"The railroad. I have thought for some time that a direct line would be put in from Carlisle to Glasgow. We are on the logical route."

"Of course, the railroad." Why hadn't I thought of it myself?

Byron declined any more wine from Dunstan and continued on the subject, which seemed to interest him a great deal.

"Of course the county will fight it. No one wants the railroad ruining the land. Sheep that get on the tracks in front of an oncoming train get killed. Grime from the trains builds up along the route. Most of all," he gave a gesture with his hand for emphasis, "local peasants and gentry alike want to avoid the city riffraff inevitable with the train."

I stiffened. I had been called city riffraff myself, but he did not seem to think he had made a slur.

"But there is a railroad here already," I pointed out.

He shrugged and tossed his napkin onto the the table. "A spur. The main line is much farther east."

"But wouldn't the railroad be good for the local merchants and farmers? Surely with more traffic, more services could be provided — another inn, for instance."

"Of course what you say is true. I am just trying to give you the picture of a provincial people set in their ways. People here resist change."

For some reason the talk about the railroad interested me. Previous to my recent journey here, I had made only a few short trips with my parents when I was younger. Therefore railroads were quite romantic to me. I was surprised that Byron was so suspicious of seeing a new line built through this part of the country. Glasgow had always sounded like it was at the top of the world. The idea that one might get on a train here in Hevingham and speed northward into Scotland was very fascinating to me indeed.

"Enough talk of industry," he said rising. "Will you join me for a stroll?"

I was surprised he did not suggest coffee in the parlor as had been our habit. I treasured my conversations with Byron, for through them I was getting to know more and more about him. At first he had intimidated me, for I did not begin to know how to converse with anyone above my station in life. But he had a way of putting me at ease, always listening with interest to what I had to say, as if my opinion on a new breed of sheep or plans for Christmas festivities really mattered.

"Get your coat," he said. "It is a fair night out. I feel penned in. Fresh air would do us good."

I fetched the coat with the beaver trim and joined him in the entry hall. Instead of leading me out the front, we returned to the painting gallery and he opened one of the French doors leading me out onto the terrace.

I took his arm and we descended the steps to the gravel paths that led through the now barren garden. A silvery three-quarter moon acted as a backdrop to the shadows of shrubbery and fruit trees in the carefully landscaped setting. Statuary seemed an intrinsic part of the garden, which stretched farther than I had seen before. I couldn't help but think what a contrast this part of the Worthington estate made with the wild gorse and peat bogs of the moors above.

"My grandfather Alfred, named after our illustrious ancestor Alfred, was fond of statuary. He had this bronze equestrian statue done of himself."

We stepped nearer the bronze, which had been kept polished by the indefatigable Effram, no doubt. Sir Alfred stood in his stirrups as his steed reared, paws flailing, muscles rippling. We made a tour of the other statues then. Not all of them were replicas of the ancestors I had already become acquainted with inside. Nymphs cavorted in the marble fountains, and a few Grecian figures danced on their pedestals. We stopped before one.

The night was mild, and I had not been cold until I heard a rush of wind that sounded like it was coming down from the moors. It gusted over the valley, and I pulled my collar closer. At the same moment Byron stepped nearer, his arm going around my shoulders for added warmth.

I was smiling up at him in the magic of the intimacy that seemed to form around us. He kissed my hair, and I turned my head to press it against his shoulder. Then my eyes flew up in horror as the marble statue above us began to topple. The blank eyes of the Grecian lady bore downward and I cried out.

"Byron, watch out."

I jumped backward at the same moment he flung his arm upward to protect me. Then my scream pierced the silent night as the statue seemed to fly off its base and take Byron with it as it fell to the ground.

Eight

I thought he was dead, for the statue had caught him across the chest, forcing him backward to the ground. Crushed by a statue. I could only think how aptly the phrase fit into the litany of deaths of the Worthington heirs. At the same moment, I dropped to my knees, crying his name, looking into his white face, his eyes closed. The statue lay across one shoulder, its face near his head.

"Byron, Byron," I sobbed as I tried to lift the heavy statue. Then someone else was beside me, and Effram was shoving me aside. He wrapped his thick arms around the statue and moved it off Byron, dropping the thing to the ground.

Footsteps sounded on the gravel, and Robin appeared.

"Heard a scream," the groom said. Then, seeing Byron's inert form, "Oh, my God."

"Sir, sir," cried Robin. "Can you hear me?"

Robin started to lift him up, but I stopped him.

"Wait. Don't touch him. His shoulder looks broken. Quickly, get the doctor. Send Mrs. MacDougal to me. Have her bring blankets."

Robin dashed off on his errand, and I set about loosening Byron's collar so he could get more air. I laid my ear to his chest and heard his heartbeat, steady. I saw that he was breathing. But already a lump was forming where the statue had grazed his temple. I opened the coat as far as I could, but I was afraid to move the arm.

In minutes, Mrs. MacDougal came and we spread blankets over Byron. It seemed like hours, but he began to come around just before the doctor came running down the gravel path, his coat flying about him.

Byron groaned, and I cradled his head in my hands. His eyelids fluttered, and he looked up at me. His lips moved, but I could not hear what he said. Doctor Morebattle gave a "hrmph," and slit Byron's sleeve so he could set the dislocated shoulder. I was thankful that no one chattered uselessly while the doctor did his work. Byron shut his eyes again and gripped my hand like a vise against the pain.

"There, that's done," the doctor said, after making what looked like a wrenching movement on Byron's arm and shoulder, setting the arm back in the socket. Then he tied a sling over Byron's other shoulder so it would support the right arm. "You all right, sir?" asked the doctor.

Byron's color was slowly returning and his voice was strong now. "I'll mend. Thanks."

"Now let me take a look at that head."

The doctor examined the head wound, but didn't think it was as serious as it looked.

"Let's get him inside now. Don't anyone touch that arm."

I helped him up, and he put his good arm around my shoulder for support. The blow to the head seemed to leave him a little dizzy. Mrs. MacDougal went ahead to prepare his bed, so when we got there a peat fire was blazing and the sheets were turned down on a bed warmed with coals in a warming pan.

Byron sat on the edge of the bed. The doctor placed his bag on the night table. "I've given Mrs. MacDougal something to put in a hot drink for the pain. Some torn ligaments. But you're healthy. You'll mend. Just keep that arm in the sling until I say you can take it off. I'll look in again."

"Thank you, Doctor," said Byron. "I'm sure your expert job prevented me from being deformed for life." He grimaced. "I'll have that drink now."

I helped Byron lie back against the pillows, then followed the doctor to the door of the bedchamber.

"Thank you, Doctor. Is there anything else I should know?"

He drew his bushy eyebrows down. "Just keep him down tomorrow. And keep him off his horse. Don't want to take a chance on another fall."

He turned to the door, then paused, turned around and looked hard at me. "How did that statue fall on him?"

I wrung my hands together as Mrs. MacDougal slipped past us with a steaming mug on a tray.

"A wind . . ." I said. But I knew as well as he that no wind would blow a marble statue off its pedestal unaided.

"Hmmmph," said the doctor, then opened the door to go out. I shivered, wondering if the doctor knew about the curse. He had practiced in the county ever since he'd graduated from medical college. Surely he must know.

I turned back to Byron, but Mrs. MacDougal was helping him out of the one remaining sleeve. She turned and stood protectively in front of the bed as if shielding Byron from me. Her look said it wasn't seemly for me to assist a man getting undressed and into bed.

I resented her prudery. Byron was hurt. He needed me. But arguments would do no good. I hoped he was at least in capable hands.

"Good night then. I'll look in on Sir Byron in the morning." The last was said for his sake.

Before I shut the door behind me I glanced at the bed once again. She had pulled the covers over his chest and his head lolled on the pillow, the drug already taking effect.

In my room, I did not go to bed directly. Rather, after Annie had come to help me out of my gown, I donned a quilted dressing gown and sat before the fire, an unopened book in my lap, Hadrian purring on the floor at my feet.

Someone had tried to kill Byron. Had there been anyone in the garden with us? I tried to remember what happened just before and after the statue fell, but it all had happened so fast, I could no longer be sure just who had arrived at the scene first. I remembered Effram removing the statue from Byron. Robin had come running, and on his heels,

98

Mrs. MacDougal. I had sent Robin to fetch Mrs. MacDougal, but she had appeared sooner than he could have roused her if she had been in her quarters, especially if she had already retired. Then Annie had brought the doctor. Cook had been on hand boiling hot water and brewing tea. But something bothered me about it all.

I got up, the book sliding to the floor. "Someone tried to kill your master," I said to Hadrian, lifting him up and cradling him in my arms, more for my own comfort than for his. I took him to the window seat with me and cranked open the window.

My room was on the side of the house facing the stables, so I could not see the garden. Still, I watched the trees sway, saw a lantern being carried to the stables—Robin most likely. A voice called from the kitchen below. The lantern stopped, moved back toward the kitchen. The household was not yet settled down after the excitement.

Had someone pushed the statue? It seemed the only likely answer. Or else someone had loosened it from its base. But even so, how would anyone know that we would be standing beside that very statue?

Then I froze, my grip on Hadrian making him meow loudly and jump onto the window ledge. I knew now what had bothered me so much. My scream had brought everyone running to the scene. Effram had been the first to reach us. But he was deaf.

I shuddered, rose, faced the window. Effram? Had he been lurking in the garden, waiting for us to come near the statue? If anyone was strong enough to crack a statue at its base, it might be he. But why? And would not someone else notice? I was not quite sure how statues were mounted, but surely from the sturdiness that allowed them to withstand all kinds of weather, they were built for permanence.

I walked from one end of my room to the other, suffocating from the fact that I could not talk to Byron immediately. But he was drugged and in pain or else sleeping. Was it the curse? Byron had been so cavalier about it. I thought of Rosa. Her prophecy had said there would be great danger, but she had mentioned nothing about a curse.

I had worn a path in the carpet and the fire was dying down. Hadrian came back in the window, jumped to the floor and skittered to a stop before leaping onto the chair by the fireplace.

Great danger. But her prophecy was meant for me. Great evil, great fortune, great danger and great love. I remembered her words clearly. The only person who knew that we would stand before the statue was Byron himself. He had led me there.

I was shaking now from head to toe and knelt in front of the chair, my hands on Hadrian's thick fur. "It can't be that," I whispered to the cat, who blinked at me. "No, no, not that."

Was I so overcome by my infatuation that I could not see the danger in front of my very face. Byron knew I had designs on the Blackstone property, even though the subject had been shoved to the back of our conversation. Had he been leading me on? Was it actually his intention to get rid of me? Had that statue been meant for me?

My head spun, and I wished I had some of the hot drink that was putting Byron to sleep, for I knew I would not shut my eyes this night. I thought of tiptoeing downstairs and pouring myself some sherry from the decanter in the parlor, but the thought of creeping about the house this late filled me with even more dread.

Hot tears moistened my cheeks as the confusion spun in my head. Hadrian seemed to sense my distress and licked my salty tears. I curled up in a heap for some time, but then when my tears seemed to run dry, I swallowed and sat up. I could make neither heads nor tails of what was happening. I wanted to leave, but I had nowhere to go.

As dawn began to break in the metallic sky, my grief turned into a numbing solitude. The wind had died, and the air was quite still now. No one could be awake but me. There was one thing I knew. I was not harmed. Byron lay injured in his bed, but he was not dead. His injury would heal. Whatever evil lurked here, there was a slim chance that it could be discovered.

By me? a small voice asked. *There's no one else,* I said aloud. I could not even be sure of Byron right now. Annie seemed to be a good friend, but I hardly knew her, and Mrs. MacDougal, with her odd-looking eye, made me feel as if she disapproved of me, though I tried to tell myself that physiognomy was not really a reliable way of judging character.

Eliza was far away and couldn't help me anyway, even if she were here. I wished more fervently for Rosa. She would know what to do. In the end it was thinking of Rosa that gave me the courage to face what I had to face. She had warned me against danger, but also of fortune and love. I might have been falling in love, but there was no sign of the fortune she spoke of. She had wanted me to come here. She had given me the money to come. I knew Rosa loved me and she wouldn't have wanted me to come on a journey that would end badly. Perhaps, then, she had meant me to face the danger, root out the evil.

Some sort of consolation settled over me as the sky turned a moulten pink. I pulled the curtains shut and climbed into my bed, pulling the covers over me. Hadrian settled himself on the pillow by my head, and I reached up to let my hand rest on his silky fur. If I were to find out the answers to the many riddles that had assailed me during the night I needed sleep. And at last, sleep came.

No one woke me—perhaps it was thought that I needed rest after the ordeal of the night before. One person, I thought grimly when I rose late in midday, knew just what an ordeal I was going through. Even curses have their human agents. None of the Worthington heirs had been struck down by lightning. Each had met an all too human adversary. Whoever had made that statue fall did so with a human body, and whether the culprit meant to knock the breath from my body or Byron's, it had to be someone on the estate, or someone near enough to watch us. It was my task to discover who harbored such a murderous heart and why.

By the time I dressed and went to look in on Byron, he was not there. Mrs. MacDougal was fluffing up his pillows. When I came in she turned and shook her head, clucking her tongue.

"If it's the master yer lookin' for, he's not here. Refused to stay in bed past noon. Said it was useless to stay in bed, that he could recuperate just as well downstairs."

"I see." I slipped out and went downstairs.

I found him in his big leather chair, poring over some correspondence.

"Good morning," I said. "I didn't know you would be working today. The doctor said—"

He tossed the papers he had been reading onto the desk with a grunt. "I know what the doctor said. Damned nuisance this thing."

He winced with pain as he moved. If he had purposely lured me under that statue, he had certainly been the one to suffer for it. He glanced up at me.

"I can see by the circles under your eyes that you did not sleep well last night."

I moved rigidly, as if guarding myself.

The pain on his face was so real that my heart constricted. I decided that my suspicions that he himself might be somehow at the bottom of the accident were entirely foolish. I had to stop myself from reaching out to smooth his brow.

But someone had pushed the statue over. Who?

Byron got himself into a more comfortable position, and I crossed to look out the window. He cleared his throat.

"You . . . one of us could have been killed last night," I said. I saw no reason to mince words. When I turned, I saw the grim line across his forehead.

"I am aware of that," he said. "I am looking into it."

"How?" I didn't mean to challenge his authority, but I needed to know what he was doing.

"I am questioning all of the servants, for one thing. And anyone who might have been on the estate."

"I see."

102

I would have liked to have been in on these interviews, but I doubted there was much chance for that. I told him Effram had been the first one to the scene after my scream.

"Is Effram completely deaf?" I asked.

Byron nodded. "To my knowledge. You raise an interesting point. However, Effram has been known to prowl the grounds at night as well as during the day. He seems to regard the gardens as his. If there was something he wanted to see to, no matter what the hour, he would do it."

He went on. "I don't believe there is cause for alarm. I would take ordinary precautions, if I were you," he said. "But other than that . . ."

His attempt to reassure me sounded weak, even to himself it seemed. I met his gaze.

"If you think that a single incident such as this will send me running back to Nottingham, then you are wrong. I am of course more than interested in what is going on here. We have not determined which of us that statue was meant to harm."

"Then you are not convinced that last night was an attempt to carry out the so-called curse hanging over my head?"

I cocked my head. "It might have been."

"But you're not sure."

"No, I am not. It might have been that someone wanted to harm me. Perhaps someone does not want me here."

Instead of a heated denial, he pulled the corner of his lip back in a gesture of irony. "I have thought of that."

"Who might that be?" I said slowly.

"I cannot imagine."

My eyes narrowed slightly. Ridiculous as it might be, there could be someone besides Sir Byron who was threatened by my supposed claim to Blackstone Castle.

He lightened his tone. "Take today off from your work," he said. "I am in no mood for business. Perhaps tomorrow."

Tomorrow—after he had had a chance to finish inter-

103

viewing the servants—I thought. "Very well. I believe I will take a walk."

"I would feel better if you stayed within sight of the house then, until this little matter of the accident is cleared up."

"If you wish." As I recalled, the house could be seen from almost any spot up to the moor.

I left him rearranging his desk with one hand, and as I was on the way to my room to put on sturdy walking boots I ran into Annie. She had been dusting the chair rail, almost as if she had been waiting for me, for when she saw me, she put down her rag and approached me, twisting her hands as if she didn't know what to do with them.

"What is it Annie?"

"Well, I was wondering something, miss. About your lace."

I smiled at her. "What about the lace?"

"Well, you know how to make it."

I nodded.

"Well, Sophie and me, we was wonderin', if it wouldn't be too much trouble, that is. Could you show us how to do it some time?"

Her face was red, as if it had cost her a great effort to ask, and I immediately tried to put her at her ease. "Of course, Annie. I would love to show you and Sophie. When you're finished with your work? After dinner?"

She nodded vigorously. "Yes, yes. We'd be ever so grateful."

"I just purchased some new thread and bobbins."

I thought perhaps we could work in my room by the fireplace, but Annie's screwed-up expression told me that idea was not appropriate. I had to do some wheedling to understand why.

"Well," she finally said. "Mrs. MacDougal overheard us talking about it. She didn't come right out and say, but I think she wouldn't mind learnin' something of it herself. Not that she would ask outright. She said she didn't mind if we watched, that it wouldn't hurt none."

"Oh, I understand. Well then, I'll bring my things down to the kitchen after supper. There'll be more room there, and Mrs. MacDougal and Cook can watch, too, if they please."

The big table where the servants took meals would be a good place to work. Annie seemed pleased, and the matter of where we would work being resolved, she returned to her dusting with a smile on her face.

I put on sturdy walking boots, my coat, and a furry hat and went outside. I went first along the path that led to the fallen statue. I did not see Effram anywhere. The statue had been dragged over near its pedestal.

I looked at conceivable places to hide. There were several shrubs. It had been night, even if moonlit. It would not have been hard for almost anyone to conceal themselves behind the statue and crouch beneath the pedestal after Byron had been knocked to the ground. But if the statue really had been intended for Byron, then why? There was no jealous heir to the title waiting in the wings that I knew of. Had Byron done something to someone now wanting revenge? How would I ever find out?

If, on the other hand, the accident had been meant for me, I had to consider that someone wanted me out of the way. My claims to Blackstone Castle seemed so flimsy, even to me, that I could not imagine anyone taking them seriously. Byron certainly did not. This brought me again to the idea that perhaps Byron did not take my claims as lightly as he seemed to. Was I so enamored of his charm that I was unable to see any malice in him?

I circled the statue until my footsteps had nearly worn a path, but all my speculations were merely that. I had nothing else to go on. The only glimmer of a thought that occurred to me that day was this: Perhaps I had more claim to the Blackstone estate than I knew. Besides a moldering ruin of a castle, perhaps there really was something of value. Were I to win my claim, might it be worth something, after all? There was the estate, of course. The pastures and the fields that Byron rented out to tenants. I could understand that he himself would not like to be unseated from even such a modest claim. But when I tried to match the kind of covert evil that had to accompany an act such as that of last night with the warm, dry humor of the man I was coming to know better all the time, I failed to rouse myself to point an accusing finger.

No. It had to be someone else. If so, this someone must know something of the Blackstone claim, perhaps even something Byron did not know. I had widened my path around the statue until I made a tour of the gardens. The steps seemed to help my logic. Finally, I left the gardens through an opening in one of the hedges and struck a path along the woods behind.

The path I took led eventually into the woods. I was deep in thought and giving little heed to where I was going until I heard the lilting sound of a flute. Drifting to me through the trees the music almost made me feel as if I had lost my way and had wandered into some fairyland. I followed the entrancing sound, sometimes losing it, then hearing it again.

The trees thinned again, and now, in between the melodies played on the flute, I could hear a voice I recognized, singing. I ducked under a branch and stepped into a clearing where I saw Raoule, sitting on the ground, his back against a thick tree trunk, singing and waving the flute. He put the instrument to his lips and poured forth some dancing notes. As he saw me approach, a smile lit his eyes as he moved his head in rhythm with his song. When he stopped, I clapped and sat down on the ground beside him.

"I should have known it would be you," I said. "Did you lure me here like the Pied Piper?"

He laughed. "I had hoped my song would find you," he said.

"Do play something else," I said. "The music is soothing."

"As you wish."

He put the flute to his lips and this time played a haunting, slow melody. The tune had the yearning quality I always associated with Gypsy music, and I was quite able to forget myself as Raoule's spell dropped over me. The last note died away, and he put the flute in the leather scabbard he had for it.

"Enough music," he said. "Come. You are out for a walk, are you not? We shall walk. And you will tell me what is on your mind."

It was easy to talk to Raoule. He seemed the nearest thing to a friend that I had in this place. I told him what had happened, and he stopped to stare at me when he realized how near I had come to harm. He uttered a string of words I did not understand.

"Sorry," he said. "I speak in the Gypsy language, Romany, when I am angry. I thought you would be safe with Sir Byron." He shook his head. "I have been remiss, then. It was Rosa's wish that I watch over you."

I gave him a little laugh. "But, Raoule, you cannot possibly watch me every minute, especially when I am at the manor. You are with your sheep, are you not?"

He gave me a sidelong glance I could not interpret. "I have ways. But, alas, last night I was elsewhere. And Sir Byron, is he all right?"

"He will mend."

While I had been feeling so comforted a moment ago, now a fearful thought occurred to me. Raoule himself seemed to slip about the region unexpectedly. Could he have been in the garden last night? But I did not dwell on this horrid possibility, for we had come into the open and Raoule was pointing out the direction we would go.

"But first, wait."

He walked back among the trees, poking about the underbrush. Finally he pulled forth a long stick and broke off the smaller branches from it. He handed me the stouter end, and I could see it was perfect for a walking stick.

"The hills are steep," he said. "You will find that the stick, which is light to carry, is strong and will help you pull yourself up."

He was right. For we began an ascent over rather rough

terrain, and the stick was a great help. We left the trees far behind and climbed upward through bleak pastures, bordered with stone fences. We came to a very deep ditch, grassy now, but we crossed it where it had been filled in and beaten down. I was so intent on keeping my footing that I didn't look up until we were on the other side where the remains of a road ran along a steep embankment. I looked up, realizing now where we were. Of course, we had come to the Roman Wall.

"This way," said Raoule. "There is a plateau up there from where you can see everything."

We climbed the last embankment to where it leveled out. Here were large square blocks cast about what Raoule explained were the ruins of a mile castle, one of the stations along the Wall where the Romans had garrisoned and kept supplies. The Wall itself, about six or seven feet high by about the same width, stretched across the ridge where we stood, disappeared for a few yards in a belt of stunted, bristling woodland on the verge of a precipice, buttressed by a natural cliff, then it dipped. It reappeared, dipped down and then rose again, following the line of hills as far as the eye could see in both directions. I could see now the abrupt declivities and sharp crags over which the Wall marched relentlessly. A line that marked the edge of the Roman Empire in its time, and the end of civilization.

Raoule led me up some remaining steps of what looked like had once been a tower. There was a flat space where we could stand and contemplate the impressive sight, and Raoule refrained from intruding on my thoughts. I had not realized how immense the country looked from here, both to the north and south. Far away in the cut of the hills, I could see rooftops, but so small I felt as if we stood in a world where humanity counted for little, where nature and the mysteries of the past were everything. And why would humanity want to venture farther northward than this, I asked myself.

Clumps of heather and moss grew in large patches, but the barren waste stretched endlessly. The wind sighed, and I could almost feel the presence of the Roman sentinels that had paced this lonely summit guarding the frontier. I shivered, thinking of the claims that they still did.

To the west I could see the clear lake we had passed on the way to Blackstone Castle, and I pointed it out to Raoule. Now, the westering sun had turned it to a sheet of gold.

"Aye, 'tis clear by day, but black as pitch at night," he said. "That's when the specters dance on the ice." He said it matter-of-factly, as if they were merely part of the landscape.

Raoule returned down the steps and bent to poke among some loose rubble. I could imagine that this must have been a treasure trove of artifacts left behind by the Romans when they finally gave up the defense, but surely everything of value had been carried off by now. Raoule muttered to himself, then stood, turning something over in his hands. I went down the steps to see what he had found.

He held out the arrowhead, and I took it in my hand. Though worn from weather and time, its shape was unmistakable. I almost imagined I held the entire arrow used by some infantryman. Or perhaps the arrowhead had been shot over the Wall by one of the Picts. I handed it back to Raoule, who tossed it up and caught it in his fist, then put it in his pocket.

"Might fetch a coin or too," he said. "A souvenir."

If I were to believe that the spirits of the long gone Romans still hovered, it would be in such a place. Yet how could one fear such ghostly sentinels, bent only on duty and keeping the savages out.

"I've never seen a place like this," I said to Raoule.

He lifted his face to the endless expanse before us. "It is a good place to come to."

I wondered about the Gypsies and their ways, and on our descent, I asked Raoule about them, confessing that I was fascinated with the Gypsy customs I had learned from Rosa, but that not being a Gypsy I supposed there was much about their culture I would not understand. Raoule was not at all offended by my questions and was quite loquacious on the subject.

His band was mostly shepherds and tinkers. They were tolerated here in this part of Britain because of their ways with animals. They had skills that the Northumberland farmers needed.

"You must come to our camp one night," he said. "You can sing and dance with us."

I promised I would, for I was always deeply moved by Gypsy music. We neared the fields again. Raoule bid me good-bye and turned off into the woods near where I had found him. From here the path led directly to the gardens. I remembered then that Byron had bid me stay in sight of the house. For the most part I had, for the manor was visible from the top of the wall. If someone had cared to watch me, they would know I had ascended the heights with a Gypsy shepherd.

"How shall I find you?" I asked, remembering his invitation to visit his camp.

"A signal. A light in your window and I will come to the end of the garden."

"Then you can see . . . ?"

He gave a nod. He had said he would watch over me. I wondered now just how closely he watched.

As I walked back, it seemed to have gotten colder, and I was glad to reach the house. Upstairs in my room I sorted out the things I would need to show the other women how to make lace. I dined in my room, and then went down to the kitchen.

Annie awaited me eagerly, having cleared off the work table for us. Sophie smiled shyly and looked with great curiosity as I laid out the stiff parchment on which the pattern had already been drawn, pins, bobbins and finally the pillow, the rounded board stuffed to form a cushion. I had brought enough for all of us.

Mrs. MacDougal already sat by the fire, embroidering. She gave her odd sideways glance as I showed the two girls what everything was, but then she returned to her work.

Louisa joined us, and we all sat down and placed the pillows on our knees. I showed them how to pick out the outline of the drawing, sticking the pins at close intervals. Then we took up the bobbins and wound the thread around the pins, twisting and crossing to form the various meshes and openings. Then we took the heavier thread and interwove it.

At first Mrs. MacDougal simply glanced our way each time I introduced a new step. Finally she laid down her embroidery and watched, her head tilted at an angle so she could see better. I knew she wouldn't ask, so I handed her my piece and let her have a try.

There was much pricking of fingers and tangling of threads, and Louisa kept exclaiming in French, but I could see that Annie had the knack. I told them that if they practiced, they could become accomplished. Besides being a livelihood for those in the factories, lacemaking was a pastime of gentlewomen who had the time and patience to produce real works of art. Just how much Annie and the others could accomplish on their free time would depend on their dedication.

Somewhere in the house a clock struck ten, and Annie dropped her work, looking up in surprise.

"I must go . . . to bed now, if you'll excuse me."

From her bright, rounded eyes, I did not think she looked sleepy, but I said of course she must go. I told her to take her work with her to her room. I didn't need the bobbin just now.

"Oh, I . . . all right," she said. "Well, I'll just leave it here for now." She got up, wiping her hands on her apron. "I must just see about something . . . in the pantry."

I blinked—she left so suddenly. Sophie bent farther over her work, but I thought from her expression that she must know where Annie was going. Mrs. MacDougal furrowed her thick brows and drew her lips into a firm line. I mumbled something about it being late and got up.

As I was gathering up my things I caught a flash of white skirt going out the door. Annie. She must be going to a

111

rendezvous. That would explain the reactions in the kitchen. I had seen her with Robin once or twice, deep in conversation.

Were they courting then? Somehow I had felt displeasure imagining the spritely maid with the distant stablehand who always looked at me as if he were taking my measure. But it was none of my business. If she found the young man attractive, who was I to criticize? Hadn't I lost my own head over a man I suspected was not right for me?

Mrs. MacDougal handed me back the pillow with the piece of work she had tangled up.

"Takes nimble fingers, this. I'll stick to my embroidery, thank you."

Nine

Byron was impatient with his arm, and much of my time working with him was spent trying to make his paperwork easier without making him feel the invalid. We spent the mornings taking care of business, and I became more and more fascinated by the complex workings of an estate the size of this one.

In the afternoons he consulted with me about some redecorating of the house. When he had first asked me about making lace for him I thought it might be because he felt sorry for me and, knowing that I would not take charity, he saw how he could make me feel useful. But now I saw it was more than that. Many of the rooms were badly in need of redoing, for some, particularly on the third floor, had not been used for some time. Some of the curtains were faded and needed replacing. Tablecloths of various sizes were needed. My imagination took hold, and I spent many an hour sitting with my work in the informal parlor, in the kitchen or in my room.

Those were pleasant days. I was being productive and I felt that Byron needed me. I was never entirely easy, but I grew used to the strange sounds at night and managed to put the Worthington curse at the back of my mind. I remained watchful, using my time spent over the lace to listen to other people's conversations, to observe the goings on in the house. But besides Annie's slipping out sometimes at night, I noticed nothing untoward.

At the end of two weeks, I found myself with a morning free, as Byron had gone to Carlisle the day before to see about some business there. I decided to ride out alone. I thought perhaps I would run into Raoule, but even if I did not, it did not matter. I was used to Theo now, having ridden her to the village several times. So I went to the barn to ask Robin to saddle her for me.

"Ridin' out alone, are ye?" he asked.

"Just for a short ride."

I still felt as if he did not approve of my horsewomanship. He saddled her for me, and I watched carefully, thinking I might need to do it myself someday. Then he led Theo to the mounting block in the stable yard and handed me the reins. The mare stood still while I got to the seat.

"Thank you, Robin," I said affecting a manner of dismissal.

I thought his look mocked me and wondered if perhaps he did not like me because in truth we were not of dissimilar stations in life, but I was being given more privileges than I deserved.

I did not see how Robin could harbor such a resentful manner all the time. Animals he worked with did not seem to be mistreated. I was thoughtful as I rode Theo out the gate and took the path that led up to the sheep pastures.

I knew servants had a way of knowing things even their masters did not tell them, and they loved to gossip.

Maybe he knew my claim to the Blackstone heritage and disliked me for it. I shook my head. I did not really know. I got along well enough with the two maids, and Louisa seemed pleasant. Mrs. MacDougal tolerated me as long as I demonstrated I was not afraid of a good day's work. But I had yet to win over Robin.

I rode up to the pastures, Theo's hooves crunching on the frosty ground. But for once the sun filtered through a hazy sky, and there was little wind. I saw a flock of wooly

114

sheep on a distant hill, but I could not see a shepherd. If Raoule was aware of my presence he did not show himself. But I did not care. I had been couped up with people for a fortnight, and I rather relished the time alone.

The gentle mare and I had a good rapport, and I barely had to use the reins. She seemed to know where we were going. As we left the neatly cultivated fields behind and went up to the moorlands, I let her pick her way, so she wouldn't twist her ankle in a hidden hole. Finally we came to the path that led to the castle. We slowly closed the distance, crossing the bare pastures where gorse and low scrub struggled against the west wind.

We came to the footbridge over the moat and I reined in to take in the sight of the towering ruin above me. A wind wafted over the moor and I thought I heard flute music. I could see no one, but it sounded like Raoule. Of course in these wide spaces, sound might carry a great distance.

I crossed the moat and rode around the slope that encircled the castle, for I wanted to observe it from every angle. Although it still filled me with a sense of pride to be standing before the home of my ancestors, I had to admit the castle was quite moldering. Still, with some repairs, parts of it could be put back to use. An idea had formed in my head that I wanted to broach with Byron, but I had wanted to make a closer observation of the part of the castle in the least disrepair before I said anything.

From what Stanley Symmes had said to me and what Byron agreed must be his purpose here, it seemed reasonable to assume that the railroad was going to be extended into Scotland at this point to compete with the eastern line. If that happened, the railroad would bring hundreds of travelers into Hevingham. What if the castle were made into an inn for visitors?

A carriage could meet guests and drive them to the castle. From here they could tour the Roman Wall. There was enough nature about to attract outdoor types, and I could imagine the colors of the wildflowers on the moor in summer. As I dismounted and climbed over some rubble to the steps leading to the main arched entry, I became excited over the idea. I made my way across the courtyard, smiling to myself.

I was in the main entry hall when I heard the music again. It seemed to come from above me, and I peered upward, half expecting to see Raoule perched on some ledge. He had a way of turning up unexpectedly, and I was so used to the sly Gypsy ways that it would not surprise me in the least if he appeared out of nowhere.

I still saw no one, but the main staircase seemed in good enough repair that I held on to the stone banister and mounted to the second floor. The music wafted in and out as if changing direction with the wind. Then I froze. I distinctly heard the sound of a tambourine, the plucked strings of a lute, and the long, low moan of a viol.

I knew instinctively that the sound was coming from behind chipped and peeled double doors in front of me, and I moved forward slowly. I grasped the rusty door handle and pushed inward.

Voices laughed. Rich turquoise, crimson, gold, purple flashed. A courtier in a dark purple doublet, hose and silver ruff bowed, his long dark hair falling over his shoulder. I gasped, so real was the scene. It started to fade as I stepped onto the ballroom floor where the wood was rotten. Then I screamed as I fell into emptiness.

A bundle of straw broke my fall, but my shoulder hit the edge of a trestle table, and I rolled onto the stone floor, stunned.

I must have lain there some time until the pain turned into a dull throbbing and I caught my breath again. I could move my limbs, and could turn my wrists, but I was shaken. I pulled myself onto the straw to rest, frightened that I could have been killed. I looked at the hole in the floor above me. If it hadn't been for the strange vision I had had I would have watched where I was stepping, and I chastised myself for being so careless. What had I been trying to do, step back in time?

The answer to that question, when I considered it later was yes. One does not have such strong psychic connections with some time past without trying to explore them. But as I lay there, hurting, all I could think about was making sure I had not been seriously injured.

The light on this floor was considerably less, and as the day lenghthened, the shadows became deeper and deeper. Finally I pulled myself up, standing beside the trestle table, testing my footing.

Then to my great surprise I heard an insistent "meow," and looked up to see Hadrian sitting in the doorway to the room.

"Hadrian," I said. "How did you get here?"

He shifted his weight on his paws and reseated himself, looking into the room, his fur arched. I was surprised that he had walked this far. But I had not seen him at the manor in the last few days, and thought that possibly he did wander far and wide.

"Come here, Hadrian," I said, reaching out a hand. But in the independent way cats have, he ignored me and circled the room, sniffing at corners.

When I persuaded myself that I was whole, I limped toward Hadrian and lifted him up. "Come on, my friend. We can't stay here forever."

Going out, I found that we were in a series of chambers that led one to the other. There were no windows here, but some gray light filtered through from the holes in the walls and the floors overhead. Forgetting my scrapes, I felt a renewed interest in the place.

The hinges had rusted off most of the doors, but I came to one heavy timber door with wrought iron hardware that looked newer than the rest. I tried the door handle and the door squeaked open. Steps led downward. I was not tempted to go there, but Hadrian leapt out

117

of my arms and crying loudly, he ran down the stairs.

"Hadrian, come back here."

But he simply sat on the bottom step and looked back at me as if beckoning me to follow. He would not come, so I finally stepped onto the stone stairs that wound downward. They seemed in good repair, so I went down to pick up the recalcitrant feline.

I heard the squeak of hinges and turned just in time to see the door close above me.

"Hello," I called. "Is someone there?"

My heart bounced against my ribs. Could the wind have shut the door? I tried to tell myself so, even though I was aware of the weight of the door. Or was someone else in the castle?

I tried the steps again, my hand on the cold stone wall as my shaking legs carried me back up.

"Hello, hello," I called as loudly as I could, but the sound seemed to bounce back at me from the thick wooden door. It wouldn't budge.

I had momentarily forgotten Hadrian, and when I felt the tickle of fur on my leg I jumped. But his loud "meow" gave me comfort, if only to let me know I wasn't absolutely alone in this pitch black chamber. For here, no holes let through any light whatsoever.

My apprehension turned to terror, and I pressed my head against the door. Then I took several breaths, willing my mind to think. I had to find a way out. Perhaps the door would open from the inside.

There was no handle, but I felt along the edge for a hold. The door was rough, giving me many splinters, but after a great deal of time, I had to admit that I couldn't get it open. Pushing did no good. It felt as if it were bolted in place from the other side.

"All right, Hadrian," I said to the cat, just to hear my own voice. "We can't get out this way. Perhaps there is another way."

I reasoned that the lower chamber had to lead somewhere. Perhaps I would find another passage. Or I might come to a hole in a wall. If this dungeon was anything like the rest of the place, the likelihood of breaking out was great. I picked up Hadrian, and he clung to my shoulder, digging in with his claws. I did not think he liked the darkness any better than I.

Feeling as if I were stepping into my own grave, I held Hadrian with one hand, used the other to guide myself down the stairs and walked downward, step by step.

I did not stop where Hadrian had waited for me. The staircase curved around, ever downward. I wished I had brought a lantern. It had been stupid to come here without one. If I had expected to move toward more light, I was mistaken. We came to the bottom of the steps, and I moved slowly along the passage, clutching Hadrian to my shoulder. I tried to keep myself from panicking, repeating to myself over and over again that we would come to another way out.

Eventually we did come to a corner where the passage seemed to turn, and the very change encouraged me to some degree. From somewhere in the distance I could hear water dripping, and I moved in that direction. The sound grew louder, and at last the ground under me began to rise.

Then all the hope drained away as I thought I heard a rustle behind me.

"Hello," I called tentatively.

Hadrian tensed, and I decided that what I had heard must be a rat. I held onto the cat, not wanting to let him get into a confrontation. The rustling stopped and I moved forward again, this time more quickly. But the sound continued to follow me, and I began to hurry even more, as if whatever it was was pursuing me.

Fear now gripped me uncontrollably as I came to some steps leading upward. I fled up them, hardly noticing that this passage seemed lighter. When my hand scraped along a door I almost dropped the cat in relief. But though I tugged at the handle, it would not budge.

A sob of hysteria rose in my throat and I struggled to breathe deeply. Surely if there was one door there would be others.

"This way, Hadrian," I said, carrying him up more steps.

I was right, for a crack of light ahead told me there was indeed a way out of this tomb. I reached the door, grasped the rusted handle and flung it open to a dimly lit chamber. So great was my relief that I dropped Hadrian and closed the door behind us, falling against its splintery surface, sobbing in the aftermath.

As soon as I recovered, I wiped my hands on my skirt and walked around the room we were in. Some beams lay across the stone floor, and looking upward I could see where they had once supported the ceiling. An open archway led into another chamber, so I gathered Hadrian, who was by now meowing, but did not resist coming with me.

My troubles were not over, however, for the chamber I found myself in led to another and another. There was no central passage, rather a series of small rooms that seemed to lay in a circular pattern, leading me back to the room where I had started. I thought I would never find a stairway upward when I finally came to a dim passage I had missed before.

I hesitated to venture into darkness again, but as soon as I set my foot on the bottom steps, I saw a shaft of light above me, and clinging to Hadrian almost as hard as he clung to me, I climbed. The sunlight came from a small window at ground level, and I almost cried for joy when we reached it. If I had to, I could crawl out this way.

But I saw ahead of me that this would be unnecessary. A few more steps above me was a heavy oak door, and I ran toward it. I heard what sounded like someone wearing heavy boots walking quickly on the other side, and with a cry, I flung open the door and nearly collided with Byron.

We both gasped and stood for a moment staring wide-eyed at each other. He was dressed in a tweed riding clothes and carrying his crop.

"Heather, where have you been?" he asked.

Then I was in his arms, sobbing in relief. "I . . . I got lost. Hadrian was with me. A door shut behind me and I couldn't get back out that way."

I babbled on, making no sense, as Byron held me tightly. Hadrian circled our feet meowing.

"You're all right now, Heather," he said, his hands caressing my face, wiping away my tears. "Though you should not have come here alone."

It was only then that I noticed his arm was no longer in the sling.

"Your shoulder," I said. "Why aren't you wearing the sling?"

"Damn nuisance, that. It's been two weeks. The shoulder is well enough."

I stood back from him now, examining him as if he were the patient. "But the doctor said you should not ride. He told me—"

Byron cut me off. "That was last week. I'm not about to sit around like an invalid. I've too many things to do."

Then we touched each other tentatively, as if assuring ourselves that the other was all right. Finally he led me out of the castle. I blinked in the sunlight, and as we crossed the courtyard and walked down the slope to the edge of the moat, I was never so grateful to be in the light of day.

We sat down on the short grasses, and I told Byron my idea about restoring part of the castle and making it into an inn. At first he listened to me with a modicum of seriousness, then he laughed.

He grasped my hand as he chuckled. "My brave Heather. No sooner have you escaped the dungeons of the castle than you want to renovate it." He shook his head.

121

"What a study in contradictions you are, always full of surprises."

I was miffed that he did not really take me seriously, and I tried to argue.

"If the railroad is going through to Scotland, surely there will be more visitors to Hevingham. You said yourself you would not mind seeing tourism boost the economy of the village. Why not offer visitors a reason to stay here?"

I shook my head, gesturing to the shades of nature that surrounded us, the blue of the sky melting into the gray-green of the distant hills, the translucence of the lake far below us.

"You take it for granted," I said. "You have not been confined to a small, dirty space in a filthy, noisy city all your life. You do not know what it is to escape to these endless spaces, stark as they may be to some."

There was more resentment in my voice than I had meant to show. I stopped talking, not liking to reveal so much of my feelings when he was not about to understand, but I had underestimated him.

He nodded more soberly, looking about us at the folds in the hills below, the long line of the ancient Roman Wall crawling dauntlessly across the ridges. "You are right," he said. "It is beautiful."

He chuckled softly. "For fifteen hundred years this land was fought over by Roman, Viking, Saxon, Norman and Scot. Now the Northumbrians and the sheep have it to themselves. Perhaps you are right. We should share it."

I breathed deeply, glad that he could share my appreciation. Something about the clear air and the height made the spirit rise, and awareness began to flow between Byron and me. The feelings that had ignited between us when we'd first met had not died. Here on the moor, unhampered by the strictures and civilities in the manor house, my plans and dreams took over, and they spawned the lush craving that flowed between us.

122

He must have felt it too. The wind blew at my disheveled hair, threatening to loosen the remaining pins. His eyes fastened hungrily on mine, and a surge of desire blossomed within me. In spite of all the dangers that had threatened us, it seemed at that moment as if we were destined to be together.

I had not slept a night without waking up, aware of his presence in the house, my body warm with unspoken desire that I suspected he could fulfill as he almost had that night in the gallery.

We leaned into each other then. His mouth covered mine, and my head bent back as he scooped me into his arms. I pressed against him, only then realizing how constrained I had felt in the house and how watchful I had been of touching him since his injury.

"Heather," he said, as he lifted his head, his kisses dusting over my face. "You don't know how badly I want you," he said.

The deep rich words plumbed my soul, and I responded. I had been badly frightened. Byron was a refuge, and I wanted nothing more than to quench the thirst I had for him.

Then he gave me his ironic smile. "Being trussed up like a chicken has kept me away from you. But I'm free of that restriction now."

"I . . ." my voice came out breathlessly, but I did not have the words to express what I was feeling. He knew though. He saw the desire in my eyes.

"Heather," he said, his voice full of emotion. "I cannot keep myself from you, from what's grown between us."

He pulled his fingers through my hair as we kissed hungrily. His urgency growing, he fumbled with the buttons on my bodice, and my hands moved of their own accord inside his jacket.

"Come," he said, pulling me up and gesturing with his chin toward a stand of trees across the footbridge.

I followed him, and we led the horses. He took a blanket from where it was tied behind his saddle, and laid it on the ground. There he discarded his jacket and we sank onto the blanket, cushioned by the soft moorland grass. He leaned his back against a tree trunk and I reclined beside him, my elbow supporting me. For a while we remained silent. Then he reached to run his fingers through my hair.

I did not know if it was right to take such joy in his presence, but I could not describe the thrill I felt beside him. Then he turned me so that I faced him as I wrapped my arms around his neck.

I clung to him as his mouth and tongue worked their magic on mine and his fingers on my bodice finished what they had begun. The fire began to burn in my flesh. His voice was deeper, more husky now as he murmured into my ear, pushing my bodice off my shoulders.

The wind brushed across my naked shoulders, but my blood warmed me, and I felt one with the nature around us. When he gazed upon me, his face filled with emotion, and I could see the desire flooding through him.

"Lie beside me," he said, enticing me to spread myself on the blanket where he held me.

My hands sought him as he sought me. I shook with pleasure. We became flesh upon flesh, pleasure seeking pleasure. Finally he lay on top of me, calling my name. "This will hurt a little, my darling," he said. "But love will overcome the hurt."

My body throbbed at his words, so that the pain was quickly numbed with the newness, and the joy I felt at giving him so much pleasure surmounted my own discomfort as I accustomed myself to this new wonder.

I clung to his back as he held me tightly, his own body moving, thrusting, drinking in what he had waited for for so long.

"My beauty, you set me on fire," he said as he moved faster and faster until I thought he would drive me into the ground with an immense shudder of release.

We both breathed heavily, and then after some moments, he lightened his weight on me and pulled aside, still caressing me, kissing me gently, arranging my skirts, brushing my hair with his fingers. He curled an arm over me, and I lay against him, speechless.

So I had finally given myself to this man. I supposed now I was his mistress. The thought that he was, in a way, still my rival did not change anything.

After a length of time I could not guess, he rolled on his other side and plucked a wildflower, turning back to me and twirling it by its stem. He smiled into my eyes.

"Heather, what joy you have given me." Then he laughed that deep laugh I had come to treasure. "And I can see by the glow about your face that it was the same for you."

I blushed as he held me against him, my head tucked under his chin. "Ah, glorious days," he said.

At length, he let me go and leaned on one elbow musing at me. "The castle," he said. "It means very much to you, does it not?"

I lay on my back, looking through the leaves above us at the metallic sky above. "I have strange feelings when I am there," I said. "It's as if . . ." I hesitated. "As if I've been there before. In some other lifetime."

I turned my head to look into his face. "Have you ever experienced such a thing?"

He looked at me whimsically for a moment, then raised his eyes to look at the castle dominating the hill above us. He narrowed his eyes thoughtfully. I would have paid a dear price to know what he was thinking. But then he looked down at me again and smiled.

"No," he said. "That would be impossible."

I studied his expression, but what he was really thinking was unfathomable. I sat up, leaning on my elbows. I came back to my idea of restoration.

"You may laugh," I said. "But it is a good idea. It could pay for itself. If I had money . . ." I said.

125

"Hmmph. I am not laughing. It is not a bad idea. But the truth is I haven't any capital for such a project. The Worthington fortunes have long since gone the way of my ancestors. I'm afraid my hands are full managing the tenant farms on the estate."

I did have to admire his dedication to running the estate smartly. If it were true that his ancestors had squandered the fortune, he was making up for it by his careful attention to financial matters.

I sighed. I supposed he was right. It was just a dream. Only my stubbornness would not let me give up. I thought again of the Blackstone claim. Was it perhaps no more than legend? I would perhaps never have the proof. I could not make Byron do anything with the castle. But what if it were mine?

Ten

December brought colder weather. It was too cold to walk on the moors, but there was so much to do in preparation for Christmas festivities I did not miss my outdoor excursions. Together with Annie, Sophie and Mrs. MacDougal, I helped put up boughs of green cut by Effram and Robin.

We fashioned Christmas decorations out of dried berries, ribbon, nuts and pieces of felt. Annie was quite talented and designed some quaint little figures with painted faces on wood carvings that Robin had made. Angels, elves, and fairies danced about the greenery. But as I was handing the decorations up to her, I picked up one little figure that looked more like a troll than an elf. He was nearly square-shaped, and the face she had painted was twisted with a hateful look.

"Annie, did you make this one? He looks so unhappy."

She took it in her hand and gave a little gasp, nearly dropping it. "Why, no, miss. I never would have painted such a bad-looking face."

Her face seemed to go pale, and I was afraid she would teeter off the bench she was standing on.

"Here," I said. "Give it to me."

She handed it down. "I wonder where it came from."

Her lips seemed to tighten, and her brow furrowed in agitation. "I can't imagine. I'm sure I've never seen it."

And she turned back to her work. I put the little troll back into the box of decorations, covering it with some cotton. I should have thrown it in the fireplace. I was curious as to where it had come from, but there was so much distraction about the house that I didn't have time to think about it.

With the holiday season approaching, Byron began to entertain the other gentry in the county. When he was a guest, he would be gone for several nights, for the distances between large estates was often great. I told myself that the hollow feeling in my chest that I felt when he was gone was my longing for his presence. We had not had a rendezvous since the day by the castle, and I told myself he wanted to be discreet about our affair.

But he spent little time in my presence for the next two weeks, and I began to wonder if he regretted what had happened between us. Our conversations in his study were very formal and often interrupted by servants or callers. I tried to satisfy myself with all the blessings I seemed to have, and I reminded myself that Christmas was not the season to be greedy. Indeed I entered into preparations for the festivities with great enthusiasm. But there were moments when I was alone in a passage when I would hear a door slam, or see Byron's coattail disappear around a corner ahead, and I would feel a yearning in my heart that was hard to deny, for I was by now hopelessly in love with him.

We put off any further discussions about the castle. I knew that my future was in a sort of limbo. But there was much to think about, and I decided I need not worry about what to do with the rest of my life just yet. I thought perhaps I should forget Byron as a man and simply regard him as an employer. Certainly I had all the comfort and security here I needed. Byron would never marry me. I was too far beneath him in rank, and I had come to know that he was ever the traditionalist, even with his sometimes cynical views. I felt like a beggar, longing for a few crumbs of affection. I didn't even care about the trappings a real mistress had.

I remembered with distaste the proposition put before me by Mr. Biggleston. Such a business arrangement turned my stomach. No, it was only Byron himself that I wanted. But I had to force myself to face the fact that he did not love me. He was a man like any other man and had been tempted by the feelings that passed between us. Once satisfied, perhaps he did not need me in that way anymore. It crushed me to think so, but I had to consider the possibility that this might be true. I should have felt humiliated, but I didn't. Instead, as I lay in my bed every night that he was gone, I listened for his carriage to roll up to the door, listened for boot heels on the stairs and waited for a soft knock on my door. But he never came.

I had gone to the village with some fresh-baked bread for the vicar and his wife when I ran into Stanley Symmes again. He was standing on the church steps taking his leave of Reverend Brown. As soon as they both saw me, Mr. Symmes came to the road to help me down from the four-seated phaeton in which Robin drove me.

"Why, Miss Blackstone, what a pleasure to see you," said Mr. Symmes. "You are looking well. This cold Northumberland weather seems to agree with you."

"Thank you, Mr. Symmes. I am surprised to see you."

He handed me into the churchyard. "As a matter-of-fact I have just returned to Hevingham. Since we last spoke I have been traveling quite a bit. Er, um, on the business I spoke of."

"Of course." I tried not to show how interested I was in his business. "I am glad your work has brought you back this way."

"Are you now? Well, then I am flattered." He bent to kiss my hand.

"Are you staying long?"

"That depends." He gave me a sly look as if we had a secret between us.

I decided he must come to the manor house and talk to Byron. Perhaps if the two of them spoke, Byron would be more convinced that my idea of turning the castle into an inn was a good one.

"Then you must pay us a call at Worthington Manor. You must meet Sir Byron."

His brows shot up and his blue eyes widened slightly. "I would be honored."

"Please tell me where you are staying," I said, "so that I may send a proper invitation." I knew I could not ask him without Byron's approval.

"You can reach me at the Black Rook. I will be here until the day before Christmas Eve. Then I must return to Nottingham to be with my dear old mother."

"Of course."

"Well, now I'll be getting along. You will be wanting to talk to Reverend Brown. I had no intention of interrupting your visit."

He bid the reverend good-bye once again and then turned into the lane. He passed by the phaeton where Robin sat, straight as a rod on the front seat. I could not tell if Robin enjoyed his role as driver or not. His manner was still so distant with me I could never tell what he was thinking. Mr. Symmes walked past him without looking up.

Mrs. Brown had come out of the rectory, a small stone house with a slate roof, and bustled across to the churchyard.

"Why, Heather Blackstone, how are you, dear. Come in, come in. These men will keep you standing out in the cold."

"Good morning, Mrs. Brown. I've brought you some bread from the manor. Cook made it early this morning. It's still warm."

"Why then we must cut a slice and have it with tea."

I told Robin I would stay at the rectory awhile, for I knew he had to see to business at the blacksmith. Ladies

130

of fashion might keep their driver waiting in the cold while they took their ease in front of a warm fire, but even if Robin would pay me such deference, I would never do that. The three of us walked back to the little rectory. Inside, I hung my coat on the coat tree and took a seat by the cozy fire she had going in her stone fireplace. Reverend Brown had not been wearing an outer wrap, and he stood on the braided rug and rubbed his hands over the fire, as I admired the knicknacks on the oak mantle.

"I hope you don't mind the cold," he said. "People who haven't grown up in these parts aren't used to it."

I made myself comfortable in a cane rocker while Mrs. Brown puttered in her kitchen.

"I don't mind it," I said. I didn't go on to explain that since I'd lived at the manor house I always had warm clothes to wear, something I had not grown up with, and so I was always dressed for the cold climate.

"It's a busy time at the manor house, I imagine," he went on. "Christmas brings the village to life in our otherwise quiet winter," he said. "Much to do, much to do."

"I hope you and Mrs. Brown are coming to our party this Saturday evening." I knew they had been invited. "Cook is outdoing herself with goodies to taste. And there will be two punches, one with spirits and one without."

He gave me a wink. "You don't need to make a punch without spirits on my account," he said. "I don't mind imbibing in the name of a celebration. You can't have drunk as much communion wine as I have without developing a taste for it."

I smothered my laugh. Mrs. Brown brought in a tray and set it on the low coffee table. The sliced bread smelled heavenly, and we melted pieces of butter over it, topped with generous knifefuls of homemade preserves. I ate so much I would not need lunch, and I felt glad I had brought two loaves, since we had just made quick work of nearly all of one.

We talked with some enthusiasm about the party planned for the manor and about the village celebrations. Of course, Reverend Brown had many special services, and I thought that even as we sat there, his mind was wandering to the sermons he had to prepare. Indeed, he excused himself as soon as we had finished our refreshments, leaving me to gossip with Mrs. Brown.

I did not mean to be nosy, but she was so free with her information that I found myself leading her on and on about the Worthingtons. She asked me how I was getting on with the rest of the staff, and when I said that I still had the feeling that Mrs. MacDougal didn't approve of me, Mrs. Brown knit her brows.

"She's a strange one that. Always did rule the house with an iron hand. Don't take it to heart if you don't get on with her, dearie. It's nothing you're doin' or not doin', you can be sure of that. Some people just don't like any interference."

I told Mrs. Brown about Byron's accident. I suppose I wanted to know if she would see any evildoing, and if so from where it might have come. But she simply shook her head and clicked her tongue on her teeth, falling back on the Worthington curse as the cause of all the ill that befell the house.

"It's dreadful, the evil that's come upon that house. Poor Erlinda," she said, referring to Byron's late sister. "You know how she died, don't you?"

"No, I don't know."

"She was thrown from a newly broken horse up on the moor. Horse ran away with her and stumbled in one of those dreadful holes."

"How awful. I didn't know."

"Sir Byron had intended to ride the new gelding that day. He had it saddled up for that very purpose. But Erlinda was quite the horsewoman. She got to the stable, and seeing the gelding saddled, decided to take it out. She didn't know there was a burr under its saddle. Sir Byron

132

blamed himself, I daresay. But it wasn't his fault. It was that headstrong sister of his, may she rest in peace. She was always doing whatever came to her mind."

My jaw slackened as I listened to the narrative. "Then the horse was meant for Byron."

She took my meaning. "The curse, you see. The hand of destiny reaching out for Sir Byron that day. Only his sister got in the way."

The hand of destiny or the hand of some very human evildoer.

"But surely you don't believe this curse just happens. Someone must have put the burr under the saddle. Didn't Sir Byron try to find out who?"

"Indeed he did. Fired his groom for negligence. Even if the groom didn't do it, he should never have allowed anyone close enough to the horse to do the evil deed."

"Then you do see that someone meant Sir Byron harm. It can't be just fate."

She shrugged, took another sip of tea and set her cup and saucer back on the tray. "Fate, destiny, the hand of God. Call it what you will. It works through man sometimes. That's just the way of things."

I pursed my lips. For all their hardworking, well-meaning virtues, the Northumbrians I'd met could be very set in their ways, and superstition played no little part. I was troubled about the way Byron's sister had died, even if the burr under the saddle had been accidental, and I felt even more empathy for the burden he must have carried since that day. It explained some of the reason he sometimes reached out to me. He must miss his sister very much. While I did not for a minute think he had a brotherly affection for me, surely in some ways I must fill some of that void of companionship.

I had hoped my outing to the village would lift my spirits. I always enjoyed the spirit of giving that came with Christmastime, though the gifts I had always given were simple and homemade. Being part of the holiday

133

festivities at Worthington Manor was yet another blessing for which I should be thankful. And yet I could not forget that life at the manor was not quite right. I carried the uneasy weight of knowing that some evil lurked, the more troubling because I knew neither its source nor its intended victim. Did someone want to kill Byron, using the age-old curse as the excuse? Or did someone hold a grudge against me and want me gone?

I tried to shake off these gloomy thoughts as we turned our conversations to more cheery subjects. I was about to leave when Mrs. Brown commented that she was going to wrap up some of her dried herbs and take them to Mrs. Herdman, whose husband was ailing. The water avens would do his chill good.

I had seen Mrs. Herdman in church, and when I learned that the elderly couple lived on the other side of the lake, I volunteered to take Mrs. Brown's package.

"Well, it's quite a distance," said Mrs. Brown doubtfully, but I could see that for her to make such an effort would not be easy.

"Oh please, let me take it. I'll take a loaf of bread from the manor too. If Mrs. Herdman's tending her husband, she probably has little time for baking. It's no trouble, really."

I could see the relief in her face. I waited while she wrapped her package. Besides the avens, she sent wild basil, fenugreek, and sweet cicely, with a note of instructions as to the best ways to use them. I hated to leave the warm cottage, but I bundled myself up and stepped outside.

I followed the flagstone path to the road and then turned toward the village. The cold must have kept everyone indoors, for there was no one out, even when I reached the heart of the village. It might have been the cold that made the skin prickle on the back of my neck, but I sensed I was being watched. When I stopped in front of the grocer's, I turned and caught the movement of a curtain on the second floor above the clerk's office across the street.

But it was too cold to tarry outside, so I went in. Here, the smells of fresh-ground coffee, cinnamon and other spices made me forget my concerns, and I had the fun of buying cranberries, apple cider and other staples for Cook. In a moment of whimsy, I bought a box of silver tinsel for decoration. I came away with so many packages that the proprietor had to help me out.

We carried everything to the phaeton and deposited the packages on the floor. My next step was at the drygoods shop where I bought enough red velvet to make myself a party gown for Christmas. I lingered for some time, running my fingers over the nap. It was still hard to believe I was wearing such rich materials.

I bid Mrs. Goodson good day and left the cozy shop. Then I pushed open the door of the blacksmith's to find Robin. Sparks flew off the ringing anvil, where Robin was watching the brawny blacksmith at his work. Neither looked up, so I cleared my throat and moved farther into the darkened interior.

"I'm ready," I said to Robin, who looked up suddenly as if seeing a ghost. Then, seeing it was me, the expression closed over his face and he nodded slowly.

"All right then. If you'll just wait outside, I'll be along in a minute."

"Very well."

I turned and went back toward the door. I resented the way he ordered me out. He must have known it was cold outside, and I knew he would take pleasure in making me freeze for the length of time it took him to finish whatever he was doing. I was not about to be such a victim. So I sat down on a bale of hay and waited by the door.

Robin had left some tools for the blacksmith to mend. He finished showing the man what was wrong, and I thought he took his own sweet time about taking his leave. I was sorry I had never succeeded in making friends

135

with Robin. I had tried to treat him in a friendly manner, but he persisted in doing things to aggravate me, as if he knew exactly what would annoy me most.

As I watched him talk with the brawny blacksmith, I wondered if it really had been Robin who had knocked the statue over that night. I could not see why he would want to harm his employer. But he obviously did not like me. Neither did he look like he had the strength to shove something so heavy. But his muscle-bound friend, the blacksmith, did. Would the man have done such a favor for Robin?

I did not like such glum thoughts, but there were still no answers, so I had to consider every possibility. I decided then to spend more time watching Robin's actions. Maybe if I found out more about how he spent his time and who he spent it with, it would give me insight into what he wanted, and possibly why he didn't like me.

He finally finished his business and started toward me. As we took the little side door to the street, I heard the ringing of the anvil behind us.

Since Robin never bothered to strike up a conversation with me, I remained silent, lost in my own thoughts during the ride back. It was a relief to drive through the wrought iron gates and pull up the gravel drive to the back of the house.

The kitchen was a place of bustling activity when I brought my packages in the back door. Cook exclaimed gratefully over the spices I had brought, and Mrs. Mac-Dougal stiffly approved the cranberries, but sniffed at the tinsel, saying it was a waste of money. However, Annie winked at me and made a humorous gesture behind the housekeeper's back. I was at home helping with the work that took place in the big, toasty kitchen, and it made me forget my more solemn thoughts. Surely the good cheer of Christmas would dissipate the evil that had hung about the house like an ugly cloud.

I went upstairs to put on a work dress, and when I

136

entered my room, I noticed that my family Bible was lying on the pillow.

This was curious, for I certainly hadn't left it there. I walked over to the bed and picked it up. Had whoever made my bed thought perhaps I should spend more time on devotional studies? My eyes narrowed in suspicion. Was this Mrs. MacDougal's way of insinuating something about my morals? Did she know what had happened between Byron and me?

I went to the chest and put the Bible in the top drawer where I had always kept it. I had not forgotten the first time it had been "borrowed." Had the same person taken it out and then left it carelessly on my bed? I expelled a sigh of frustration. Was there no end to the odd happenings in this house? I would give my eye teeth to know who was at the root of them.

But there was too much to be done to ponder it now. I quickly changed into a plain brown woolen day dress and went back downstairs to don an apron.

I was sitting with Louisa, threading a needle with which to string cranberries, when I thought I heard the sound of horses and carriage wheels outside. Probably more visitors. Byron was being called on by many acquaintances, most of whom I never got to meet. It being the holiday season, many of them would only stay for an hour or two, leave some token, toast the season with Byron in the parlor and leave.

Though I tried not to be envious, my curiosity about who Byron socialized with made me wish I could be introduced. But it was a further indication of the gulf between us that he did not think fit to introduce me to the gentry. But what could I expect?

I was droning on to myself in such a manner, when a door somewhere in the house banged shut. Then Sophie flew into the kitchen, arms akimbo, gibbering in a dialect so heavy I couldn't catch a word of what she was saying. Mrs. MacDougal turned a shade paler and knocked the

137

potpourri off the edge of the table. Dried petals floated to her feet. Cook grabbed a broom from the corner, but instead of using it to clean up the spilled leaves and petals, she brandished it about the kitchen ordering everyone out.

"What's happened?" I asked the air, for no one was paying the least attention to me.

The thunder of boots on the back staircase preceded Robin's appearance, and he flew across the kitchen and out the back door, buttoning his trousers as he ran. Moments later Annie appeared down the same stairs, her cheeks flushed. It was no secret what they had been doing, but no one seemed to notice. I decided the best thing for me to do was to get out of everyone's way. An important guest must have arrived unexpectedly, and the entire household was now rushing around to greet them properly.

I went up the back stairs toward my room. Before I turned into my wing, however, I stopped at the front landing, and leaned out the casement windows to see what I could see. The elegant dark green carriage with the monogramed crest emblazoned on the side was turned out with four identical dappled grays. The top-hatted coachman was just shutting the door, from which he must have handed down the visitor. The groom held the horses. Then the coachman mounted the box, gave a word of encouragement, and the coach rolled forward, presumably to the stable.

I couldn't help imagining how these two formally dressed servants in their velvet collars, dark burgundy tailcoats and silk hats would put Robin in his place. But then I wondered. Robin had a way of letting you know that he was subservient to no one except his master, and then only by accident of birth.

I was so lost in my musings that I jumped when Mrs. MacDougal spoke behind me. I had not heard her approach, but she looked up at me from the half flight of stairs below.

138

"Sir Byron requests your company in the formal parlor, at your convenience."

My eyes widened. "He does?"

Her perfunctory nod did nothing to conceal the disapproval in her eyes. She went on to say, "You'll be needing to look presentable," making me glance down at my woolen day dress as if it were one of the rags I used to wear to the factory.

"Yes, of course."

She sighed, as if letting me struggle into my gown alone would be less acceptable than sending anyone to help me dress in clothes that kept me acting above myself, but she said she would send Annie to me.

I selected the blue-gray grosgrain with the large fan pleats and back drapery. I was in my dressing gown and petticoats when Annie hurried in, the curls spilling out from under her cap. I smiled.

"My goodness, Annie, what is all the fuss? Are we entertaining royalty? I've never seen everyone so upset about a guest. Who is it?"

"Practically royalty, miss. Though I've never seen her myself. I have it from Mrs. MacDougal herself that she married an earl. That makes her a countess. We're all to address her as Lady Liddicoat, never Lady Margaret, which is her first name. The nobility don't like it if you get their titles mixed up."

"No, I'm sure they don't," I said, as Annie pulled the dress over my head and fastened the back.

"Now, miss, we must do your hair up right." I thought she had an impish gleam in her eye as she stuck the curling iron under the coals.

I grinned back at her. Perhaps I should have been more patient with Byron, if he now saw fit to introduce me to such a distinguished visitor. From the nature of the invitation to appear in the formal parlor, and from the preparations we were making for my appearance, it seemed I was not being summoned as a servant.

My excitement mounted as we put on the finishing touches of my toilet, and then Annie held the door for me as if I were some grand lady. My blue velvet slippers carried me noiselessly to the stairs, where I floated down.

Dunstan stood at attention at the front door, and as soon as he saw me, he walked stiffly to the parlor doors and opened them. The formal parlor was much larger than the one I usually met Byron in. The room stretched along the front wing of the house, with brocaded furniture set in clusters.

I slipped in to see Byron at the far end of the room lifting his glass in the direction of a short, stocky woman of mature years, the generous folds of her purple and black velvet skirt spread over the blue brocade sofa. Bright little blue eyes gazed out from under the black netting she had pushed back on her hat, and a sharp nose lifted slightly as if to inspect me.

Momentary relief passed over me. I suppose in the back of my mind I was afraid that Lady Liddicoat would be a young widow, come to turn Byron's head. But I could see there was no possibility of that.

Byron set down his glass on a small side table, and crossed the Persian carpet to me. Though he only glanced at my attire briefly, I saw the look of approval in his eyes. I knew I had done him proud. But in the next moment, my confidence fled, for he led me to the center of the room.

"Lady Liddicoat, may I present Miss Heather Blackstone."

My mouth felt chiseled out of stone as I tried to smile at the powdered, hawk-like face before me that bore traces I began to recognize.

"Heather, this is my mother."

Eleven

He had never mentioned his mother, and having been so preoccupied with the strange deaths of the male side of the family, I had spared little thought for the erstwhile Lady Worthington. But of course Byron had said that his father had died at the age of forty-nine, so why shouldn't his wife remarry?

All of this flashed through my mind as I stood there tongue-tied. What did you do in front of a countess? My knees seemed rusted together, but I forced them to bend in a brief curtsy. I panicked, realizing I would have to address her. Was she "your ladyship?" I was doubly angry with Byron for not having prepared me for this, but as the sounds in my ear began to register as his words I got at least half the explanation.

"Mother has honored me with a surprise visit, Heather. She seldom leaves her home in Sussex."

"That's true enough, Byron," she said, waving a hand. "But please drop the formalities, and pour me some more sherry. I am determined to do nothing more this day but relax after that horrid ride over nothing but bumpy roads. I declare the roads up here haven't been repaired since the Romans left."

My face, already burning from shock and embarrassment, now must have registered my reaction to her earthy tone. A giggle bubbled up in my throat, but I swallowed it in sort of a hiccup. I hadn't yet said anything, and I did

141

not want the lady to think I was a simpering fool.

She curled her index finger toward me. "Come here, dear. Let me see you. Byron says you're his new secretary."

The word secretary was filled with sarcasm, and I felt even hotter. She wasn't fooled for a minute, and I thought she was going to drop all remaining decorum and ask how long Byron had had me in his bed.

I managed to move toward her, and when she patted the seat beside her on the sofa, I sat down.

"That's right," I said, in a rather squeaky voice. I cleared my throat, struggling to regain my composure, for I was determined to make a good showing. "He was kind enough to employ me, when I . . ." I lost my way, and would probably have further embarrassed myself if she hadn't waved my explanation away.

"He already explained. I understand you've come from Notthingham, and that you're a very talented lace-maker."

"That's right." I didn't say more, not knowing what Byron might have said about my background exactly.

Her beady eyes drilled into my face. "Sounds very interesting, if you ask me. Says you're a Blackstone. Family came from around here. Lost the property because they were Roundheads. But that the line carried on."

"Yes, that is so."

She leaned closer, frowning, then looking me over from head to toe. Then she leaned back, slapped her knee and laughed. "Bloody good joke, I'd say. Come marching right up to the house and announce yourself as the rightful owner of the old Blackstone property."

Byron intervened, obviously realizing that I would not know what to make of his eccentric mother's ways.

"Mother, I told you it was not exactly like that. She was curious, of course, about what was once her family's. I daresay when I showed her the remains of Blackstone castle she was disappointed."

142

"Hrumph. Pile of rubble's all that's left, though I suppose it was grand enough in its day. Been falling down and rebuilt ever since Norman times. But no one can afford to live like that anymore." She gave another laugh. "Not even my husband, and I married him because he had more money than anyone else in Sussex."

I smiled. I was becoming very curious about this outspoken lady who had married "up." How had she achieved it, I wondered. I began to relax enough to speak.

"Will you be staying for the holidays?" I asked.

"Might do, might do. The earl is being well taken care of by my stepdaughters, the doting girls. He won't lack for entertainment. Thought it was high time I looked in on this standoffish son of mine to see if he was still the recluse he used to be. Can't get him to the south of England for the world. Hates London. Doesn't even like to go to the theater or the opera. You'd think I raised a barbarian."

"Mother!"

"Sorry, Byron. More sherry. But you know how I feel about your not mixing with society." She gave me a sly sideways glance. "Though this time I can perhaps see why."

I blushed. But she carried on.

"Haven't you any other house guests? Who am I to talk to if I do stay here, besides Miss Blackstone, that is. I wouldn't want to wear her ears out, and I know that as soon as you've done your familial duties, I'll be left to my needlework and other such boring poppycock."

He gave a laugh and addressed me. "She is hopeless, Heather. You can see why she hates the North. Hasn't the appreciation of nature one must have if one is to live here. Not enough balls and parties for her. Not enough matchmaking to do in our thinly populated county."

"Hrumph," she said again.

I thought mother and son would continue sparring, but Dunstan entered, pushing a table on wheels laden with a

143

silver tray, a tea service, a mound of sandwiches and cookies. My stomach rumbled at the sight of food, for it was teatime. Now I could see why Cook had flown around the kitchen in such a state. She had accomplished a lot since I had left her domain.

"Now this is more like it," said Lady Liddicoat, reaching for a sandwich. "I'm glad to see there's decent fare here."

Dunstan poured tea and handed cups and saucers all around. We ate and drank for a few moments, and I was so amused by Byron's mother that I began to enjoy myself. He had resumed his slightly cynical air, but I could see that he must be fond of his mother in spite of, or perhaps because of, her eccentric ways. With the exception of Lady St. Edmund, I had never been in the presence of the aristocracy—and she had always held herself quite above the commoners who worked for her.

Lady Liddicoat, on the other hand, asked me about my lacemaking and said that she would love to have some handmade lace to replace that on some of her gowns. I agreed to take a look at the wardrobe she had brought with her to advise her on what needed repair and what I might replace with newly made lace.

When she had satisfied herself with the refreshments, she made a grand gesture indicating that she was finished with us. I was intrigued by the way she could so casually use mannerisms that left one in no doubt as to her position, while at the same time being so unique in character. She seemed to have the viewpoint that since she was a countess, she could be and do whatever she pleased, and everyone else was supposed to grant her wishes and behave accordingly.

"You must carry on with whatever you were doing before I came. No doubt old Dunstan will have dragged my trunks up the stairs by now. Marie can unpack for me. She's my new maid. Brought her from France. Everybody has to have a French maid these days. Got the ugliest one

144

I could find, though. Didn't want her philandering with the earl's cronies."

She chortled. "No doubt my sudden arrival gave Mrs. MacDougal something to snap and pop about. She always did pride herself on her iron hand running the household. We'll see if she's up to her old standards."

I was on my feet, aware that I was being dismissed.

"Very well, Mother," said Byron. "I do have some business to attend to. I am sure you will be able to make yourself quite at home. Dinner is at eight."

"Well, I hope Miss Blackstone will join us. We'll be running out of things to say to each other by the end of the week."

"Thank you," I said.

I left the other two, promising to look into the matter of lace for Lady Liddicoat as soon as she was settled. Then I decided to take the afternoon to carry the herbs and spices from Mrs. Brown and the fresh bread Cook had made this morning to the Herdmans' as I had planned. It would be a good excuse to get out of everyone's way, since the arrival of Byron's mother and her entourage had set the household buzzing. There would be extra linens to air out, and her servants would have to be put up in the servants' quarters as well.

I changed into the green woolen riding habit and gathered the parcels together that were to go to the Herdmans' and carried them out to the stable. Robin was nowhere to be seen. Lady Liddicoat's team of grays had been stabled and were hungrily munching oats, but the coachman and the groom were absent. Probably Robin had taken them to the kitchen or down to the village for some ale and horse talk. So I saddled Theo myself the way I had seen Robin do it and tied the parcels on behind. Theo and I were getting to be old friends, and I felt quite comfortable handling the horse without Robin's help.

I headed up toward the lake, for I remembered Mrs. Brown saying the Herdmans lived on the other side of it.

145

I passed through the forest where I sometimes found Raoule playing his flute, but he was not there. The woods were quiet except for the sound of Theo's hooves crunching on the frosty ground. My thoughts turned to Lady Liddicoat, and I felt a great desire to get to know her better.

I supposed I would see even less of Byron with his duties as host, and I tried again to lecture myself about my relationship with him. Already in the back of my mind was the notion that I should leave Worthington Manor. I admitted I was in love with Byron, but he was not in love with me. It would not matter if he was. He would never marry me. And I wondered if one of the reason's Lady Liddicoat had come to see her son was to marry him off. And why hadn't he married? Surely he wanted an heir.

Then a grim thought struck me. Perhaps he had not married because he believed in the Worthington curse and was afraid it would strike the child he sired. The horror of living with such a fear brought a weight to my heart.

I came out of the woods and we climbed the path that led up toward the lake. Already I could hear the shouts of children, and when we emerged alongside the lake, I could see three little boys skating with glee across the frozen ice, their bright scarves flying behind them. I watched them as we skirted the reedy shallows, home of innumerable small black-headed gulls.

I had not given a lot of thought to having my own children. I still felt so much the child myself, that I had never seriously considered the idea seriously. And it was probably only because I had at last experienced the joy of a man's embrace that the thought crossed my mind now.

Emotions churned in my stomach as I rode along in the crisp air, and I scolded myself for being so melancholy. This was the season for joy, not sorrow. Why then could I never seem to shake the gray forboding that seemed to follow me everywhere?

The boys skated away, and I concentrated on where I was going. We were on the other side of the lake now, and I looked for the turnoff that led to the Herdmans' cottage. When I found it, we turned into the woods again. Here I had to duck to avoid overhanging branches, and I was again filled with the sense that I was not alone.

I hastened Theo, for I was anxious to get through the thick woods. We were still on the path, but here and there branches had fallen across it, and once I had to dismount to remove them.

Soon, however, the trees cleared, and before me was a neat cottage homestead, built, I could guess, of purloined Roman stone and thatched with heather. The smoke rising from the chimney promised a cheerful fire. I got down and tied Theo to a tree, and taking my packages I knocked. I heard the shuffle of footsteps and then a wizened little woman opened the door. She looked at me in great surprise, and then opened the door wider.

"Mrs. Herdman? I'm Heather Blackstone from Worthington Manor. Mrs. Brown gave me some things to bring you, and I told her since you lived this side of the manor I would bring them. I hope I'm not intruding."

She waved me in. "Come in, come in. Didn't expect visitors on such a cold day as this."

Though the cottage was small, it was immaculate. And evergreens graced the stone fireplace. There were even stockings hung from the wooden mantle. Kitchen cupboards lined one wall with a gateleg table on one side. A set of stairs led upward.

"Who is it?" called a voice from above.

"Someone come from Mrs. Brown," called my hostess with a sharp voice that could carry across a field. I had noticed from the farm implements around a small shed outside that the Herdmans must farm grains.

"I understand your husband is ill," I said. "I hope it is not serious."

"If it ain't his stomach, his head ails him."

I told her about a concoction I remembered Rosa once making for someone who once had the same chronic problems. Mrs. Herdman seemed intrigued with the recipe, which required calamus.

I tried to remember the herbs that grew in the manor garden. "I'll see if there is any calamus at the manor. If Cook has some, I'm sure she wouldn't mind my bringing it to you."

"Wouldn't want to put ye to no trouble, but what with this cold weather, his head just gets worse."

If I could find some, I promised to bring it tomorrow. She made me stay for a cup of hot milk, and then, concerned with the hour, I bid her good-bye.

But when I got to Theo, I could see something was wrong. She was holding her right foreleg up, and when I went around to see if I could tell what was the matter, she whinnied and wouldn't let me touch it. I returned to the cottage.

"I think my horse has gone lame," I said when Mrs. Herdman opened the door again. "Would you mind if I left her in your barn and sent our groom to see what is the matter? It's not far, and I can walk home."

"Oh my, don't worry about your horse. There's plenty of room in the barn, and fresh hay. My grandson came yesterday to see to that. Pity the pole broke last week on the wagon, and we haven't got to fix it yet. But you could take old Nell, long as your groom brought her back in the morning."

"Oh, no, thank you."

I didn't tell her that I didn't feel accomplished enough to deal with another horse. Indeed, the fact that Theo had gone lame was a great disappointment. I had fancied that I was not such a bad horsewoman when on the docile mare. But to try to ride a workhorse that didn't know me would be too much to attempt.

"It isn't far, really. I can walk."

After putting Theo up in the barn and making sure she

had plenty of hay, I set off on the path through the woods. It was still early, but there was hardly any light in the thick forest of ash, birch and oak. I made my way as quickly as I could through the woods, but the many tangles and branches that had slowed Theo down, slowed me down as well. I had to admit I was glad to emerge from the thick woods to where the path led alongside the lake.

A wind had come up, and I could see by the sullen clouds rolling in that a storm was on its way. A drop of rain on my nose told me I was in danger of a soaking if I didn't reach shelter soon. I looked back the way I had come, but taking shelter in the dark forest did not appeal to me.

I knew that if I cut directly across the lake, I would save much time and would be down out of the high country before the storm broke. I had passed a deserted cabin on the way here, and I could take shelter there.

I walked to the edge of the ice. It looked frozen solid. I remembered the boys skating there earlier, and judged the lake to be safe. Walking carefully, I stepped out on the ice. If I hadn't been in a hurry to get to shelter before the rain got heavier, I might have enjoyed the experience of being on the frozen lake. When I looked down, it was like walking on the top of crystal caverns. I could not go too fast, of course, for though the ice was not smooth, it was somewhat slick.

Gradually I began to close the distance to the other side. Then suddenly a sound like marbles bouncing off the sidewalk was all around me, and I was pelted with a sharp piece of hail. The sky seemed to open, and the hail poured down. I pulled my hood further over my face, hastening my steps. It was harder to see now, and the hail pelting my face kept me from watching where I was going. My feet began to slip under me. I grasped blindly at the air.

A dark shape moved in my direction from the shore, and I thought that one of the specters must have come out in the storm. Suddenly, the ice cracked under me. No matter how much I scrambled to try to save myself, it did no good. Then, before I knew it, icy fingers reached up to encircle me. I kicked and screamed and splashed and surely would have met my death had not strong arms, which I at first fought in my hysteria, dragged me out of the water.

"Heather, Heather," said a familiar voice, barely reaching my numbed brain. He slapped my face.

I stopped fighting, and the arms pulled me further away from the thin ice. Then he grasped me and stood up, trudging across the ice to solid ground. I could see now, but everything was blurry, and the hail still came, though the hailstones seemed smaller.

The specter turned out to be Byron, and he carried me toward his horse. I was shivering uncontrollably, and my death grip on him probably told him I could not ride. He whistled to his horse and carried me down the path that led to the abandoned cottage. As I looked over his shoulder at the edge of the lake, I saw the sign that warned all comers of the thin ice. It lay on the ground where Byron's horse had stood.

We came to the hut, and Byron kicked the door open. Here, at least, was shelter. He put me down on a small rope-sprung bed, then pulled some blankets off a shelf.

"You need to get out of those clothes," he ordered, wrapping one of the blankets around me. "Can you manage, while I build a fire?"

I nodded, dumbly, but didn't speak. He went to the small stone fireplace and rummaged about for implements to start the fire. I tried to unbutton my jacket, but my fingers were frostbitten, and I could not make them work.

I was still freezing, and I feared I would die of cold sitting on the bed. Byron glanced over, and seeing I had made no progress, quickly crossed over to me again.

"Here," he said, gently. "I'll do that."

He got me out of my jacket and threw it aside. Next, he managed to undo the buttons of my soaked blouse and stripped it off of me. Then he used one of the blankets to rub my skin. I started to pull the blanket all the way around me, but he shook his head.

"No, everything, down to the skin. You're soaked clear through."

My hands still felt like lead, so he helped me strip out of the skirt and breeches. Then his deft fingers unlaced my corset and cast it aside. He pulled my camisole over my head, and then pulled the blanket around my shoulders.

"There now," he said, chafing my clammy skin with the rough woolen blanket. "Let me get that fire going."

Soon the smell of peat filled my nostrils, and the fire blazed. Byron himself had gotten wet as well, but only now did he stop to get out of his own wet things. He found some trousers and a work shirt in one of the trunks and put them on. Then he helped me up and moved the bed right next to the fire and placed a chair next to it.

I gave him a weak smile as I sat down again. I wasn't shivering as badly now, and decided I was going to live. I sat hunched on the bed while Byron massaged my head with the blanket. I had been badly shocked, and Byron said little, concentrating on getting me warm and dry.

He fetched a kettle and boiled water, then he steeped tea he found on the shelves. The hut seemed equipped with everything for the fishermen who used it. I was grateful for that.

The wind whistled through the eaves of the cottage, but the hot tea and the roaring fire began to relax me.

"Feeling better now?" Byron asked me, refilling my cup.

I nodded. "I'm all right," I managed to say.

"My poor dear. What were you doing on the lake?"

"I . . . I . . . was taking a shortcut."

"What happened to your horse? Robin said you'd taken Theo some hours ago."

"She's lame. I left her at Herdmans' cottage."

"Ah. Well, thank God you're safe."

He sat down beside me on the bed and pulled me to him, hugging me for warmth. I rested my head beneath his chin, but my muscles remained tense.

"The sign," I said. "It was down."

"I saw that," he said, his voice angry.

"There were skaters earlier," I said. "They must've not seen the sign either."

"Luckily they skated on the other side where the ice was solid."

"But who would take the sign down? One of the specters?"

I was making a grim joke, knowing how the Northumbrians liked to find supernatural explanations for so many things.

"Who told you about the specters?"

"Raoule." I forgot I had never mentioned him to Byron.

"I see." He said it as if he knew him. "How did you meet Raoule?"

"Well, Rosa . . ."

"Ah, I had forgotten your Gypsy fortune-teller."

"She said Raoule would meet me when I came. Only, he didn't."

He gave a short chuckle. "I am aware of that."

But I wanted to talk about the sign. "Could someone have taken it down on purpose?"

"That would be a foolish thing to do. The wind was strong, perhaps the sign blew down."

I furrowed my brow as he smoothed my hair with his hand. Now that I was feeling better, my thoughts were coming back in a tumble. I had not done very well in my investigations at Worthington Manor, and I would have to rectify that.

But now Byron's lips had found my forehead, and as the blanket dropped away from my shoulders, his hands were rubbing my skin. My ears started pounding, and I hadn't the strength to pull away.

"Byron, I . . ."

But I could not bring forth the words I had wanted to say. I had not been happy these last weeks that he had ignored me, but I had pride enough to resent the fact that he seemed drawn to me now because of the circumstance. My body wanted to fill itself up with him, but my mind fought against it. Was I only to be his plaything, serving him as a secret mistress whenever it was convenient for him? Didn't I deserve something better?

Of course all such reason fled when his mouth was covering mine, his hand gently cupping my breast.

"My sweet, sweet Heather. How can I resist your loveliness now?"

Over his shoulder I saw how the flickering firelight cast our entwined shadows on the wall. Still, some part of my mind wanted to talk to him. To ask him what? What his intentions were? Did that not sound presumptuous for someone in my position? I knew, of course, that titled gentlemen often dallied with their servants.

But my words got swallowed up in the yearning for his tongue to probe deeper, for his hands to caress my skin. My breasts ached, and as he lowered me to the bed and stretched out beside me, the fire ignited between us. Again we fulfilled what seemed right between us. Afterward he gathered me into his arms and drowsiness overtook me.

When I awoke, Byron was puttering about the fire. A glance at the window told me it was dark. My stomach rumbled, and I wondered what the hour was.

I sat up, the blankets draped about me. Byron looked up and caught my gaze. He gave me a slow smile. He looked comical in the trousers that were too short and the shirt that was too big. He had our clothing arranged about the fire and was drying everything out.

"It must be late," I said.

"I don't know the time. My pocket watch stopped upon being dunked in the lake."

"I'm sorry. I shouldn't have gone that way." Now I felt foolish. Then something new occurred to me. "How did you come to find me?"

"When I saw the storm brewing up and found that you had taken the horse, I was concerned. You do not know the suddeness of change that can occur in our Northumbrian weather."

Something bothered me about his sudden appearance just in time to pluck me from the icy waters, but I let it go for the moment.

"The clothes are almost dry. I do not think we shall have to return to the manor in fisherman's clothing and blankets."

I found myself blushing. If we did have to go back to the manor dressed in such a way, I felt that every eye would be able to read what had happened between us. My chagrin over what I had done came over me again. Decent girls were not supposed to give themselves to handsome gentlemen. I could not justify it. I remembered the Bible on my pillow and again feared it was a hint from someone in the household that I should mend my ways. I did not disagree.

I did not look Byron in the eye as I put on the dry clothing. My boots were still wet, but there was nothing to be done about that. If we could both ride on Byron's mount, we could get back quickly.

We tidied up the hut, leaving it for the next visitor. Before dousing the fire, Byron asked, "Are you quite recovered? I do not want to expose you to the elements if you're not up to it. Doctor Morebattle will have my skin if you catch pneumonia."

As if to answer, I sneezed. But then I shook my head, wiping moistness from the corner of my eyes as Byron

154

handed me a damp handkerchief from his coat pocket.

"I seem to have some sniffles. But I don't think there's any danger." I didn't want to spend the night in the little hut for more reasons than one. "Your mother will be worried if we don't go back."

The corner of his mouth pulled back in a wry grin. "My mother has not been able to keep track of my whereabouts for a great many years. I doubt she will try to start now."

The storm had died down but left behind the scent of moisture in the leaves and in the mossy peat. Water dripped from the thatch, but already the air was turning cold, and by morning, icicles would hang from the corners of the little cottage, making it look like something out of *Grimm's Fairytales*.

Byron led his black gelding to a tree stump, which we used as a mounting block. I hiked my skirt about me and mounted, straddling the horse. Then Byron climbed up behind me. The moon lit our way through the trees. I was glad not to be out alone, for the tree limbs twisted and bent into odd shapes as we passed by them.

I heard the by now familiar sounds like chains clanking and the thump that might be distant marching feet or a rumble of thunder. We could no longer see the lake. But I was just as glad. For if there were specters, as Raoule had said, and they were dancing about on the black surface of the lake, I would just as soon not see them.

Twelve

Our clothes had not completely dried, and by the time we reached the house I was shivering and sniffling, so that Mrs. MacDougal ordered me straight to bed. She said she herself would prepare a toddy for me to drink. I just hoped she wouldn't put any poison in it. Byron spared me embarrassment by saying that my horse had gone lame, and I had fallen in the icy water and that we had left the horse with the Herdmans'.

Annie peeled my clothes off and took the underthings to be laundered.

"You must've taken quite a dunking," she said.

"I'm afraid I did," I said. "The ice was thin." I sneezed. "But someone had taken down the warning sign."

She pressed her lips together in a grim line. "That was careless of them."

"Yes. Unless someone did it on purpose."

She busied herself about the bed, not looking me in the eye. "I'm sure I don't know who would do such a thing. Maybe someone knocked it over by accident."

I sneezed again. "That's what Sir Byron said."

"You just rest now. I'll go fetch that toddy."

Hadrian jumped up on the bed to keep me company, but as soon as I sneezed he ran to the trunk by the foot of the bed.

"I'm sorry, Hadrian," I said. "It's only a sneeze. Come back." I patted the bed beside me.

156

But he remained suspicious, staring at me with his yellow eyes.

Annie returned with a tray and started to set it on my night table. But my Bible was lying there.

"Why is that there?" I said, reaching to move it aside to make room for the tray. "Who keeps getting out my Bible? Do you know, Annie?"

The tray clattered, and she grabbed the mug to keep it from spilling.

She shook her head. "No, miss."

"Does Mrs. MacDougal think I need to read it?"

She wiped the mug with a linen napkin she had brought on the tray. "Yes, perhaps that's it. Here, I'll put it away, if you like."

"No, leave it there. I don't mind it being out."

She handed me the mug and glanced apprehensively at the Bible. I drank down the toddy. I had to admit it was tasty. I could taste cinnamon, brandy and lemon and some other herbs I could not identify.

"Is there anything else you'd be wanting?" she asked, when I had drained the mug.

I shook my head. "No, thank you, Annie. I'll just rest for a bit."

She left me, and I reached for the Bible, deciding to thumb through it. I propped it up on the bedcovers and opened it to the pages where family births, deaths and marriages were recorded. My birth was at the bottom, the last entry, of course. I had had a sister, but she died before I was born. My father's birth was there, and his brothers, sisters and his father. The births went back to 1611, the year this volume had been printed. I read with interest all the names. By comparing the dates with the record of deaths, I could see how long they had lived, and I knew now which ones were buried in the village churchyard.

The handwriting from the early years was harder to

read, but, nevertheless, fascinating. I wondered how the Bible had come into the family, while regretting that it did not tell me what I wanted to know. For I had not forgotten my resolve to be more active in my searching for facts relating to the Blackstone heritage and the Worthington curse.

The curse. There might have been some satisfaction in thinking that the curse came as a result of the Worthingtons snatching away the Blackstone property. Perhaps one of my ancestors had uttered a curse. But such was lost in legend now.

My thoughts turned to the strange intuition I had had every time I went to the castle. I shut my eyes, trying to see the scenes I had seen again. Though the images were fuzzy, I remembered quite a bit about the clothing the people wore.

"Elizabethan," I said aloud, popping my eyes open. The tunics, ruffs and flat bodices came from the time of Queen Elizabeth. I had seen such pictures in history books at the orphanage.

I frowned. I did not know where the visions came from, but I did not discount the possibility that such emanations clung to places of great antiquity. I lay back on the pillows, trying to bring the images back again. If the visions were real and if they came from Elizabethan times, then it was Blackstones I saw, for my ancestors would have been in possession of the castle then. But the faces would not form. It seemed I had to be in the castle itself for the phenomenon to occur.

The toddy began to make me drowsy, and I decided that my sleuthing would have to wait. But I knew one thing. I would have a long visit with Lady Liddicoat as soon as the opportunity presented itself.

My wish was granted next morning after I had

breakfasted on the tray of steaming dishes Cook sent up. Annie brushed and braided my hair, which seemed to be growing longer and thicker, no doubt because of my improved diet and the care I could afford to give myself now. I was not altogether unpleased with my appearance, except for my red nose. I finished my toilette before the dresser mirror and put on a quilted dressing gown with a ruffled collar.

There was a knock on the door, and when I said, "Come in," Lady Liddicoat swept in. She was wearing a Russian green cashmere gown with appliqué velvet leaves on the bodice and skirt, with a large bow of drapery behind. The bouffant sleeves were finished with a cuff of ecru with lace.

"Good morning, child," she said. "I was horrified to learn that you almost drowned yesterday. I hear my son pulled you out."

I smiled in embarrassment. "I was fortunate. Sir Byron happened along at the right time."

She took a seat in the big wing chair, her skirt spreading around her.

"He has a way of doing that," she said. "I also understand he had gone looking for you. Now, I always did say my son is a responsible employer. But it is a bit unusual for the master of the estate to take so keen an interest in members of his staff, eh? Unless there is a special reason."

I flushed, not knowing what to say, but she spared me by raising her hand.

"Oh, you don't have to say anything. I'm not blind or old-fashioned. You've got good looks, and Byron is a healthy male. I'm not here to butt into his affairs or yours, for that matter. I'm just hoping you use a little sense. Attractions of such a nature can lead to children, if you know what I mean, an extra burden if had outside of marriage. Now, I'll say no more on that."

I swallowed the lump in my throat. There was nothing to say.

"Now, my dear, I just wondered how you were faring. I can see by your nose that you've got a cold."

"It's much better. I slept very well after a strong toddy Mrs. MacDougal sent."

Lady Liddicoat nodded. "I'll not deny the effectiveness of her remedies, the old atheist. Runs an efficient household if you keep out of her way. Though I've a few of my own methods I plan to pass on to her."

"I've been trying to do that. I'm just sorry she is so difficult to befriend."

Lady Liddicoat shook her head sympathetically. "People in your position are in a difficult spot. You're in a lesser class than the gentry for whom you work, but by your wit and skills you're above the lot of the servants. Hard to fit in anywhere, either upstairs with the master, or downstairs with the servants. It's a sort of limbo."

I nodded, as before, appreciating her directness.

"I have felt that way. I was born into a middle class home. My parents worked for Lady St. Edmund in her home in Nottingham. But when they died I was sent to an orphanage. Then when I was fourteen I went to work in the factory."

"A difficult life indeed. You are lucky then that Byron has chosen to keep you on here."

I glanced at my hands. "I'm not sure how long I will stay on."

"Oh? And where would you go?"

I hoped I didn't show my discomfort with this conversation. "I haven't made any definite plans. But, as you say, I am skilled."

"Hmmm. Well, time enough for all that."

"Lady Liddicoat," I said, steering the conversation in a new direction. "You seem to know something of the his-

160

tory of the estate, particularly the . . . er . . . um . . . castle."

"Ah yes, the castle that bears your name."

I nodded. "It's very fascinating to me."

"And well it might be. I know more legend than fact, I'm sorry to tell you. The Blackstone name is remembered because of it. They were Roundheads as I understand it, reason they lost the property in Charles the Second's time. Cedric Worthington was awarded the estate for helping Charles escape or some such thing."

"Yes, yes, I know that, with the exception that my family believes the Blackstones to have been, in fact, spies for Charles the First."

She arched one gray eyebrow, the other knotting under it. "So Byron said. I suppose you want to prove it's true."

I shrugged. "I don't suppose it would make any difference. I don't mean to insult the Worthingtons. It would bring some satisfaction, I suppose, to know the truth, I mean. My father said there was a deed, and a . . . reward."

"And you would like to find them." She did not mince words.

"Well, I, that is, it would be rather interesting, after all this time."

She chuckled to herself. "It would be rather amusing at that, wouldn't it? And then you could turn my son out?"

Her hawk eyes danced with the irony of it. "I suppose in that case he would come begging to me. Though I suppose he has enough money to set himself up as a gentleman in London."

"I thought he hated the city."

"He does." Then she looked at me as if trying to assess just how far I might go, given the chance.

"The mystery is interesting, but I wanted to ask you something else, if you wouldn't mind," I said.

161

"Of course not. I haven't anything better to do than to sit and gossip. What is it?"

"Well, the castle is in disrepair now, but I was wondering if you knew what it was like long ago, when it was in use, I mean."

She screwed up her face, thinking.

"Hasn't been in use in my time. This house was built as a hunting lodge. But the family moved into it shortly afterwards. County was drained of its economy by then, I believe, and the Worthingtons along with it." She gave a chortle. "That's the way it is with titled gentry. They don't always have the money to keep up appearances. Don't think I didn't learn to be frugal when I ran this house."

She cast a measuring glance my way. "I'll bet you've had plenty of experience with frugality. Trouble is, if you don't mind my saying so, you can't always tell when someone's plucked from poverty and set down in more fortunate circumstances whether they're going to remember their good habits or give in to greedy indulgence."

I was not sure if she was speaking in generalities or if she was insinuating something about me, but just in case, I said, "I think it's a shame to waste things, even when there's plenty. One must always make things go as far as possible. And when we have plenty ourselves, we always need to remember those who don't."

For some reason at that moment I thought of the Gypsies. None of them were wealthy. Some were frugal, others wasteful. I doubted Lady Liddicoat knew any Gypsies, but I didn't think this was the time to ask.

"I think there might be some drawings of the castle in a portfolio in the library," she said.

My interest immediately perked up. If there were drawings, why hadn't Byron mentioned them to me?

"Come to think of it, they might be stored away somewhere, but if it would amuse you to see them, I'll see what I can do. They're quite ancient, probably valuable

162

by now. Made in Queen Elizabeth's day, if I rightly remember."

"Oh?" My heart began to hammer with excitement. I was on the verge of telling Lady Liddicoat about my visions, but my fear that she would be skeptical, made me hold my tongue.

"Well now, I've probably tired you enough."

"Not at all. I'm quite recovered. This cold will go away in a few days, I'm sure."

"Probably. I'll just go along now and see what else I can do to keep Mrs. MacDougal on her toes." She chortled again as if the two of them were old rivals. "I trust I will see you this evening."

"I will look forward to it," I said, rising with her and blowing my nose on my handkerchief.

A little after she left, Mrs. MacDougal came with a formal message that Sir Byron did not expect me to work this morning—he wanted me to take care of my cold. But he did ask if I was feeling well enough this evening to join him and his mother for dinner. The housekeeper delivered her message as she usually did, her head tucked down slightly, her crossed eye accusing me.

I was pleased to be invited, and wondered what I would do to fill the time until then. I spent time going through the dresses that now made up my wardrobe, selecting something to wear this evening. I had put on a little weight from all the good food, and now gowns that had been a trifle too large before fit me in a more flattering manner. I considered asking Lady Liddicoat if I could be of help in searching for the drawings of the castle she had promised me, but decided I shouldn't make a nuisance of myself.

Finally, my eye fell on the Bible again. I picked it up and brought it to the chair by the fire. Ever since it had been appearing by my bedside, the same thought had been making circles in my mind. My father said my heritage was in the Bible. I could remember him saying it as if it were just yesterday. I had already studied the family records kept in the volume and had discovered nothing more than the tiny snatches I got of the lives recorded there.

But perhaps I was on the wrong track altogether. Perhaps the Bible did hold a clue to the ownership of the Blackstone estate, but it was not in the family records. Perhaps there was a clue elsewhere in the Bible.

As I had the thought, I felt a prickling at the back of my neck. Was that why I kept finding the Bible where I had not left it? Did someone else know it held a clue? If so, was my opponent trying to find it as well? Or did the person want me to lead them to it?

I stood up suddenly, holding the leather volume to my chest. Hadrian lifted his head at my sudden movement, and I looked down, unsure of why I had stood up. I ran my hand over the rough black leather and sat down again, opening the cover slowly. I had heard that books often contained concealed documents, and I carefully poked along the binding and felt the edges of the ancient cover, but it did not seem as if anything was hidden there. I would have to take a knife and split the binding apart to be sure, but before I demolished the binding, I would look on the pages themselves. I began to turn the pages slowly, running my fingers down the thin paper. There were some underlines and notations along the side. They'd been there since long before I'd owned it. Verses were sometimes cross-referenced with other verses, and there were many jottings, some not legible. I realized now that these notations might be what I was looking for. I had had them all the time, but had never studied them.

I flipped through the pages. The markings seemed at random, with many pages perfectly clean. I frowned, realizing I had my work cut out for me.

Then I raised my head and stared at the air before me.

I thought very possibly I was on the right track at last. But if so, the thought still plagued me that someone else thought so too.

Byron knew about the Bible. The thought chilled me that he might be the one looking for clues. Of course I did not think he rummaged in my drawer himself. But he could have asked Mrs. MacDougal, Annie or Sophie to bring it to him. They were the most likely to be in my room without my suspecting anything. One of them might have taken it to him. Or to someone else?

My head swam with the possibilities. Maybe Byron was trying to make me fall in love with him so I would not press my claim. I was confused about his responses to me. There were moments when his tenderness seemed real, and I was helpless against his advances, each time swearing I would remain stalwart the next time he came near me. I even told myself I would leave the manor after Christmas, if I had not found what I had come for. My lovesickness made me beg for crumbs from the master, and I knew my foolish heart was leading me into trouble. But I told myself it was too soon to leave. My mission had not yet been fulfilled. I had not come any closer to the Blackstone claim, and perhaps I never would, but I was not satisfied that I had looked for every possible clue.

I was not unaware of the danger I was in. But a stubborn resolve made me sit in the chair, staring at the squiggly lines and annotations various hands had made in the margins of my Bible. If there was a clue to be had here, I would find it. Whatever the Bible had to reveal belonged to me and no one else. I had not come this close to finding my heritage only to have someone else take it from me.

I thought of Raoule, who assured me I was under his protection. With the bustle of holiday plans I had been remiss about going to look for him. There was a little comfort in knowing I had a friend here. For his connection to Rosa gave me faith in what he said. But he could not watch me every moment, no matter how stealthful he was. I would have to be more on my guard.

There was a knock on my door.

"Come in," I said. It was Annie.

"Excuse me, miss. Thought I'd dust your room."

She wiped her hands on her starched apron, and her eyes darted about the room.

"Fine, Annie," I said. "I'm spending my recuperating time doing a bit of reading."

Her eyes came to rest on the volume in my hands and she gave a quick wistful look.

"You're lucky you can read so well. I don't read much."

"Oh?"

"That is, my uncle taught me a little. I can make out some words, but I never read a whole book. It's painful slow."

I cocked my head and looked at her. "Well, if you'd like to learn to read, I could spend some time teaching you."

I felt a sneeze coming on and slid my handkerchief down between the cushion and the side of the chair.

"Hatchoo! Oh my, Annie, could you bring me a handkerchief."

She moved to the chest and pulled open the top drawer. "Are they in here, miss?"

I nodded watching her. "Yes, there should be a stack on the right."

"Here they are."

She lifted out the plain linen handkerchief and handed it to me. I don't know what I expected by that little test. For her to comment that the Bible was not in its usual place? But of course she had seen it was in my hands.

If she couldn't read, it could not be Annie who was perusing my Bible. I liked her and didn't want to suspect her. But she could be following someone's orders.

I smiled at her, blew my nose, and she went about her duties, finally taking away the feather duster.

I stayed doggedly at my task until lunchtime. I read all the notes I could decipher and all the verses that had been underlined. But if there was a meaning I was supposed to discern, I failed. Then I noticed the missing pages.

I had been reading in the Book of Luke when I saw the torn edge along the binding. Looking at the passage that ended the page and the numbers of the verses that began the next, I could see that a page had been torn out.

I came instantly alert. Had the page been recently torn out? Or had it been missing for a long time? There was no way to tell. But I began the exacting task of looking to see if any other pages were missing. Finally, I found one. Someone had taken a page from the Book of Job as well. The thought was mystifying, but no matter how long I pondered it, I could not solve the puzzle.

When I finally rose and stretched, Hadrian did the same, arching his back, fur standing on end.

"Now Hadrian," I said conspiratorially. "I am going to take the Bible where no one will find it. And you aren't going to tell anyone."

He blinked his yellow eyes. I left the Bible in the chair and went down to the pantry to fetch a basket. Cook had Louisa washing vegetables over the dry sink. Neither looked up as I took the basket and went up the back stairs. Soon, the servants would gather in the servants' hall for lunch, but I wouldn't be there. I put the Bible in the bottom of the basket and covered it with the red checked linen napkin that lay there. If anyone asked, I would say that I was going to look for some mistletoe that I saw in the woods the other day. For it was in the woods that I hoped to find Raoule.

I bundled up in my boots, my brown woolen dress, knitted scarf, coat and hat and left the back way. Cook and Sophie were still hard at work over the vegetables. I heard Lady Liddicoat's voice growing louder as she approached the kitchens. I could not tell who she was talking to, but I slipped out before she saw me.

I tried to keep from scurrying, and, in fact, slowed my pace as I passed the stables. I didn't see Robin anywhere. But I heard laughter from within the stables and remembered Lady Liddicoat's servants. They must have been in the stables with Robin.

Still, I had the feeling that from somewhere in the manor someone was watching me as I took to the road leading toward the uplands. Soon I swung off the road and onto the path that went through the woods. I had not sent Raoule any kind of signal. I would simply have to look for him.

I followed the path into the trees, my boots crunching on the twigs. From somewhere ahead, I heard the sound of a flute. I came to the clearing where I had last met Raoule, but he wasn't there. Keeping my fingers crossed that I would find him, I went on. The ground rose under my feet, and I was out of breath by the time I came to the fields on the other side of the woods. Far in the distance I saw a flock of black-faced sheep grazing, not far from the Wall, and, hoping it was Raoule's flock, I trudged onward.

The wind pushed at me, unbroken now by trees, and I pulled my scarf up around my face, not wanting my cold to get any worse. When I was within hailing distance I saw him. He was circling among the sheep, his crook in his hand, and when he turned, he saw me. He waved and made a path through the sheep toward me. I stood panting near a big boulder until he came up.

"Hello, and what are you doing up here today?" he greeted me.

"I needed to see you. I have something I need for you to keep hidden for me. Do you know a place?"

His dark eyes danced with interest. "Hide something?"

I uncovered the Bible in my basket. "It's a family heirloom and valuable to me. And it mustn't get wet."

"Ah, I see." He took it in his hands. "A very valuable personal belonging. And you say you need to hide it? But why?"

"Because I think someone tried to steal it."

He turned it over in his hands as if trying to assess its worth.

"When I came here, Rosa said I would find a great . . . that there would be danger, evil, but possibly my fortune too. I think now maybe the Bible can tell me something about my family heritage and my family ownership of Blackstone Castle."

He gave me a quick glance. "It is as I feared. Your life is in danger. I can sense it." He put the Bible back in the basket.

"Come," he said. "Our camp is just over there. You must have something to eat with us."

I followed him to the edge of the sheep herd, and he went to exchange a few words with the boy who sat on the rock, telling him, no doubt, to mind the sheep while he took me to the camp. Then he ambled back and gestured for me to follow.

We made our way down the hill to a covert of trees. I could see the semicircle of barrel-topped wooden caravans, painted in bright green, red, gold, their ends decorated with fanciful designs of leaves, animals and scrollwork. As we approached I saw the other Gypsies going about their business. A man in work clothes with a yellow scarf about his neck, removed a worn shoe from a horse. Several children ran about, laughing and yelling. Two women, dressed in many layers of colorful clothing, kerchiefs covering their long, thick hair, tied at the back of their heads, were clustered around a cauldron suspended over a fire.

Raoule spoke to the farrier, who now had the shoe off

the horse. Raoule introduced the man as his brother-in-law, William.

The women looked up as we approached, and Raoule introduced me to his mother, Mia, a small woman, but with the same flashing dark eyes Raoule had. His sister, Mona, cradled a newborn infant, who grasped my finger when Mona encouraged me to play with it.

The stew in the pot smelled enticing, though I did not ask what it was, and I was handed a bowl and spoon and found a seat on an upturned crate to eat. Mona sat nearby, feeding the baby tiny spoonfuls.

"Raoule says you come from Nottingham," she said.

"Yes, that is right. My friend Rosa said I would meet Raoule here."

Mona rocked the baby back and forth, and soon its eyelids drooped. She nodded. "Raoule has told us you have come to find your family heritage."

I smiled. "A dream perhaps. I suppose I am following a fantasy."

She gave a musical laugh that reminded me of Rosa. "Do we not all follow something?"

What she said made me realize that this was what I had in common with the Gypsies. Perhaps I had their wanderlust.

"And do you stay here all the year-round?" I asked, for I knew how Gypsies loved to travel.

She shook her head. "Only when Raoule must look after his flock. But we go to the fairs. My husband can always find work with the horses."

She looked at me, her dark eyes seeming to examine me. "You like Raoule?"

I blushed. "He is a very good friend."

She nodded. "He ought to marry, have children."

I understood her insinuation, but I shook my head. "Has he not met a good Gypsy woman?"

She shrugged. "There are many women. We meet other

bands from time to time. But Raoule has been too restless."

She looked at me as if challenging me to cure Raoule of his restlessness. I smiled warmly. I knew Raoule cared about me. He was a gentle, talented man, and I felt his warmth. But I was unprepared to do what Mona suggested.

Some other men came into the camp now, and Raoule's mother handed them bowls of stew. When they were finished, William and one of the other men fetched guitars from their caravans. They started to strum a sad tune and sing softly. The others leaned against wagon wheels or lay on their blankets, humming along. One of the men picked up his carving, which I saw was going to be a shepherd's crook.

After a time, Raoule separated himself from the men and came to where I sat with Mona. He bent to kiss the baby and then reached out a hand to help me up. We walked a little away from the others.

"Heather," he said, as we walked slowly, "will you not consider something?"

"What is that?"

We had come to the end of the trees, and he looked past me, squinting his eyes. I turned to follow his gaze and was surprised to see that the manor was visible from here. In fact I thought I could pick out my room. If I sent him a signal from my window, he would have no trouble seeing it from up here. I turned back to him, and he lowered his gaze to mine.

"Leave the manor. Come stay in our Gypsy camp. As a friend of Rosa's, you would be welcome here. Come with me tonight. You will see."

For a moment I was tempted. "Thank you, Raoule. But I can only stay to visit. I . . . I think my place is at the manor."

"But why?"

171

I exhaled a frosty breath. "I am, after all, an employee there. I cannot just walk away."

"Even when your life may be in danger?"

I looked at his intense black eyes, his ruddy cheeks. "How can you be sure of that?"

He waved his hand. "Things have happened, have they not?"

"Accidents, that is all." I hoped the shiver that ran up my spine as I said it was from the cold.

He squinted his eyes again, looking in the direction of the manor, but I had the feeling it was not the setting he saw. Rosa used to get such a look when she was seeing the future.

"Someone means you harm, but I cannot tell who."

I turned and looked back at the manor, dollhouse-sized from this distance. I felt its pull on me even from where I stood. There were too many unanswered questions. Lady Liddicoat had promised to show me the drawings of the castle in its former state. And Byron? Did he have feelings for me beyond the passion we both seemed to be fighting against? I gave a little shake of the head.

"I would like to stay, Raoule, but I cannot. Please try to understand."

He gave a melancholy smile and raised my hand to his lips. "You are drawn to him aren't you, my little dove. He has you under his power, does he not?"

I'm sure he read the admission in my eyes, and I placed my hand over his. "I'm sorry. I did not plan for it to be so. But I must go back. I must find out the truth."

When I looked into his black eyes I felt that I was looking into a world of perception beyond my understanding. I was sure Raoule had something of Rosa's second sight. Standing there with him, I felt as if I could almost look into the future myself. But what I sensed wasn't clear, and then I pulled myself back. Perhaps it is not good to know one's future before it happens, for then one would stop creating it.

I took both of Raoule's hands in mine and gave them a squeeze. I knew he had feelings for me, and I cared for him as a friend. But for all that the Gypsies had become a part of my life, I was not one of them. I did not feel that I was meant to live among them.

"Thank you, Raoule," I said.

He kissed my forehead, and then he led me back to the camp. I said good-bye to his mother and sister, then waved as I started back toward the manor. The afternoon had drawn on and I had one more errand to perform before I dressed for dinner.

Hastening back the way I had come, I went into the house through the kitchen and proceeded to the library. There was no one about, so I went in. I scanned the shelves, running my fingers along some of the leather-bound volumes. Finally, I came to what I was looking for.

Satisfied, I left the room. I did not need to take any books with me now, for I would return later.

Thirteen

I was glad I spent the time on my appearance that I did, choosing to wear the indigo velvet off-the-shoulder gown.

As Annie was dressing my hair, there was a knock on the door. She went to see who it was and stood for some moments out of my sight. She came back alone, carrying a long velvet case and handed me a note.

There was no question as to the handwriting. "I would be honored if you would wear these this evening," Byron's scrawl said. "They belonged to my sister. Such jewels do no good lying about in vaults. Surely you will add to their beauty."

My heart fluttered at the words.

"Why they're lovely, miss."

"They certainly are. He means me to wear them."

She considered my appearance in the mirror. "Here, miss, let me wind them through your hair. A very pleasing effect that would make."

I agreed, and as she worked the pearls in and out of my chignon, I could not still my excitement. Finally, I was ready.

When I entered the parlor, I saw that there were guests at the far end, and as I traversed the length of Persian carpet, the heads turned to look at me.

Byron turned as I approached, broke off his conversation and lifted an eyebrow as he watched me. Then he drained his sherry glass and set it on the mantle.

174

Lady Liddicoat turned, her eyes flitting from Byron to me as he examined my appearance. From the look in his eye, he seemed pleased.

The two other gentlemen, one portly, the other young and blond, smiled blandly, while the petite yellow-haired lady between them, appraised my appearance, her cold blue eyes taking in every detail of my dress.

"There you are," said Byron, giving me his arm. "I would like to introduce my guests."

He made introductions to Mr. Allan Bothwick and his nephew, Carver and daughter, Claire. They were neighbors from the other side of the county, and I could tell from their thick accents that they were native Northumbrians.

Before resuming her monologue with Bothwick, Lady Liddicoat's sharp eyes traveled the length of my costume. She cocked her head for a moment, looking at the pearls I wore, and then as Dunstan appeared at my elbow to hand me a glass of sherry, she cornered her prey again. Byron, Carver, Claire and I stood apart in a circle.

"Byron says you come from Nottingham," said the young lady.

The accent, which made the men sound like farmers, rolled off her tongue in musical tones, and I thought there was something of the challenge in her manner. Nor was I blind to the feminine effect she created in her emerald green satin gown, wrapped in lace drapery. Green satin flowers adorned her hair.

"That's right," I said cautiously. "This is the first I've seen of the north country."

"Sir Byron says your people were from around here," interjected the blond young man. He had a thin face and a wide mouth, but his eyes held genuine enthusiasm. And I thought he held himself rather rigidly, as if he weren't used to the clothes he wore.

"Your line goes back before King Charles's time, does it?" he said.

I could not help the amusement I felt. Evidently my lineage proved convenient, even to Byron at times, to be brought out and displayed like the best china, when appropriate.

"That's right," I said, standing straighter. "The Blackstones left the area due to a misunderstanding with Charles the Second."

I thought Lady Liddicoat's eyes twinkled at that, for she paused long enough to glance my way.

"Fascinating," said Carver.

Dunstan announced dinner, saving us from further discussion of my ancestry. Lady Liddicoat led the way in on Bothwick's arm. She still chattered away, and I could not help but wonder if he would be deaf by the meal's end.

Byron led Claire in, and she batted her eyelashes up at him. I took Carver's arm and asked him about the part of Northumberland he was from. Apparently they lived very far north in the border country.

We all paused in the anteroom before entering the dining room. Bothwick had stopped to examine the German rhinestone dagger lying on silk under glass. Carver was especially taken with the multicolored wood handle of the Viking dagger, and as I stared at the three-foot long double-bladed battle-ax, I blinked. I had been in this room many times, and though I had never stopped to give the weapons more than a cursory examination, I knew something was out of place.

I felt Byron's gaze behind me, and I turned to catch his eye. He was staring at the same spot I had just been looking at. Then I realized what was wrong. The battle-ax was one of a pair that had crossed on the wall. The other one was missing.

Byron's eyes narrowed slightly, and then he met my gaze. I knew by his look that he was not going to speak of it to his guests, but as the others admired the collection, he disappeared in the direction of the dining room, presumably to speak with Dunstan about the missing weapon.

While Carver pointed out details of the weapons to me, I

half listened. I was aware that Lady Liddicoat knew a great deal about their history, which confirmed her keen interest in the past. It was possible that someone had taken down the battle-ax to clean or repair it. But already my mind was leaping ahead with more gruesome suggestions.

I leaned on one of the cases and shut my eyes briefly, trying to stop my head from throbbing. Then Byron reappeared, touching my elbow briefly as he passed by to the others.

"Well," he said to the gathering. "Shall we?"

We left the anteroom and proceeded to the dining room, taking our places, Lady Liddicoat at Byron's right, Claire at his left. I sat beside Carver and across from Bothwick, who was seated on Lady Liddicoat's other side. The room glowed softly with candelabra on the table and side tables, leaving the vaulted ceiling above us in darkness.

Cook had outdone herself in preparing roast venison, roast pigeons, fillet of rabbit, spinach, cucumber salad and macaroon pudding with cognac and cream, and the conversation proceeded to become more lively as the evening wore on.

Claire saved most of her glances for Byron, but he seemed quieter than usual throughout the meal. She was a pretty girl, and I felt a rise of jealousy when Byron did lean his head toward her to catch her words. But I could tell from his expression that he had not been satisfied with whatever inquiry he had made about the missing weapon from the collection, and I could not keep it out of my mind.

I felt little relief when I followed Lady Liddicoat and Claire back to the parlor, leaving Byron and Bothwick and his nephew to their port. Though Lady Liddicoat kept up the conversation, rambling on about her travels in Europe and the fashions she had seen there, the paintings at the Louvre and the people she had met, I was hard-pressed to participate.

Claire plied the older lady with questions, no doubt trying to learn anything she could that would help her put on airs. But from the pink that tinged her cheeks when the doors opened and the gentlemen joined us, I knew that she had been waiting for Byron to return.

For the rest of the evening he was attentive to her, and Carver did his best to entertain me with card tricks he had learned. But I was tired of the company, filled with a dull anxiety I could not shake and I longed to go to my room.

Finally Lady Liddicoat yawned, and as if on cue, we all rose. The company was staying over, and we all retired to go upstairs, Dunstan coming to extinguish the lamps behind us.

I followed Lady Liddicoat to the top of the stairs, bidding her good night as she turned into her room. Claire gave a little titter and commented with emphasis.

"My room is so lovely, looking out at the garden from the end of the wing." She gave a little sigh. "It's such a big house. I could get lost in it."

I did not miss her meaning, and I wondered if she expected Byron to take the hint and visit her in her room. I clenched my teeth. I had told myself a thousand times that such a thing might happen. That I had no claims on him. But when I glanced at him to say good night, I saw the same worried, distracted look he had in his eyes before.

He did not even look at Claire or me, throwing a casual good night over his shoulder. Then he clapped Bothwick on the shoulder, leading him in the other direction to his room.

I felt restless, and once in my dressing gown, my hair braided for the night, I did not feel I could sleep. I had left my Bible with Raoule, but, still wondering about the pages that had been torn out, I slipped out into the hall.

The house had quieted, and I presumed everyone had gone to bed. There was no trouble about slipping back downstairs and into the library where I located the Bible I had seen on the shelf earlier. Back in the hall, I made sure there was no one about and carried the volume to my room.

If anyone saw me I could simply say I could not sleep and had gotten something to read. My sudden devotion to Biblical studies might surprise some of the household. But there was a more important reason for keeping my reading secret. I didn't want whoever had been borrowing my Bible to know I was reading it. If we were both looking for clues therein, the closer I came to them the more I would be in danger.

I had just carried the lamp to the chair by the fireplace in my room and was about to sit down when a scratching sound at the door made me jump. My heart raced to my throat and I froze as I watched the door push inward slightly.

I braced myself as my mind spun with gruesome images. Was whoever had taken the ax from the weapons collection coming to use it against me now? I moved stealthily toward the center of the room, ready to scream and run toward the door and attempt to get around my attacker.

The door squeaked on its hinges as it opened further, and Hadrian slipped around its edge. I exhaled a breath.

"Hadrian, you scared the life out of me."

I knelt to pet him as he came to rub my ankles. I couldn't blame him for not knocking first.

I picked the cat up and took him to the chair where we sat. Then I picked up the Bible I had borrowed and turned to the Book of Luke. Running my finger along the pages, I came to the section that was missing from my Bible. I vaguely remembered a verse I thought had been marked in the other Bible.

Luke 11:44 said, "For ye are as graves which appear not, and the men that walk over them are not aware of them."

I turned the phrase over and over on my tongue. It brought forth many images, but nothing I could fit directly into my situation. Was some ancestor trying to leave a clue? Graves. Was there a secret at the bottom of a grave?

179

I thought of the old graves in the cemetery by the village church. Parson Brown would hardly appreciate my asking to dig them all up.

Hadrian curled up at my feet and was soon purring. The other page missing from my Bible was from the Book of Job, Chapter 38. I turned there and sought the part I had read before the missing section. I scanned the rest. I could not remember which verses were marked here, but I kept coming back to verse twenty-five: "Who hath divided a watercourse for the overflowing of waters, or a way for the lightning of thunder."

I thought of the watercourses I had seen here. There was a stream in the village, but not very near the cemetery. There was a small trickle of a stream that had to be crossed between here and the castle, and, of course, there was the lake. Had any of them overflowed at one time?

I studied the pages again, trying to discern if there might be another reason someone had torn them out of my Bible. But I could not decipher anything.

I committed the verses to memory, and then tiptoeing to my door, I opened it slowly, wincing with every creak. I had to return the Bible to the library so as not to draw notice that I had borrowed it.

Making my way along carefully, I came to the stairs. I was about to turn on the landing when I heard a soft tread below me. A white petticoat flashed around the corner below and I froze, my hand on the newel post.

Then I choked back a scream as a hand covered my mouth, and a voice whispered, "Not a sound."

Fourteen

I smothered an instinctive scream, shaking with terror even as one hand took the Bible from me and the arms pulled me back into an alcove.

"Shhh!," he said, holding me until he was certain I would not cry out.

Gradually, I stopped shaking and looked at Byron's face in a shaft of moonlight that poured in from the casement window. I tried to swallow.

He let go of my mouth tentatively, but when I did not scream, he relaxed his grip. He held a finger to his lips then turned to pierce the darkness with his eyes. He must have been satisfied no one was about. Then he took my hand and led me down the stairs. We silently crossed the hall to the nearest room, which happened to be the weapons room.

He closed the door behind me, and I let out a sigh. I was still trembling, for I did not know why he was about. And the skirt I had seen going down the passage. Had it been Claire's? Had there been a rendezvous, after all?

Byron crossed to the doors leading to the dining room. Satisfying himself that no one was there, he came back to me. His hushed tone was urgent.

"What are you doing up?"

My lower lip trembled as I explained, "I was returning the book to the library. I couldn't sleep."

He glanced at the volume, which he still carried. "I did

not know you had the inclination. Did the passages put your mind at ease?"

"No," I snapped in a whisper. "I mean, yes." I glared at him. "It is none of your business what I read."

He shook his head, letting out a breath. "It seems we are not the only ones about tonight."

"I suppose you will tell me that is none of my business."

Even in the darkness I could hear the humor in his tone as he said, "If you think I was chasing that petticoat that flitted down the passage, it was not for the reason you might suspect. I was about to follow and see where she went, when you surprised me by coming out of your room. I nearly gave myself away."

"Perhaps the lady wanted you to follow her," I said irritably.

"I don't think she realized I was even about. But I could not help a certain curiosity about why the upstairs maid would be about so late at night."

I blinked, realizing we were talking about different people. "Annie?"

He nodded. "I saw her face in the light on the stair landing."

This was puzzling. Then I remembered Robin. "She has a beau," I said. "She often slips out to meet someone. I think perhaps your groom has been courting her."

This gave Byron pause for thought. "Possibly," he conceded. "But wouldn't she use the back stairs? What was she doing in this part of the house?"

He paced the room, coming to stop before the battle-ax and its all too evident missing mate. He turned.

"There is one way to find out."

"How?"

"A visit to the stable. But you must go back to your room. I'll take you."

"No."

He grasped my elbow, my hand was on his chest. I did not want to be led along to my room like a child.

"I cannot sleep. I'll come with you."

"Heather . . ."

But he must have sensed that arguing would do no good. He sighed in exasperation.

"Very well. But we must be very quiet."

I nodded. I followed him to the door and after making sure there was no one in the passage, we slipped out. Keeping to the shadows next to the walls, we proceeded to the foot of the stairs and then took the passage where he had seen Annie go.

Listening at each room, and then opening the doors, we ascertained that there was no one in this wing. Coming to the end where the passage turned toward the picture gallery at the back of the house, we paused.

"Look there," he said, pointing to the sliver of light that spilled across the floor.

The side door had been left open a crack. Byron and I looked at each other. It looked as if Annie had gone this way. Byron pulled a brown and black table-covering off a table by the wall.

"Wrap this around your shoulders," he said.

I was grateful for the makeshift shawl. I would freeze if I went outside dressed as I was, and the dark tablecloth would conceal the lighter color of my dressing gown.

We crept to the door and slipped out, staying near the bushes at the edge of the path. We saw no one and so cautiously followed the path around the house to the gardens.

"She could be anywhere," I whispered.

"Yes," he said grimly. "But this tells us one thing."

"What?"

"This is the longest way to get to the stables. If she is meeting Robin, as you suspect, they are not meeting there."

I remembered his mother's retinue. Robin would not want to carry on an amorous meeting under the eyes of Lady Liddicoat's coachman and groom. Perhaps they were meeting somewhere in the garden, after all. But it was a cold night for an outdoor rendezvous.

I realized how tense I was, for when Byron whispered in my ear again, I jumped.

"Follow me."

He took me by the hand and we followed the path. He was staring at the ground, and when I followed his gaze I saw what he was looking at. There had been a light snow, just enough to dust the path with white. And clearly visible were footprints the size of a woman's shoe.

We crept along, watchful for signs of anyone ahead of us. After traversing nearly the entire length of the garden, the footsteps leading us, we finally stopped.

"We'll wait there, next to the hedge."

A few feet away was located a stone bench next to a hedge. I sat down while Byron stood. I began to shiver, in spite of the tablecloth shawl. But I did not complain, for then Byron would make me go back inside, and my curiosity surpassed my discomfort.

We had not long to wait. At the other end of the section of garden where we sat, two figures emerged through an opening in the hedge. We stayed behind our hedge, but there was an opening in the branches through which I could see. Annie was talking to a man, whose face I could not see. She turned suddenly and started this way, and I felt Byron move closer to me in order not to be seen.

Then the man grabbed her and pulled her back. I could hear their voices now, raised in anger, but I could not hear what they said. Annie shook her head no and then yes, and finally he let go of her. She gestured with a shrug, exchanged a few more words with him, then turned this way.

Byron gripped my shoulder. We had to move, for she

would pass right by us. I glanced once more through the branches in time to see the man's hat come off, caught by a branch. He reached up and put it back on, but not before I saw the back of his fair head in the moonlight.

Robin was dark-headed. And this man seemed bigger than Robin, though at this distance it was hard to tell.

We hastened along the hedge and turned another corner, waiting for Annie to pass. When she had gone by, in the direction of the house, Byron motioned for me to follow him. We circled back to the opening in the hedge where Annie had held her clandestine meeting.

We searched for signs of where the man had gone, but there were none. There were no footprints, for we had come to the gravel drive which he could have taken in either direction. Or he could have crossed to the woods on the other side.

"Go back to the house," Byron said. "See if you can find out where Annie has gone. I'm going to see if I can track our friend."

"It's dangerous," I told him.

I did not argue about going into the woods where the moonlight failed to penetrate, but I did not like the idea of Byron going alone either.

"I have this."

From his pocket he produced a revolver, the metal glinting in his hand. I nodded. I wanted to find out who Annie's fair-haired friend was, but something told me to obey Byron's orders this time. I started back to the house, still walking softly. I turned back once, but Byron had retreated.

My heart rattled in my chest, and I tried to keep my mind on my task. I must find Annie. I tried to ignore the shadows that now seemed to loom everywhere. Though I could see the house ahead of me, it seemed a greater distance going back than when we had come. I began to run and did not stop until I was back to the corner of the manor. I crept along to the side door where we had started.

It was closed now and locked. Annie must have returned this way. I would have to find some other way in.

My heart still in my throat, I went around to the kitchen door and found it open. Moving carefully, I slipped in. I felt only slightly more secure having come this far. I did not know where Annie had gone or what I would say to her if I met her. And I did not know who else might be prowling about the house this night.

I crept up the back stairs, and only after I was safely in my room, the door shut behind me, did I lean against it and sigh in relief.

My eyes darted quickly around the room. Hadrian was curled up in the same spot where I had left him. I could not go to bed yet, however. I had to wait until Byron was safely back.

That Annie was meeting someone in the garden was not a sign that she was guilty of anything. I had thought that Robin was courting her. Had she found another lover? It looked as if she had been quarreling with the man in the garden. I distinctly remembered the glint of moonlight on blond hair. Who was he?

Then the sound of a gun going off thundered through the night. I was instantly at the window, but I could see nothing. Another shot rang out. I ran out my door and down the stairs, this time caring nothing for the noise I was making. From somewhere behind me I heard doors open, then the voices in the hall above me, but I didn't wait for anyone.

I fled down the passage to the painting gallery. Turning, I collided with someone. I screamed. The arms that grappled me released me instantly, and Robin jumped backward.

"Sorry, miss."

"Robin," I said. "What are you doing here?"

He picked up his cap from the floor. "I heard something. Goin' to see what it was."

I was too surprised to respond. Then as if we had the same thought we both went to the French doors and out onto the terrace.

"That way," I said, pointing toward the end of the garden.

I fled down the steps, Robin at my heels. My heart was pounding in my chest, and I was breathing hard by the time I reached the last rows of hedges. Ahead was the opening to the gravel drive, and when I saw Byron come out of the woods and walk across the drive, I sank down onto a stone bench in relief. He did not appear to be hurt. Robin went ahead.

"Are you all right, sir? We heard a shot."

"Quite all right, Robin. A poacher. He shot a rabbit, that is all. My shot frightened him away. I don't think he'll trespass again."

"You're not hurt then?" asked Robin.

"No, no, everything is all right. You go on back. I expect we've roused the house. Tell them to go back to bed. I'll take Miss Blackstone back."

"Very well, sir."

Robin turned and went back through the hedges and Byron came to me, dropping onto the stone bench beside me.

I knew the story about the poacher was an effort to allay suspicions. Byron would not want to draw the entire household into what was going on.

He put his left arm around me, but it became apparent that he was leaning for support rather than trying to keep me warm.

"Byron, what's happened?" I barely had my breath back and my words came in gasps.

"Just grazed, right side."

"Byron . . ." I gasped, reaching around to open his

jacket. Blood had saturated his white shirt.

"Quickly," I said. "We must get the doctor."

He shook his head. "Truly, it is a surface wound. The bullet just nicked the skin. If you'll be so good as to cleanse the wound when we get back. I don't want anyone to know about this."

I got to my feet, and he used me as a lever to hoist himself to his feet. He could walk all right, but it seemed to pain him to put much weight on his right side. He didn't waste his breath talking, but we concentrated on walking back through the garden.

When we got to the house, we went in through the kitchen. Lady Liddicoat rose from a seat by the fireplace, in which a fire was licking the bottom of a pot hung from a hook. Her quilted dressing gown was laced to her throat, and an enormous cap covered her hair.

"Well," she said as we came in. "Your orders didn't fool me, but I sent the others back to their beds. Now what has happened?"

"Nothing to worry about," said Byron. "I just got a scratch, that's all. Whoever I was following evidently saw me and fired."

"Well, let's see to it then. Come over here by the fire."

With my help, Byron walked to the Windsor chair and sank into it. His face was pale, and his mother and I helped him out of his coat, then opened the shirt. She clucked her tongue, then motioned to the clean linen cloth she had laid out. I dipped the cloth into the warm water and bathed the skin around the wound.

The wound was a nasty gash, and he had bled quite a bit. When I had done what I could, his mother examined the wound, then she stood up, hands on hips.

"I have a tincture of arnica. We'll put that on it. You didn't take the bullet anyway."

He shook his head. "I heard it lodge in the ground behind me."

She soaked a pad with the arnica and held it. "This will sting. We'd better have you drink something first. Heather, pour my son a generous glass of that whiskey," she said, pointing to the bottle and glass on the table.

I did as I was asked, impressed that she was so prepared with the herbal disinfectant. Then I saw the thread and the curved needle from her embroidery set. At first I did not realize why they were there, but as Byron was draining his glass, I caught Lady Liddicoat's gaze, and I got her meaning. I blanched, leaning on the table. She meant for me to sew him up.

The color returned to Byron's face and he set his glass down. I refilled it. He sipped it, then his mother bent to her task. He grimaced when she touched the soaked pad to the wound and gulped another glass of whiskey. A moment passed, and he seemed to relax a bit.

"Now," she said. "That's got to be stitched up."

She held the needle, which had already been threaded, and with the other hand picked up a long wooden match.

My eyes widened. "But I've never—"

"You're handy with needle and thread," she said. "The skin won't mend unless it's stitched."

"But surely the doctor . . ."

"I gather my son doesn't want the whole village to know he's been shot at. Better this way. Do you agree, Byron?"

His eyes had taken on a bloodshot haze, and I gathered he was getting drunk as quickly as possible so as to be able to stand the pain. They really meant it.

Byron reached out a hand to mine. His grip was warm as he squeezed it. "Go ahead."

He gave me a bleary-eyed wink. "My life is in your hands."

My head reeled. Then I fetched a cup from a nearby cupboard, returned to the table and poured myself a stiff whiskey. I swallowed it, letting the heat run down my throat, bracing me. Then I washed my hands in the basin into which Lady Liddicoat had poured warm, sudsy water. She had thought of everything.

Lady Liddicoat struck the match and held the needle over the flame, sterilizing it. I steadied myself as I took the needle and sat down with the light of the fire on Byron's wound. He grasped his left shoulder with his right arm, so as to keep it out of my way.

I swallowed, waiting until my hand was steady. Then I concentrated on the job before me, trying to focus on the loose flaps of skin, not thinking that they belonged to a man I cared for.

Somehow I got the skin to lay as it should. Holding it there with my left hand, I pierced it with the needle. Byron groaned and rolled his head, but he did not move.

"Go on," I heard him grunt.

Gritting my teeth, I pierced the other piece of skin, then ignoring the tears that came to my own eyes, I proceeded to gather the skin together, drawing the thread neatly behind the needle. The skin puckered where it came together as I sewed six more stitches. Finally I tied off the knot.

Lady Liddicoat's hand appeared in front of me holding a pair of gleaming scissors. I dropped the needle in my lap and cut the thread close to the wound. Then I slumped back, letting the breath out of my lungs.

"Done," I said in a small voice.

"You'd better have some more of this," said Byron's mother, handing me another glass of whiskey. I swallowed thankfully.

I saw that while I had been stitching Byron up, Lady Liddicoat had been busy making a poultice of yarrow leaves soaked in hot water and wrapped in cheesecloth. Now she leaned over Byron and applied the poultice to his side.

"We'll need to bandage this up," she said to me. "Bring that roll of gauze from the table."

Braced with the whiskey, I fetched the gauze from the table. He had to lean forward, so I could wrap it around his chest, and I saw the beads of sweat rolling down his face. His eyes were closed. My heart contracted at his stoicism.

I tried to wrap the bandages so the poultice was kept firm against the wound, without binding him too tightly. When we were finished, I helped Byron back into his coat. Lady Liddicoat disposed of the water and bundled his bloody shirt to be burned later.

"You take him up to his room," she said. "I trust he can walk that far. I'll get rid of the rest of these things."

I nodded, impressed with her efficiency. She was far more capable than one might expect of a grand lady. Her years running the household at Worthington manor must have served her well. No wonder she sometimes clashed with Mrs. MacDougal. Each was like a military commander, and I was sure Mrs. MacDougal preferred to give orders than to take them.

I got Byron to his feet, and he leaned on me as we walked across the kitchen. He mumbled a few words, but the liquor had had its effect, and his words were slurred. We got to the foot of the back stairs, and I wondered how I was going to get him up them, but enough of his strength returned that he was able to get up the stairs. There was no way to be quiet, and I expected bedroom doors to open any minute and the guests to peer out, wondering what was going on.

Lady Liddicoat came up the stairs behind us, carrying the bunched-up, bloody shirt. She passed us on the landing and went along to Byron's room, evidently to turn down the bed and stoke the fire.

When we came to the door, it was partially open and we pushed through into the sitting room. A few steps more and we crossed to the bedroom. The bed was in the center of the room, with a fireplace at one end, the fire bright. We hobbled to the bed, where I was able to lower Byron to sit.

His mother must have decided it would be too difficult to get a nightshirt over his head, so she had laid out a quilted smoking jacket. He put his good arm into the smoking jacket, which I held for him. I could see the pain in his face as he struggled with the other arm, then he lay back on the pillows.

Lady Liddicoat had stuffed the shirt into the fireplace, and she approached the bed.

"Thank you, my dear," she said to me. "You have been most helpful. I will see that he gets to sleep."

I knew I was being dismissed so that she could remove his boots and trousers, a job that would not be proper for me to do. I glanced at Byron's head on the pillow and could see that exhaustion from the pain was overtaking him. He would need strong coffee in the morning. Perhaps Lady Liddicoat knew an herb mixture that would cure a hangover.

My heart turned over in my chest. I wanted to stay and minister to him, but I knew that would not do. At least I had the comfort of knowing he was in his mother's capable hands.

She walked with me to the door.

"Good night," I whispered.

She nodded and closed the door behind me.

The next day was Christmas Eve, and I dragged myself out of bed, knowing that we must not make it look like we had had any change in the household routine. I dressed and went down to breakfast. The Bothwicks were breakfasting, and the men rose as I entered. We exchanged good mornings. Dunstan slid about serving coffee and refilling plates from the sideboard. Carver held a chair for me.

"Did you sleep well, Miss Blackstone?" he asked. "Thought I heard a shot in the night."

"Was there? Oh yes, poacher as I understand," I said, trying to act unconcerned.

"It woke me too," said Claire, her eyes large with curiosity. "I'm sure I heard doors opening and closing and such."

"Poachers can be a problem," said Bothwick, buttering another biscuit. "Probably some poor fellow out shooting his Christmas dinner on Worthington's land." He chuckled. "Can't let 'em take advantage, though. Start winking a little here and there and they'll think they have the right to cross where they have no right, any time they please."

Dunstan cleared away plates, then stood beside the table.

"Will there be anything else?" he asked.

"Not for me," said Bothwick.

"We can help ourselves in any case," said Carver, good-naturedly.

Dunstan bowed stiffly and then took himself away.

Claire grew bored with the conversation about the poacher and turned to more social matters.

"It's a shame Byron had to go out so early."

I blinked.

"Dunstan told us he personally delivers turkeys and hams to the tenants today. That he left already."

"Oh, yes, that is so," I said, not looking anyone in the eye. "It's quite a busy day today."

Tonight other neighbors had been invited to a party at the manor. I had to finish some of the decorations for the ballroom. The servants would have their own celebration below stairs in the servants' hall.

I gulped down my coffee. I had to see Byron as soon as he was awake. I could not imagine that he would be fit

193

enough to entertain, let alone, dance.

The Bothwicks had planned to go for a ride this morning. Then Claire offered her assistance with the party preparations this afternoon.

"Thank you," I said. "I'm sure there will be things to do. Lady Liddicoat can direct you."

I excused myself as soon as I could without being rude and then hurried upstairs. I paused at Byron's sitting room door, not wanting to wake him. I heard footsteps inside and knocked tentatively.

Dunstan answered the door. He must have slipped up here after serving breakfast.

"I . . . I wondered if Sir Byron needed anything from me," I said stupidly.

Dunstan nodded, his expression blank. "I will inquire." And he shut the door in my face.

I only waited a few moments when the door opened again and Dunstan admitted me. Byron was not in his bed, but in a large wing chair in the sitting room, his smoking jacket tied at the waist.

"Thank you, Dunstan," he said. "That will be all. Take the tray down the back stairs."

"Yes, sir."

I could see that Byron had breakfasted here, and that he had not indeed been delivering hams and turkeys. Evidently Dunstan had been taken into his confidence and had informed the guests that their host was not on the premises so that Byron could rest.

The door shut behind me, and we were alone. I pressed my lips together as he let out a sigh. But then a hint of a smile played about his lips.

"Come closer," he said. "Don't just stand there like a statue. I'm not a complete invalid, thanks to your expert doctoring last night."

I crossed the room and sat on the hassock at his feet. "How . . . how do you feel?" I said.

194

He gave me a smile, but the pain was still in his eyes. "Right now I can't tell you which hurts worse, my head or my wound. That was a lot of whiskey my dear old mother poured down me last night."

I could not hold back the tears that came into my eyes. He reached for my hand and squeezed it.

"You must continue to help with our charade, eh? I think it's best the guests do not know what has happened until we catch our culprit."

"Then you believe that what we witnessed last night was more than just a lover's tryst?" I said.

"I suspect it may be."

"Someone means harm."

He nodded. "I'm afraid so. I do not know what it is the culprit wants, but I intend to find out."

"Then you think it is more than the curse."

He gestured with his good hand impatiently. "The curse may be a convenient excuse for someone to make trouble here. But I intend to catch whoever it is."

"Will you cancel the evening's festivities?" I asked. "Surely you cannot—"

But he cut me off. "On no account. We will go ahead as planned. I will be a fit enough host tonight."

"Surely you cannot dance."

"Perhaps not. That will not be necessary."

I didn't disagree with him, though I very much wondered how in the brief hours that remained until tonight he would mend enough to play host to a large party. Of course Lady Liddicoat could take over much of that burden.

"Now, my dear, you must help me."

"Of course."

"You must help keep our guests entertained. I've already sent word that I am wishing my tenants a happy Christmas. Dunstan can be relied upon to keep our secret. I shall spend the morning resting. This afternoon I shall descend to greet my arriving guests. I've no doubt that between Mrs. MacDougal and my mother, nothing will be forgotten." He gave a chuckle. "Perhaps it is a blessing that she turned up just now, after all."

I smiled. "She does seem very capable."

His look sobered. "One cannot live in the north country and not be capable. Do you think you can help entertain the guests? Find things for them to do so that they don't become too curious about my whereabouts?"

"Of course, Byron, but—"

He placed his fingers on my lips. "How sweet my name sounds on your lips."

We gazed at each other for a moment, and I was aware of how much I cared for him. Whether he was growing to care for me, I still did not know beyond the physical need he had, and now his reliance on my help since he'd been wounded. I tried to turn my mind to what must be done.

"We'll need to change the dressing," I said. "If your mother is busy, I can do it."

He winked at me. "I suppose I can tolerate your ministrations, since I trusted you to sew me up last night."

I got to my feet. "I'll consult Lady Liddicoat. She will tell me where to find the supplies."

He kissed my hand and pressed it against his cheek, which felt very warm. I began to worry that he had a fever, and thought we should consult the doctor after all. But Byron brushed aside the idea.

"There is nothing the doctor can do that good home remedies can't take care of. I've lived in the country too long not to believe that."

"All right," I said, taking on the role of nurse, once again. "Then you must get back in bed. I will bring the dressing."

Byron obliged me and got to his feet. He could walk without my assistance, but I followed him from the sitting room into the bedroom and pulled back the covers. Dunstan must have helped him into a nightshirt, for he now shed his dressing gown, which I laid over a chair. After pulling the covers up over him, I left.

Downstairs, I sought Lady Liddicoat and learned she was in the ballroom, supervising preparations for tonight. I sought her there and pulled her aside.

"The dressing will need to be changed," I said.

"I had thought of that. If you could take care of it, my dear, I would be so grateful. As you see, my presence is needed here if this room is to be in decent form by tonight."

She broke off to give some directions to the servants who were scurrying about. Then she lowered her voice to me. "You will find the yarrow leaves in a jar in the pantry. Far left as you turn in, eye level. Cheesecloth will be at your feet as you stand. If anything's been moved, ask Cook. Say you burned yourself on the curling iron."

I took myself downstairs and found what I needed just as she had left everything. I dodged Cook, who raced back and forth between boiling cranberries and kneading dough while keeping up a constant stream of conversation with Louisa, who was dressing turkeys in the center of the table. I dashed up the back stairs with no one noticing me.

Fifteen

I changed the dressing and thought that, to my inexperienced eyes, the wound looked like it was healing well. I left Byron to rest and after burning the old bandages in his fireplace, I threw myself into the household preparations for tonight's festivities.

By five o'clock I had exhausted myself and I returned to my room to rest and get ready for the evening. Carriages and carts rolled up the drive now at steady intervals. I donned my new red velvet dress trimmed with my own Honiton lace, wearing the pearls in my coif. Then I descended to the formal parlor where guests were already milling about sampling hors d'oeuvres from a tray that Dunstan passed around.

I said hello to the Bothwicks, and Carver introduced me to several of their friends. I was scanning the sea of mostly unfamiliar faces when a voice behind me said, "Miss Blackstone."

I turned to stare at Stanley Symmes, who stood before me in evening dress, his hair smoothed back and his moustache waxed in place. I blinked. So much had happened lately that I had forgotten about him. I vaguely remembered extending him an invitation to the party and mentioning it to Byron, who must have sent one along.

"Good evening, Mr. Symmes," I said. "How nice to see you."

"Likewise. My, that color does flatter you." He chuckled. "Each time I see you, I am more convinced that your journey here from Nottingham has brought nothing but good fortune."

I tried to smile at the compliments, but I was very distracted.

"Thank you," I said.

Just then I caught sight of Byron, standing with a group of guests, and I excused myself from Mr. Symmes, promising to see him later.

I made my way toward Byron, not wanting to interrupt his conversation. I saw that he had the good sense to be using a cane. It was smoothly polished with an elegantly carved ram's horn head. The color and smoothness of the wood reminded me of the shepherd's crook one of the Gypsies had been carving at the camp, and I felt guilty for not sparing a thought for how the Gypsies were spending their Christmas eve.

But I had no more thoughts for the Gypsies, for I gazed at Byron's face. His color was a shade paler than usual, but he was keeping up a conversation with one of his guests.

He saw me at the same time the group broke away to circulate, and I went toward him. Even though the effort of being here must have cost him, he managed a smile.

"How lovely you look, my dear. You are brighter than the gayest of the decorations."

I blushed. "Thank you. But I am concerned about you," I said in a low voice.

"I will see that the party has a fitting start then disappear for a bit before supper. Do not worry. Your job is to act as if everything is normal. I have already made the excuse that an old injury is bothering my foot. I shall beg out of the dancing."

"That is wise, I think." I tried to erase the worried look from my face.

Allan and Claire Bothwick approached, and I tried to

199

smile convivially. Claire batted her eyelashes at Byron.

"I have so looked forward to this evening," she said. "I am so glad I could be of some small help today. Lady Liddicoat instructed me on hanging the holly. I think such touches are important in a home. Lady Liddicoat seems to have a great many such skills. She must be a very capable lady of the household."

"Indeed."

Her insinuations were not lost on me, and I tried to stem the jealousy that rose in my throat when Byron returned her smile. Surely he could see she was of marriageable age and looking for a proposal. She was from a good family, and would consider it a good match if Byron married her. Evidently she had spent some time with Lady Liddicoat, and I had not forgotten my suspicions that Byron's mother might be looking for a suitable wife for her son.

Such thoughts spun around in my head as I stood with a rigid expression carved on my face. At the same time, I was concerned for Byron's well-being, so that my own emotions were so enmeshed I did not know how I would get through the evening.

The doting Carver insisted on getting me refreshments and then plied me with questions about how I liked being employed at Worthington manor.

I answered stiffly, swallowing great gulps of punch from a fluted goblet. Carver was fascinated with my family history, and he persuaded me to tell him the Blackstone legend and how it had been passed down from generation to generation.

"I should like you to show me this castle of yours," he said. "I have seen it only from a distance, and that very long ago. It is not far from the great Roman Wall, if I remember correctly."

"That is true."

The doors opened and the party proceeded to the ballroom. I took Carver's arm, and we fell in with the group going upstairs. As we entered the ballroom, I had to admire its appearance. The greenery was festooned along the molding of the ceiling and the railing of the balcony that surrounded the room. Red ribbons and holly draped the four pillars.

Musicians on the raised platform at the end of the room tuned their instruments. Then Byron stepped up to the platform and gestured for silence.

"Welcome, ladies and gentlemen," he said to his guests. "It is my pleasure to gather together friends from far and near for our annual Christmas Eve celebration. As my fathers before me always welcomed Christmas guests, may this tradition continue until long after I am gone. Let there be no stint of merrymaking this evening. Without further adieu, let the grand march begin."

I followed Carver to a place in the line. I had never been in a grand march before and said as much to Carver.

"Don't worry," he said. "Just do what the other ladies do. You'll see."

Byron and his mother were at the head of the line, and as the music began, and they led the others around the room. I was relieved to see that all one was required to do was walk. Byron had laid down his cane, and moved to the music with only a slight limp.

The room spun with color and rang with laughter, and I envied those who could forget themselves and have such a good time. I followed the others as the ladies circled and met up with our partners again, but I was glad when it was all over.

The musicians went right on to the next dance and Carver tried to lead me out. But I held back.

"I'm not a very good dancer," I told him. While there

had been times in the orphanage when we girls had played at dancing, there had been no formal instruction.

"Then we will keep to the simple steps. Here, I'll show you."

At least he did as he promised, and I was able to follow him without getting my feet in his way. But it required a great deal of concentration, and my head began to throb from the effort. At the end of the dance, I begged to sit down.

His father approached. "Ah, there you are, son. If Miss Blackstone will excuse you, there is someone I want you to meet."

"Of course," I said, for I had grown tired of Carver's attentions.

Mr. Bothwick bowed to me. In his parting look I thought I saw something of uncertain deference. I realized in a glimmer that I was being included in the Bothwick's circle only because I had claims to ancestors of distinction, even if they were thought to have been on the wrong side, politically. But Mr. Bothwick must have been none too sure where this claim left me. His son was gentry. At the moment I was a seamstress and secretary, with no dowry. Perhaps Bothwick wanted to use this very social occasion to introduce his son to wealthier young ladies than I. Carver promised to meet me again later and allowed his father to usher him away.

I did not see Byron, and I hoped he had had the sense to escape. I was wondering what I ought to do next, when Stanley Symmes approached.

"Ah, there you are, Miss Blackstone. Would you care to dance?"

"Thank you, but I have just been dancing. I prefer to rest."

"Of course. Would you care for any refreshment?"

I had had enough punch, I thought, but I remembered

the coffee urn downstairs and said I would enjoy a strong cup of coffee.

"It would be my pleasure to get it for you," he said.

"No, I'll come," I said. The room was beginning to feel stuffy, and I wanted to get away from the swirling figures before me.

He offered his arm and we left the ballroom. Downstairs, several card games were in progress, and the refreshment table had been refilled. I took a plate of fruit and cheese, and after Mr. Symmes filled a china cup of coffee for me, we found seats in the corner where a draft from the window helped me cool off.

"I fear I shall be leaving Northumberland," said Mr. Symmes. "My business here is nearly completed."

"Oh?"

I remembered my interest in his business and how it might affect the local economy. I hadn't even had time to consider my grandiose plans for an inn at the castle, these last few days.

"And when will you be leaving?"

"Possibly next week. There is still one thing yet to be done, but I believe that all will be concluded neatly very soon."

He gave a self-satisfied smile, and I could not help but envy a man who had his business affairs in such good order. His smugness served as an ironic contrast to the distressing turn my own affairs had taken lately. I tried to turn my thoughts to gayer topics, but without much success. I'm afraid my conversation must have sounded stilted and uninteresting.

Stanley laid his plate aside and leaned closer to me. "I will tell you, Miss Blackstone, that I had hoped to have a private word with you before I left. The longer I have spent in the county, the stranger things I have heard about er, um . . . your present abode."

I tried to keep a neutral expression. "Whatever do you mean?"

He cleared his throat, and his eyes shifted as if he wanted to make sure no one else was listening.

"Worthington Manor seems to carry with it strange legends."

I smiled weakly. "I may have heard something of what you speak."

"I am not a superstitious man, but I only mention it because I would hate for you to be caught in a dangerous position."

I tried to sit straighter. "Surely these things you speak of have to do with the Worthington family itself, not with its employees."

His eyebrows arched. "Ah, I see you know something of what I speak."

I shrugged. "I have heard stories about Sir Byron's ancestors. It seems many of them died by violent means. Such occurrences lend themselves to legend."

"Of course, that is the rational attitude to take. I would not wish it otherwise."

He shook his head and gave me a wry expression. "Perhaps I have been among these superstitious Northumbrians too long, for I have listened to many a tale over a glass of ale at the Black Rook."

"Yes, I do know what you mean," I said, thinking of the odd visions I experienced whenever I went to the castle. "What sort of tales?"

He signaled Dunstan, who passed near with a tray of punch. Stanley took another glass, but I declind, asking for more coffee. I needed to regain my clear-headedness.

"Tales of the moors being haunted by the Roman soldiers who once guarded the frontiers," he said after we had our drinks. "I must admit I nearly believe them, such strange things I've heard at night. I'm used to an evening walk, but I soon found I dared not stray far from the main street of the village for the frightening clanks and screeches that seemed carried this way by the wind."

I tried to smile noncommittally. "I too have heard such things. Perhaps what they say is true. I don't discount the possibility of the spirit world."

"Perhaps. Food for thought."

"Tell me," I said thoughtfully, "have the villagers spoken much of Blackstone castle? Surely there are, er . . . such legends connected to a building of that age."

"Oh, assuredly."

I leaned forward eagerly. "What have they said?"

He took off his spectacles and polished them with a handkerchief he removed from his breast pocket.

"My dear, you are turning me into the village gossip. If I did not feel that we had a special acquaintance, I would not repeat such wild tales. But then I know that your name is Blackstone, and I have concluded that perhaps this was why you ventured to Hevingham after all."

My cheeks colored. "You are partially correct. When I, um, had an opportunity for employment here, I took it, thinking it would be interesting after all, if I did find out more about my own ancestors, since they came from here."

"Most certainly. One must return to the place of one's ancestors. Only I am confused. Some say the Worthingtons stole the land from the Blackstones. Others say the Blackstones were spies for the crown during Cromwell's time. I must confess I am confused as to which king favored which family and how it came that the Blackstones left the county some hundred years ago."

"You know as much as I, sir," I said. I shook my head. "I had hoped to learn more, but I have failed at that. There seem to be no written records."

"No?"

"Not that I have found. The vicar . . ." I paused, thinking I was talking rather a lot.

It had been my habit to pursue my quest alone, and some sense of self-protection made me hesitate to gossip about my family history. Though Stanley Symmes had been quite friendly to me, I did not consider him an intimate friend. I turned the conversation again. I wanted to know what he had heard about the castle.

"But perhaps you have learned something that I should know. What else do the villagers say about my family or the castle?"

He replaced his spectacles and laughed. "I am a man of fact. All my life has been spent poring over dry factual documents and seeing to other people's business affairs, making claims when one party has been done in by another. And you wish me to satisfy your curiosity for legends hatched on cold, dark nights by people who long for a macabre tale."

"You put it very descriptively," I said, disappointed that Stanley Symmes, keen observer that he must be in his profession, had gleaned nothing that would help me.

"They do say," he said at last, just as I was about to make an excuse to get up, "that though the owners of the castle left in disgrace and poverty, a great fortune is hid among the ruins."

My eyes opened wide and I stared at him. Besides Rosa, no one else had mentioned a fortune and I had told no one about that part of her prophecy.

"A fortune?" I said.

He nodded soberly. "In gold."

My mouth opened, and I could feel the blood pulsing through my veins. He must have noticed my look, for he patted my knee.

"Now, my dear, I only told you because you were so

206

insistent. You mustn't give any credence to such tales. Such things lead to fatuous dreams. It is most likely that any fortune would have been found and spent by now. Probably by the unscrupulous Worthingtons who came after, eh? If some of the baronets in the family line lived as extravagantly as they say, or as their portraits show, they would need a ready-made fortune in gold, would they not?"

I nodded, but my mind was racing. Never mind that Stanley Symmes was skeptical. He was a solicitor. As he said, such men dealt in the dull stuff of life, fed on family arguments. But this did nothing to stop my imagination from racing forward.

"There could have been a fortune," I murmured, almost to myself. "The Blackstones were very gay and wealthy in Queen Elizabeth's times."

He blinked, not comprehending. But I only smiled, thinking of the castle the way I had seen it in my visions. Rich fabrics and gold jewelry did not come of poverty.

"Ah, well," he said, evidently tired of the subject. "I am sorry you have not found any old documents. Should you do so and should you need them deciphered for you, I could of course perform such a service for you."

He gave a half-smile as if he meant not to encourage me too much. "Such an occurrence, unlikely as it is, would be most interesting, would it not?"

We returned to the ballroom, and I looked around for someone I knew. I did not want Stanley to feel burdened with me.

My timing was fortunate, for at that moment, Byron, who must have returned after a brief respite, was making a circle of the room and came our way. The two men shook hands.

"Thank you for your invitation, Sir Byron," said Stanley. "A most lavish celebration."

"I'm glad you are enjoying yourself. Has Miss Black-stone been keeping you entertained?"

"Most assuredly," answered Stanley. "I'm afraid I have been keeping her to myself for the last hour."

"I see," said Byron. I thought he was struggling not to show the discomfort of his wound. "I can only imagine the subject of your conversation."

Stanley laughed good-naturedly. If he sensed any of Byron's impatience, he did not show it.

"Since we met, I have been most intrigued by her story of Blackstone Castle."

"I hope you have not been putting ideas into her head. She already wants me to rebuild the ruin into an inn for travelers."

Stanley glanced at me. "Oh really?" He looked at Byron again. "I see. And do you plan to pursue this possibility?"

It seemed to me that the two men measured each other. Byron, to see if he could tell by Stanley's reaction whether the nature of his business might affect such a project. Stanley to see whether Byron was sniffing out his business. If Stanley thought Byron knew what he was up to, word might spread, and then, as Stanley had told me on the train, land prices might soar.

"Well," said Stanley, relaxing his pose. "I believe I will circulate."

He turned and bowed to me. "Miss Blackstone, I hope I have the pleasure of dancing with you later this evening."

No sooner had he turned his back to us than Byron slipped his arm through mine. "Come, my dear, accompany me to the refreshment table."

To anyone watching us, we looked like we were simply strolling along the ballroom. Byron nodded to his guests pleasantly, but I could feel the pressure on my arm and I realized he was tiring. We turned into the passageway and proceeded down the staircase, Byron surrendering my arm for the banister.

We passed Claire coming up the stairway with a gentleman I had met earlier. When she saw Byron, she radiated a smile, which cooled as it swept over me. I was both worried about Byron and annoyed with her, and I thought at that moment that she might have been the one to push the statue in the garden over, trying to get rid of me. Of course she hadn't been within miles of the manor house then, but if she had been, I wouldn't put it past her.

At the bottom of the stairway, we did not turn into the refreshment room, but instead, turned into the anteroom where the weapons were kept. Another couple was bent over the glass case, admiring the collection. Byron and I smiled at them, and then he led me to where the crossed battle-axes hung. Where one ax had been missing, it had now been replaced. The pair hung as they had originally.

Glancing over my shoulder to ascertain that the other couple were not listening, I whispered, "Did Dunstan have it cleaned?"

I already knew what the answer was, for I remembered Byron conferring with the butler when the weapon had first been missing.

"No," Byron answered in a low voice. "He was most concerned that something was missing from the collection."

"Then you don't know who took it?"

"No, I do not."

His hand grew heavier on my arm, and I remembered that he probably needed rest. Having been shot in the side only last night, he couldn't possibly be fit to act the genial host he was pretending to be.

We turned, and I thought to help him to his room, but

after we crossed the foyer, he paused at the bottom of the stairs.

"You must go back to the party, Heather."

"But surely—"

He cut me off with the raise of a hand. "There are guests about."

He favored me with an overly lascivious look, and I do believe he was teasing me. "You would not want to create a scandal, now would you? That is all the house of Worthington needs to go with our bloody curse."

My cheeks colored. "Of course not. It is just that I . . ." my lips trembled, and I could not help the emotion that flooded over me. Truly I was coming more and more under Byron Worthington's spell. I knew he was attracted to me, and the dark look of desire that replaced that of teasing drew me to him.

He held my hand for a moment, then turned and with the help of his cane, ascended the stairs. I did not see how I could face the party again, so many were my concerns. But I ascended the stairs, a discreet amount of time later, and re-entered the ballroom.

What happened after that is a blur. I plastered a smile on my face and chattered with the guests I met, for Lady Liddicoat caught up with me and saw to it that introductions were made. I danced a little, always pleading that I was a poor dancer. Carver hung onto me longer than I would have liked. His sister cast me curious looks when she saw me, and I was certain that the displeasure on her face was caused by Byron's absence.

Some time after midnight I slipped out of the room. The musicians would play for one more hour yet, but I felt I had done my duty. I found my way to bed, struggled out of my dress and sat for a while in the window seat, my lamp out, looking over the dark moor.

After a while I noticed several small points of light

that I had first taken for stars. But they were too low for stars, and I realized that they must be coming from the moor. The lights flickered so that I could not always be sure that they were there.

I could hear nothing but the music from the ballroom below, so even had I opened my window to listen for the strange sounds that so often blew down on the wind, I do not think I could have heard anything. I left the window seat and went to bed then, wondering whether the points of light came from the Roman soldiers loyally guarding the Wall and keeping the empire safe, or whether the lights were made by the Gypsies.

Sixteen

Byron was much stronger on Christmas Day. He presided over the sumptuous meal with no apparent strain. The guests who had been invited to stay over, left after the meal and many thank you's. In the evening the household gathered in the formal parlor, and Lady Liddicoat helped her son hand out gifts to each of the staff. Mine was a lovely cameo broach, a proper gift for a secretary.

Then everyone bid Byron and his mother good evening. I followed the others out and started up the stairs. I had not been asked to stay, and I thought perhaps mother and son would like to share a few moments together on this holiday.

In my room, Annie presented me with a gift, a handmade sachet filled with spices to scent my linens. I in turn gave her bobbin, thread and a pillow with which to make lace, for I wanted to encourage her.

She was brushing out my hair when I noticed that her hands were shaking.

"What's wrong, Annie?" I asked her. "You do not seem yourself."

Her eyes met mine in the mirror, and the brush fell to her side. "Oh, miss, I'm so worried. I didn't want to talk about it, but I can't help it."

Her face screwed up, and her hands flew up to cover it.

"Annie, what's wrong?"

She shook her head, then pulled out a crumpled piece of paper from her pocket. I took it and pressed it out on my dresser. The warning was scrawled in big, printed letters. "Leve here if you no whats best," it said.

I started to tremble as I stared at it. "Annie, where did this come from?"

She dug a handkerchief out of her pocket and pressed it to her eyes and nose. "I found it on your bed. I didn't want you to see it. What does it mean?"

I shook my head. "I don't know. But I'm glad you showed it to me. Someone wants me to leave the manor."

She sank to her knees, clasping my hands. "Perhaps you should leave," she said, obviously frightened by the message. "Bad things have been happening in these parts. This house is dangerous."

I held her hands firmly. "What bad things do you mean, Annie? You must tell me what you know."

"Well, the master bein' laid up by that statue fallin' over. And them shots last night. He said it was a poacher, but . . . I don't believe it. And then there's the specters up on the moors. Everyone says to stay in the house at night. You don't know what's up there to get you."

"All right, Annie, I can understand your concerns. But these incidents all have different explanations. Taken one by one, it isn't so bad."

By convincing her, I must have been trying to rationalize the strange events to myself. But I wanted to know what Annie knew that I should know.

"There could be a poacher, or someone trying to rob the house. Sir Byron and I may have surprised him in the garden that night, and he pushed over the statue so he could make a run for it."

Plausible, but not very likely. However, Annie's round

213

eyes began to take on the expression of someone willing to listen.

"And the spirits that roam the moors. Have any of them been heard to come down and bother us in our houses?"

She thought for a moment. "I don't know about that. Not that I've heard."

"Good." The thought was comforting. I hoped it was true. "Now, Annie, you must tell me if there's anything specific that you know of that's happened. If there is, I might be able to help you."

She shook her head from side to side, but her eyes were still wild with fear. "No, no, miss. But it isn't safe. I know it."

I observed her carefully. Something had brought on these hysterics, and I was almost certain it was from more than just the note. It was time to find out whom she had met in the garden. She knew that he was the "poacher."

"Annie, look at me."

She bunched up the handkerchief and dabbed it at her eyes, but she raised her face to me.

"I want to ask you something, Annie. It may be very important. You were in the garden the night of the shot, weren't you?"

Her face colored, but she nodded.

"Who did you meet there?"

She shrugged and looked at her lap. "Just a man I met in the village. We didn't do nothin', really. He bought me my tea a few times, that's all."

She looked up at me apologetically. "Says he's from London, and he might take me there. He has a nice house on a square. Oh, miss, surely you understand. I ain't seen anything but here and the village where I come from. A chance to go to London don't come every day.

So when he asked me to see him, I didn't see the harm in it."

"What is his name?"

"Walter Bailey?"

I frowned. I had heard of no one by that name. I would have to ask in the village. But her story needed some checking. Of course it was not uncommon for a man to gain favors from a young woman by promising to take her away. I didn't even know who Walter Bailey was, but I very much doubted he had a house in London. Or even if he did, Annie would never see it.

"Annie, you must be careful. Surely you know the ways of men by now." I sighed. No one had ever explained these things to me, but life in a factory had taught me more, perhaps, than a mother would ever have told me.

"This Mr. Bailey may not live up to his promises. Has he," I hesitated, clearing my throat. Such things were not easily discussed. But the fact that I had to find out what Annie had to say drove me on. "Has he made any advances to you?"

Her face gave her away even as she shrugged. "Well, I didn't do anything I didn't want to."

"I see."

She got up from her kneeling position and straightened her skirt.

"Annie, I'm not here to give you a moral lecture. It's just that, as you say, there have been some unusual incidents at the manor. I'm simply trying to get to the bottom of them. I just want to know who this Mr. Bailey is and what he wants from you."

She wrapped her handkerchief around her hands. "I'm not an innocent, if that's what you mean. I've had beaux before."

I tilted my head at her. "Yes, I thought so. In fact I

215

was under the impression that you and Robin were courting.

"Oh that. Not no more."

"What happened?"

She shrugged. "We just don't get on."

I shook my head, feeling I had come to a brick wall. I knew only too well that what a woman would do with a man very much depended on how the woman felt. Hadn't I been repulsed by Mr. Biggleston's advances, whereas I only too willingly gave myself to Byron? My own misgivings interfered with my train of thought, and I had to try to concentrate again. I took a new approach.

"This note," I said, picking it up. "Are you sure you don't know where it came from?"

She nodded. "It was lyin' on the bed when I came in to sweep up the ashes. I could read enough to see it was some sort of threat. I wanted to get rid of it before you saw it."

I could understand her simple logic. What wasn't visible wasn't a threat. But it hadn't worked for her. She knew there was some threat here. But after talking to her, I believed she didn't know where it was coming from any more than I did.

"I'm glad you showed it to me, Annie. I will take precautions. And so must you."

"Then you aren't going to leave."

My heart dropped in my chest and I stared for a moment at the flames from the burning peat in the fireplace.

"I cannot leave."

"Why not?"

I tried to put on an acceptable expression. "I have nowhere else to go. I cannot return to the horrible factory where I worked in Nottingham. I have no family." I thought momentarily of Rosa, but I did not need to tell

Annie that I did not think the Gypsy life was for me.

"But surely you could go to another home. With your skills at lacemaking, and you can read or write."

I nodded. "Yes, perhaps I could seek employment elsewhere. But I cannot leave now, at the height of the winter holidays."

She looked worried, as if she actually wanted to help me find a position elsewhere.

I tried to smile. "Do not worry, Annie. I will try to take care." I took a deep breath and let it out. "Besides, I must stay for another reason."

"What is that?"

I had to put it in a way that she would understand. "I came here because my family comes from here. I wanted to find out if there was any truth to the legends that had been handed down from generation to generation."

She nodded. "The Blackstone legends."

I nodded. "Yes. It's hard to explain. I know the property's no longer ours. It isn't that so much as . . ." I drifted off, I couldn't explain it exactly, only that there was a mystery here that was not yet solved.

I wanted to know so many things. Where my visions came from. Who had lived in the castle during Queen Elizabeth's reign. If Charles the First had really promised Blackstone Castle to my ancestors, what had happened to the deed at the restoration? And last, though I tried not to dwell on it, whether there really had been a fortune in gold, and if so, where it was now?

I dragged my thoughts back to Annie. "I guess it is a little hard to explain." I could never mention my other reason. The reason that I should both stay and go, and that was Byron.

"It's late now, Annie, you'd better go. But do be careful."

"I will, miss."

I finished preparing for bed and then, after turning down the lamp, I crawled into bed. Hadrian joined me on the pillow that had become his, and we eventually both got settled.

The next day was the first chance I had to go to the village alone. Christmas day being past, the household returned to a semblance of normal. The holidays were not over, for the New Year was a very special time in Northumberland, I was told. But for the moment I was free to slip away.

I had memorized the verses from the missing pages of my Bible, and I was going to see if I could find any clue as to what they might mean. The riding habit had been steam-cleaned and pressed, and while it had shrunk a little, I could still wear it.

The day was cold and crisp, with little of the dampness that seemed so often to sink into my bones. I bundled up and went to the stables to ask Robin to saddle Theo for me. Her leg had healed under Robin's care. He was in the stable yard throwing horseshoes with Lady Liddicoat's coachman, whose name she had told me was Charles, and the younger groom, Richard. Both were in undress livery, their roundabout coats of a sturdy brown serge. Their low hats had been set aside. The latter two turned to watch me approach, but Robin pretended to ignore me, going on with his game.

I waited until he had thrown a shoe, missing by a yard, and then interrupted him. "Robin, I need to take Theo out."

I had planned to ask him to saddle her, however, I suddenly decided I was not in the mood to put up with his attitude.

"I'll saddle her," I said, "so you don't have to interrupt your game."

Richard was openly staring at me, and I did not miss the lecherous look in his eye. The older coachman maintained better decorum, brushing his hands and busying himself with the horseshoes as if not paying any attention to a conversation that was not addressed to him.

Robin said nothing, so I proceeded to the stable. I had realized for some time the inconvenience of not knowing how to drive the trap. For many of my errands to town, I ought to take the trap so as to bring back more packages. The tension between Robin and myself had grown so that I did not think I would ever ask him to take me in the phaeton again. Perhaps I could get Byron to teach me to drive. If I stayed on here, I had to add, reminding myself of my decision not to think of my position here as permanent.

I shook my head as I lifted the saddle from the wall of the tack room and then carried it along the row of stone-built stalls until I came to Theo's. She must have heard me coming, for she had her head over the wooden stall door and gave me a soft whinny.

"Hello, old girl," I said, giving her the sugar I had brought from the kitchen. "Ready to go to the village with me? You can help me in my quest."

"And what quest might that be?"

Robin startled me, and I swung around, the stirrups banging on the stall door.

"Robin, I didn't know you were there."

"I shouldn't have said anything. Looks like you were havin' a fine conversation with yer horse."

I heaved the saddle to the top of the stall door. "I thought you were playing your game outside."

He drew out a piece of straw that stuck out from the edge of the stall and put it between his teeth. He leaned on the end of the stall.

"Ye said ye were goin' to the village."

"I also said I would saddle Theo myself. You didn't need to stop your game."

He didn't look at me but chewed on the straw.

I was tired of our cat and mouse game, so I confronted him, hands on my hips.

"Robin, why don't you like me?"

He gave no indication that he had heard me for some seconds. Then he took the straw out of his mouth and shifted his weight to the other leg. When he did look at me it was with a narrowed gaze.

"I never said I bore ye any ill will," he said.

I exhaled a breath in frustration. "No, you haven't, but I think I have some understanding of people. You must admit you have not been exactly friendly to me. Have I done something to offend you?"

He cocked his head slightly, his eyelids dropping further. "Things changed after ye came here."

"What things?"

He shook his head just slightly. "Things."

I took a step nearer. He was so closemouthed I doubted I could get him to say what was on his mind, but my self-assigned role as interrogator must have made me more aggressive. For I would not let him get away with his vague insinuations.

"Robin, you must tell me what you are talking about. It's important."

He replaced the straw between his teeth and leaned on the stable post again. "Why should it matter to ye?"

"It just does, that's all. There are things going on here that I don't fully understand. I am determined to find out what they are all about."

The directness of my statement seemed to jar him out of his covert hostility. He blinked, his eyes open wider. Anger flared in them, and he threw down the straw.

"Ye put ideas into Annie's head, that's what."

"Whatever do you mean?"

He shrugged, and I was afraid he was going to slip back into his shell again. "Things was fine between Annie and me before you came, if you know what I mean. Now she ain't got the time of day for me."

My shoulders sagged. "I'm sorry, Robin. I thought you were courting her. Believe me I never said a thing to her about you." I couldn't say I'd never said anything to Annie about her love life, for that would not be true anymore, but I had never criticized Robin in her presence.

"I'm sorry if you've had a falling out with her. I only yesterday learned that she'd met a man she's seeing. She said he's from London. Robin, you must believe me. I told Annie myself not to trust this stranger. Whatever he's promised her might be nothing more than fancy. I warned her not to get involved with such a man."

He looked at me suspiciously. "Ye did?"

"Yes. I don't know who he is or where he comes from." I shook my head. "He may be perfectly innocent, but there's no way of knowing. I haven't even met him."

Robin shrugged. " 'Tis no concern of mine what Annie does anymore. If she wants to put on airs and get herself all tied up with some gentleman, 'tis no business of mine, now. I don't care what she does."

I almost reached out to touch him, but the barrier he kept around himself was still impenetrable. "I think you do care, Robin," I said.

He flicked his eyes in my direction, and I could see the hurt and anger there. I could not tell if he truly loved the girl or if she had merely humiliated him, but I saw I had struck a cord. I was also very aware that it might be Robin himself who was perpetrating some of the dangers that had befallen me, if only out of malice. But I thought of a way to make him useful to my purposes.

221

"Robin, you say you do not know who the man is that Annie is seeing?"

He shook his head. "Never set eyes on 'im."

"I see. Well, I'd like to know who he is. If you find out anymore about him, you'll let me know, won't you? As I said, I'm trying to talk some sense into Annie myself. I would appreciate knowing anything you learn about this gentleman."

He shrugged noncommittally. "You askin' me to spy?"

"Well, no, not exactly. I just mean if you happen to see him, or learn his name, or anything like that."

"Don't know how that'd happen. Don't never talk to Annie no more."

There was no use pressing him, and I knew he wouldn't tell me anything unless he wanted to. I began to lift the saddle down, but he unlatched the stall door and swung it open. Then he took the saddle from me.

"I'll do that."

I repressed a grin. "Thank you." Perhaps we had become allies of a sort, after all.

He finished saddling and bridling Theo and then led her out of the stables to the mounting block for me. I gathered up the skirt of my riding habit and mounted, taking the reins from Robin. Theo waited patiently for me to nudge her with my heel. I waved goodbye to Robin and headed to the road.

Once I turned her in the direction of the village, I had nothing else to do, for she knew where we were going. It didn't take long to reach the bend in the road that led to the little stone bridge. Smoke curled up from the cottages, and the village lanes were quiet. I took the jog in the road that led up to the church, looking past the cemetery to the babbling brook that followed the road and passed under the bridge, curving around the churchyard like a consoling arm.

I dismounted and tied Theo to the wrought iron fence and opened the gate. No one was about, so I took the flagstone walk along the side of the church and into the cemetery. I passed gravestones I had seen before, and I was headed toward the section where Reverend Brown had shown me the Blackstone graves, when I was brought up short. I stopped before a grave that looked freshly dug.

The grave was covered over, but the earth was freshly turned. I glanced at the marker. It was one of the older ones, and I could not read all of the worn inscription. I heard footsteps and turned to Reverend Brown, who was hastening toward me, his hands folded in front of him, his gown flapping behind.

"Good morning, Miss Blackstone," he said. "Nice day, isn't it? I hope your Christmas was equally fine." He was a bit out of breath when he stopped.

"Good morning to you, Reverend. Our Christmas was lovely, thank you. And yours?"

"Quite the blessed day," he said. "Mrs. Brown sees that we all have more than our share of good things to eat, and games to play with the children."

I knew that, traditionally, all the children in the village called on the vicarage on Christmas Day, and I was sure none of them went away with empty bellies.

"And what brings you to the church on so fine a morning?"

I thought he looked uneasy when he said it. Gone was the joviality with which he usually carried on conversations. I came right to the point.

"I noticed there's a freshly dug grave here. Has there been a funeral recently?"

He shook his head. "No, no. The Lord has not taken anyone recently."

He looked at the upturned dirt and shook his head.

"Rabbits been giving some trouble, burrowing around the graves, though." He shook his head. "Have to set some traps out here, I'm afraid."

"A rabbit did that?"

"Oh, to be sure, to be sure. I saw one of them myself and ran out here to scare him off." He gave me a doubtful smile. "Nothing to worry about. We'll catch them and take them up to the moors if they're no good for dinner."

I said nothing but looked from him to the grave. There was no rabbit hole, and the symmetry with which the earth had been dug were proof to me that he was lying, but I saw that he was going to stick to his story. I made a tour of the Blackstone graves, looking from where they lay to the bend in the stream, a few yards distance. The vicar followed me, chattering about trivia so that I could not hear myself think. Finally, I bid him good morning and returned to Theo.

Reverend Brown bid me good-bye and went into his church. As I was leading Theo along the lane, a plump little woman, dressed in black, with a bonnet that nearly covered her face came up to me. She stopped in my path, looking out from under her bonnet with sharp, blue eyes.

"Heard what ye was talking to the vicar about."

I blinked. "Oh?"

"Yer wastin' yer breath on him. He won't speak of what goes on in that there graveyard."

"Why, what do you mean?"

"Ain't no rabbit. 'Tis the spirits at night that are diggin' up the graves."

I shivered. "Spirits? What spirits?"

"They come down from the lake, if you ask me."

I glanced at the graveyard, believing her for a moment. But then the more rational part of my mind took over and I leveled my gaze at her.

"A long way for them to come to dig up graves. What do you suppose they want."

"Evildoings," was all she said.

I looked at her. These Northumbrians put a supernatural explanation to everything they did not understand. I did not see why spirits would bother to dig up graves just to terrorize the village inhabitants. No, I decided someone very much more human than that was at the bottom of this business.

Someone, I suspected had taken the pages out of my Bible and was following the same clues I was. Someone else believed that the secret lay at the bottom of a grave and was trying to find it.

Seventeen

I mounted Theo, and nodding to the village woman, who watched me go, I made my way to the bridge. If I had been fooling myself about being in danger before, I had no such excuses now. The Blackstone heritage was real, or else why would someone be pursuing it as doggedly as I was? For me there might be simply the reward of knowing my family roots, even if there was nothing left that I could show for it but a castle that very likely would not stand for another hundred years.

But someone else believed the story and was looking for more than that. Either fortune or property might evidently be within my grasp, and someone knew it. If they found what they were looking for, I would be the last barrier to be disposed of before the fortune or whatever the reward could be was manipulated into other hands.

I shivered from more than the cold as I urged Theo forward. The babbling of the stream to my right seemed to be telling me to hurry, hurry. I must get away before the final blow struck. The forest on my left mocked me, only waiting until I came within the grasp of the dangling branches.

I tried to separate fear from rational planning. I could not fight an unseen enemy. I did not know where to turn, for I was unsure anymore who was friend and who was foe. Even Byron had something to gain by my departure. I had not felt so hopeless and frightened since the night I had fled from Mr. Biggleston's grasp.

226

I thought of Raoule and the Gypsy band. I didn't believe they meant me any harm. Certainly Raoule had been entrusted with my safety. But I had not told him everything. Gypies were very fond of gold, and if they knew there was a fortune in gold coins to be had, I could not be certain of where friendship might end and greed begin.

I knew I was not thinking rationally, and I only wanted to return to my room where, together with Hadrian for company, I might be able to sort out my situation. I had to decide what to do. If I were to leave, I must leave immediately. And if I were to do that, I needed a place to go, enough money not to starve until I found a position. Truly, there was much to consider.

Theo must have been as anxious to get back as I was, for she kept up a lively pace. At the stable, Robin came out to take her from me. I thought our talk had done some good, for he was much more communicative to me than he had been before.

I was preoccupied as I took the path to the side door, and I did not notice whether there was anyone about. I heard the meow at the same time the flying object whizzed past, causing me to jump sideways, grasping at shrubs as a brick landed with a thud where I had stood.

I looked up to see Hadrian leaning over the balcony, crying. I was too stunned to think and stood a few moments, trying to gather my wits. My heart raced, and I bent to pick up the brick and carry it inside. As I turned the corner of the passageway, I came upon Byron. We stopped short, both blinking at each other.

"What is that you have in your hand?" he inquired.

I looked at it stupidly. "A brick. I believe it came loose from the balcony above. It nearly hit me."

He frowned and took it from me. "When did this happen?"

"Just now."

The expression in his eyes was serious. "Let us go see."

I followed him up the east stairs and down the hall to the balcony above the door where I had come in. Mrs. MacDougal was cleaning the room that opened onto the balcony directly above the path. She stopped her work and stood erect when we entered.

Byron confronted her. "It appears that this brick was dislodged from the balcony and fell. I've come to inspect the damage."

"Of course, sir," she said.

I watched her face as Byron spoke, and other than her odd look, there was no sign that she might be trying to hide the fact that she herself had pushed the brick off. But then I had never seen Mrs. MacDougal register any emotion except either displeasure or disapproval.

She moved to open the doors for us. As she did so, Hadrian ran in, mewing. I picked him up. Byron looked at me questioningly.

"The cat was on the balcony."

"Yes," I said. "I heard him meow just before the brick fell."

"Perhaps he pushed it," said Byron. "Cats do have a propensity for knocking things off high surfaces."

I petted the bundle of fur, now purring against my shoulder. "I suppose that is possible."

I held Hadrian away from me so I could look at his black, white and orange face. The yellow eyes blinked.

"Did you push the brick off, kitty? Your timing was very good, for you nearly pushed it onto my head."

Byron caught the irony of my tone and pulled the corner of his mouth back. The brick was heavy, and while it was true that cats often amused themselves by pushing objects off of high places, I found it ironic that the cat would have timed it so perfectly. Yet I had heard the meow, so I knew that Hadrian had been above my head when the brick fell.

We went out onto the balcony and had no trouble locating the place from which the brick had come loose. Byron inspected the masonry around it.

"This corner is in need of repair." As he wiggled other loose bricks, pieces of mortar fell out. "I will have a mason investigate this immediately."

He stood up. "This house is old. It is hard to keep up with checking for damage. I'm sorry you had to be there when the brick came loose."

I pressed my lips together. "Surely you do not think it came loose by itself."

He glanced over his shoulder. Mrs. MacDougal had resumed her cleaning, though she would never show that she was listening to us. Still, I knew his words were guarded for her benefit.

"As I said, the cat was here. If the brick was loose, old Hadrian might not have been able to resist playing with it."

Hadrian turned his head and strained toward Byron, giving a meow.

"You see," I said. "He disagrees."

Byron looked at me seriously for a moment. I thought he was going to argue with me, but instead he said, "Perhaps you are right. Perhaps Hadrian was trying to warn you."

I looked around the sunny balcony, which led to two more rooms besides the one we had come through. The French doors had been closed when we entered the room. If someone had been up here, they had locked the cat out when they had closed the doors. Perhaps they had done so in order to make it look like Hadrian had done it. What I did not know was whether Hadrian had been wandering in this part of the house or whether the perpetrator had brought him here for the purpose.

I looked at Hadrian who blinked and jumped out of my arms. Too bad we could not ask him. Hadrian walked back indoors, his tail in the air. He sat on the rug around which Mrs. MacDougal was sweeping. She stopped her work, whisked the broom in his direction and said shoo.

Hadrian skittered through the open door into the hallway as Mrs. MacDougal gave a huge sneeze. She fished in her pocket for a handkerchief and was blowing her nose loudly when we stepped back into the room.

"Beg your padon, sir," she said to Byron. "It's the cat makes me sneeze."

"Very good, Mrs. MacDougal," said Byron. "By the way, has anyone else come in here while you were working in this part of the house?"

"Why no, sir. Why do you ask?"

"Just wondered. We'll leave you to your work now. Come, Heather."

He escorted me out of the room. So Mrs. MacDougal had a reaction to cats. If that was true, then it was doubtful that she would have carried the bundle of fur down here, or she would have been sneezing when we came in. Evidently she hadn't known Hadrian was outside on the balcony.

Byron left me at my room. I was so preoccupied I hardly listened to what he said. Something about a meeting in the study.

I shut the door and sat on the bed. Dejection overwhelmed me. I simply gave up. It was clear that my life was in danger. No matter how well-meaning were my protectors, they could not be everywhere I was at all times. A moldering castle with my name on it no longer seemed worth it. I had not seen the drawings of the castle Lady Liddicoat promised to locate for me, but I simply could not stay here any longer.

I knew I could not tell Byron of my decision. I knew what would happen then. He would look at me with the look of desire that sprang between us when we were alone. Perhaps he would even make love to me again. But what good was it? His mother would never let him marry a woman outside his class, and I was certain that her visit here had very much to do with seeing her eligible son settled. I could not settle for being his mistress forever. The day would come when he would tire of me.

As I thought about these things I began moving about the room. I opened the trunk that sat at the foot of my bed. I tossed out the linens that were stored there and began getting down my dresses. I did not take any of the gowns Byron's sister had worn, only my underthings and the gowns that had been made for me since I was here. I put in what remained of the bolt of lace I had brought here. Some of it had been used on my own gowns, and I had given a bit of it to Lady Liddicoat. Then I reached into the armoire and got out my old suitcase. It looked worse than it had when I had arrived, but then, I was probably just seeing it in a different light after the comfort I had been living in.

My only comfort was the fact that the new clothes I now had would enable me to search for respectable employment. I went to the drawer where I had safely kept the money Rosa had given me, part of which had purchased my round-trip ticket from Nottingham. I took the ticket out of the green silk purse and then put it back again. Too many bad memories colored that city for me, I hoped I would find a position elsewhere. I might return to Nottingham, however, to ask Rosa to counsel me.

I finished my packing, including my bobbins, thread and pillows for making lace. I did not have my Bible, but at the moment I didn't care. The Bible had brought only trouble for me. I pondered what to do next. I could not carry the trunk myself. I would take only the suitcase and leave so that no one would notice me. After I had settled somewhere, I could send for the trunk. Since I did not know the train schedule, I would leave very early

231

in the morning, before the house was awake. I would have to walk to the station.

Thus decided, I replaced the suitcase in the bottom of the armoire, and sat down with a bit of embroidery. I must act as if everything was normal.

I was glad I had not been invited to dine with Byron and his mother, for if I saw Byron that evening, I might have been tempted to forsake my plans. That was not the case, for they had been invited to dine elsewhere and would be home very late. I dined in the servants' hall with the rest of the staff and listened idly to Cook and Sophie gossiping, with an occasional comment from Mrs. MacDougal.

At one end of the table, Robin carried on a conversation with Dunstan. I did not miss Robin's covert glances at Annie, but when she looked his way, he ignored her. I thought she was truly sorry she had hurt his feelings.

After dinner I excused myself early and went up to my room. Soon I heard a scratch on the door and opened it to admit Hadrian. He must have gone down to the kitchen to eat.

"Hello, Hadrian," I said as he walked in and sat at my feet, licking his chops. "Have you come to keep me company?"

I felt a twinge of loss that tomorrow I would be leaving this furry companion, for since I had been here, he seemed to have attached himself to me. Then again, perhaps he had simply gotten used to living in this room, no matter who the occupant was. I bent down to scoop him up.

"You mustn't tell anyone when I leave in the morning," I whispered. "It's our secret."

"Meow," he said.

I carried him to the wing chair by the fire and sat down, holding him on my lap.

"Will you miss me?"

I scratched his chin and then rubbed the smooth coat of his back. He whipped his tail about and purred, blinking his big eyes.

"I know you didn't push the brick down on me. I only wish you could tell me who did."

He looked into my eyes. "Meow."

"Who then?"

No response. I began a little game. I knew the cat couldn't actually tell me if he had seen anyone on the balcony, but I made as if he could.

"Was it Mrs. MacDougal? She's none too friendly to anyone, and she was cleaning in the room that day."

He didn't answer, only flipped his tail.

"Who else? Annie? I think she likes me, but she has her secrets, we know that, don't we?"

"Meow."

"Robin might have done it. He's admitted to not liking me very much."

No response from the cat.

"But I set Robin straight, didn't I?"

"Meow." Hadrian clawed the material of my dress.

I sighed. This assessment of possible suspects who wanted me out of the way was not going to get me anywhere.

"Or was it Byron?" I asked the room idly, stroking the cat, no longer trying to read his eyes for an answer.

Silly of me to keep thinking Byron might be behind all this. But I had heard of warped personalities, appearing normal on the surface, but with a strain of evil that only came out when they were desperate, and he had said his fortune was not great at present.

I took a long, soapy bath in the claw-footed tub. Then I dried my hair and skin on the thick towels I had come to take for granted. Annie came in later to help me prepare for bed. I wanted to bring up the subject of Robin, and waited for an opportunity. I thought perhaps I

233

shouldn't interfere, but I would most likely not see her again, and I couldn't help but want to offer advice. When I glanced at her in the mirror as she braided my hair, her complexion looked sallow, her lips tight.

"I spoke to Robin today," I finally said. "I had gotten the feeling he didn't like me, and I finally asked him why, because I couldn't think of anything I had done to offend him."

"Oh? He can be awful standoffish. I learned that right enough." She didn't meet my eyes and acted as if she didn't care. But I pressed on.

"He was hurt, that's all. He had blamed me for giving you ideas."

She frowned, and I winced as she pulled my hair. "What kind of ideas is that?"

"It seems my timing was bad. You met your Mr. Bailey about the time I came here."

She tossed her head. "What if I did?"

At the same time I saw in the mirror that her hands started to shake.

"Well, I suppose all that's past. Still, I think Robin cares for you."

"No he don't, else he wouldn't treat me like dirt. Just cause I didn't want to see him no more doesn't mean he couldn't be friendly. Acts like I'm no good." She shook her head vehemently. "That's just like a man, isn't it? They get you to do certain things with 'em when they want it, then when you don't want it from 'em anymore, they act as if you was cheap. Robin just don't understand."

Suddenly she started to cry. Her hands went to her face, and she uttered a sob.

"Oh, Annie," I said, turning to take her hands. "What's wrong?"

She shook her head, but wouldn't say anything. I could imagine what had happened. She and Robin had

234

been lovers, then Mr. Bailey had come along, taken advantage of her, promising the sun, moon and stars. Perhaps he had left the village now, and Annie was ashamed of having been duped.

I felt sorry for her. If only she knew how close to her own situation I was. I was far from innocent myself. I held my head in my hands, fighting the constricting feeling that seemed to be gripping me. If there had been a train that left in the middle of the night, I would have taken my luggage and walked out that very moment.

As it was, I had to wait until morning. When Annie left, I picked up Hadrian, walked to the bed and got in. I extinguished the lamp and lay staring at the shadows dancing on my wall from the dying fire. I remembered my shadow in the fisherman's hut when Byron had held me in his arms, and I pushed the thought away. I fought the tears that ran down my cheeks and onto my pillow as Hadrian licked my salty cheeks.

If Byron loved me. If he wanted to marry me. If, if, if, but such things had not come to be. I turned on my side and hit the pillow with my fist, startling Hadrian, who got to his feet.

Rosa had been wrong. I had faced danger, all right, and evil. Some evil menace, the source of which I could not find. But where was the love she had spoken of. Physical love we had had together, but not lasting love. Not great love as she had said. And there was no fortune. Or if there was, whoever wanted to be rid of me could have it. No fortune was worth dying for. I could support myself. That was all that was necessary. If I married someday I could tell the Blackstone legend to my children. I would show them which pages had been torn from my Bible. Let them search for their heritage.

My drained emotions and train of thoughts finally lulled me. I awoke much later to the sound of carriage wheels. I heard voices below as Lady Liddicoat's coach rolled off to the carriage house.

I awoke before dawn, forcing my eyes open. I got out of bed and stumbled wearily to the window, opening it enough to look out. The sky had lightened a little, and the cold air on my face helped me wake up. I considered forgetting my plans, for the bed was warm and tempting. But I shook the sleep from my head and hastened into a good traveling suit, and laced up my walking boots. When I was ready, I gave Hadrian one last pat, telling him to be quiet. I was sure that Hadrian padded around the manor every morning about this hour, for most cats I had known were early morning creatures, but I didn't want him to attract any special notice this morning.

"Good-bye Hadrian. Be a good kitty for me."

I felt like I was leaving a friend, but I consoled myself that wherever I went, if I was lucky and found a good position, there might be other pets. And Hadrian had a very good home here. At least no one was threatening him the way they had been threatening me. I envied him his security.

Sophie would be up lighting the fires downstairs, but if I took the east stairs I should be able to avoid her. I picked up the suitcase and tiptoed into the hall. I took the stairs slowly, avoiding squeaky steps. At the bottom, there was no one in the passage and I crept to the side door.

Once outside I breathed easier. It was still dark enough that I could go along the path without much worry. I had a clear view of the stables, but I didn't think Robin or Lady Liddicoat's servants would be up this early. I walked lightly, trying not to crunch my boots on the gravel. Once on the hard ground of the stable yard, I walked more quickly. When I reached the road I was breathing hard.

It was a little lighter now, and I was thankful. I did

236

not want to walk in the dark beside the line of trees that followed the road. I tightened my grasp on the suitcase and set off, leaving the manor behind. I changed arms often, for carrying the suitcase was tiring. The distance was greater on foot, but I was not worried about the time. I had gotten away from the manor safely. By the time I was missed I would be on a train headed out of Northumberland.

By the time I reached the village, the sky had been light for nearly an hour. Only a little distance more to the station, I told myself, when the weight from the suitcase felt like it would break my wrist. Nothing moved in the village lanes, but smoke curling up from the chimneys told me that the busy housewives were already at work. I climbed the steps to the station and set the suitcase down by the bench outside.

The station was closed, but the schedule was posted. There would be a train in an hour. I counted myself lucky to have only an hour's wait. But in an hour I would be missed from the manor. Byron might send someone to try to stop me, or even come himself.

I suppose that I half-hoped he would, even if I didn't admit it to myself. I could have left a note, but what would it have said? "I'm resigning as your mistress and seamstress. The position has proved too dangerous for my liking."

I hugged myself as I sat on the bench in the early morning chill. My coat was keeping me warm enough, and the day looked bright. When the tea shop across the street opened, I might step in for a warm cup of tea. As I waited, the village came to life. I saw the burly blacksmith throw open his doors. Deep inside his forge, the bellows urged the red coals to life. At the other end of the street, stableboys harnessed horses and turned out coaches in the yard at the Black Rook. Then two familiar figures emerged from the inn.

I stiffened. If I saw people I knew, word might get back to the manor of my plans. I stood to move out of sight, but as I approached the corner of the little station, I heard a voice call hello.

Stanley Symmes broke off his conversation to raise his hat at me. The vicar turned in my direction. I tried to swallow the panic I felt. Running away would look silly, so I approached the edge of the platform. The men walked slowly in my direction, still conversing. When they had come level with me, they stopped. Good mornings were said all around.

"Going on a journey?" said Mr. Symmes, his eyes flickering to the suitcase sitting by the bench. Reverend Brown looked on beneficently.

"Yes," I said: "As a matter-of-fact I am."

I stood my ground. Besides, why should either of these men care whether I stayed or went? Their acquaintances had been superficial. What I chose to do had no bearing on their lives. Already I could tell that the vicar was anxious to be on his way, though Stanley Symmes displayed more curiosity. I looked at the vicar.

"Please tell Mrs. Brown good-bye for me. I will er . . . be gone for some time."

He nodded. "Going to visit friends for the New Year?"

I had forgotten about the impending holiday.

"Yes, that's right. I have a dear friend in Nottingham. She has invited me to come and stay with her."

Mr. Symmes eyed me speculatively, and I tried to remember if I had mentioned Rosa to him during our journey here. He turned to the vicar.

"I have enjoyed our discussion, Reverend Brown. You have been most helpful."

The vicar fluttered his hands. "Not at all, my dear man. I am here to serve."

"I will keep our appointment for after lunch," said Mr.

Symmes. "I will be most interested in seeing the remaining records you spoke of."

So Mr. Symmes was moving ahead with his land purchases. I felt a momentary regret that I had not been able to convince Byron that he too could take advantage of the imminent change that I was sure was going to take place in Hevingham when the railroad was extended. But that spark of enterprise in me had been extinguished along with my other hopes and dreams.

Reverend Brown bid Mr. Symmes good day and went on his way. But Mr. Symmes turned and came up the steps to talk to me. I gritted my teeth. The last thing I felt like doing was making pleasant conversation. But he smiled and removed his hat. At the same moment, the station opened.

"So you are returning to Nottingham?" he asked pleasantly.

I nodded, not meeting his inquiring gaze.

He consulted his pocket watch. "Of course. There is a train in twenty minutes, I believe."

I nodded. He would know the schedule since he came and went so often on his business.

"Ah, and now the station is open. Have you a ticket?"

I hesitated. "Yes."

He was too perceptive and must have guessed that I was using the other half of my round-trip ticket. His eyes examined my face. When he spoke, it was in a lower, more intimate tone.

"I don't mean to pry," he said. "But my guess is that you are leaving for good. Is this true?"

I stammered. "I have decided to look for work elsewhere."

His look of pity made my skin crawl. I felt as if he were guessing all my secrets. He nodded and gave a sigh.

"I see. I am sorry things did not work out for you here. I had looked forward to enjoying more of your company."

I could not help frowning at him. I did not mean to be insulting, it was just that at the moment I did not feel like social banter. Stanley Symmes had proved pleasant to talk to, especially when I was trying to decipher his business here, but I was in no mood to encourage him.

"I wish you well with your enterprises," I said rather stiffly.

He could not repress a smile. "Thank you. They are going rather well at the moment. My employers are quite pleased with what I have accomplished here."

He seemed to accept the situation that I was leaving and consulted his watch again. "I must be on my way."

He took my hand. "Good luck, Miss Blackstone. And please let me know where you are staying when you get settled. You have my card, I believe."

"Yes, I still have it. And thank you."

He smiled congenially and went down the steps. I watched him disappear into the tea shop as I heard the whistle of the train in the distance.

The next moment a hand covered my mouth. I tried to scream, but strong fumes penetrated my nostrils, and though I struggled, my limbs weakened. Then I was vaguely aware of being dragged backward as unconsciousness overtook me, and I swooned.

Eighteen

When I awoke I found myself in a soft bed enclosed in a small wooden barrel-topped cave. A window beside me looked out on a grove of trees. Outside, a guitar strummed, and something roasted over a fire. As my head cleared I realized I must be in a Gypsy caravan. I remembered standing at the station, remembered Stanley Symmes stepping into the tea shop, and then I must have been abducted.

I struggled out of the blankets that covered me. Was I a prisoner in Raoule's Gypsy camp? It made no sense. At that moment, the door to the caravan opened and Raoule stuck his head inside.

"Good," he said. "You are awake."

"Raoule," I said. "Why am I here? Who brought me here?"

He held up his hands. "Do not be angry," he said. "You are perfectly safe. I am sorry for the means with which you were brought, but Sir Byron did not think you would agree to come."

"Byron!"

Raoule nodded apologetically. "I am sorry to say he heard of your flight before I did. Luckily he was quick to act."

I kicked the last of the covers free and sat on the edge of the small bed. "I don't understand. Byron had me brought here?"

Raoule nodded. "I was as gentle as possible. The chloroform made you swoon. We carried you here in the caravan."

My head swam. "I saw no Gypsy caravan in the village."

He smiled. "You were not meant to."

Anger swept over me. Foiled by Byron again. "Why didn't he just have me gagged, tied and taken to the manor, since I am his prisoner."

Raoule laughed, reaching for my hand to help me out of the caravan. "You are not a prisoner. He simply wished to speak with you before you flew away, for we might not be able to find you again."

I glared at him. "I did not know you and Sir Byron were in league. You never mentioned that you took orders from him."

Raoule cocked his head, leaning against the side of the caravan. "Not orders exactly. No, it is not like that."

"Well, what is it like, since you have me captured and mystified?"

He chuckled softly. "Come, my little bird. You are hungry. A strong cup of coffee will help and some hot food in your stomach will do much to restore your temper."

I followed him to the circle around the fire and managed to be civil to the others there. The women inquired how I was feeling and showed me where to take care of my personal necessities. Then I was handed a plate of roasted meat and a mug of hot coffee.

Raoule was right. The food, which had been most unusually spiced, and the hot drink restored my spirits to some degree, but I still insisted on an explanation. Raoule came to sit by me.

"Your Sir Byron is a benefactor to the Gypsies," said Raoule. "He is actually our blood brother."

I must have looked at him like he was crazy. Byron blood brother to a Gypsy? I would have laughed if I had been in a better mood, and I could not help but wonder if Lady Liddicoat knew.

"How did he come to be a blood brother?" I asked Raoule.

His dark eyes were serious as he said, "He saved a child's life once, but that is a long story."

"I see."

I slumped back against the tree trunk I was leaning on. "But why didn't he come to get me himself if he was so determined that I should not leave?"

Raoule's look teased me. "Surely you can understand that it would not look right to his household if he abducted you there."

I begrudgingly agreed on that point, still I resented that Byron had sent someone else to bring me back.

"I am glad you have not suffered in the undertaking," said Raoule, sipping his coffee.

Raoule had expressed once that he cared for me, yet here he was perfectly and calmly willing to deliver me into another man's hands. Surely he must respect Byron a great deal.

"I did not know the extent of your friendship with Sir Byron," I said.

Raoule shrugged. "It is not something I speak of often."

"I see." We sat in silence for a moment, watching the activity of the camp.

"And what now?" I asked. "Now that I am not to leave of my own free will."

"Stay here with us," said Raoule. "Things have not been safe for you. This way I can keep an eye on you at all times. I can make sure you are safe."

I thought about this possibility. "If I stay here, you would not construe it wrong. It would not mean that I wanted to remain here permanently."

He leveled his eyes at me. "I understand."

A smile twitched at my lips. I was still angry at Byron for a dozen reasons. If he had wanted me to stay at the manor, why had he not simply asked me to stay. And why did he want me to stay anyway? Living among the Gypsies might make him think twice about his intentions. I suppose I was being childish, but I was half acting on emotion, not reason at the time.

"Very well," I said. "I will stay."

Raoule looked a little surprised. I suppose he thought he was going to have to persuade me. And perhaps he had been ordered to hand me over to Byron right away. He grinned.

"I will ask my mother to find you some clothing."

Mia and Mona were delighted that I was staying, and they flurried around the camp, making preparations. We all giggled as I got out of my more constricting clothing and they tied my hair back and put a scarf on my head and dressed me like a Gypsy in a ruffled skirt, print blouse, and a woolen cloak. I enjoyed their spirit and was able to set aside my worries. The warmth they always showed me, and the welcome they extended was a contrast to the formality of the manor, and I allowed myself to play the part.

There was something else that inspired me, though I did not quite recognize it at the time. The Gypsy camp was located at the edge of the woods within sight of the castle. In a way that I could not understand, I drew power from it. Perhaps because I felt it was the only thing I had that belonged to my family, even though we did not presently own it.

For one who had lived most of her life in poverty, even a tangible ruin was some comfort to me. That night after a supper of lamb stew, we sat around the camp fire as Raoule's brother-in-law worked magic on his guitar with his fingers. Sometimes he sang alone, sometimes the others joined in, their soft voices drifting on the night.

I could imagine that if there had been Roman sentries on the Wall, not so far from where we camped, they would have put down their armor, relaxed and listened. I thought of the supposed spirits on the lake, and of the visions I had had of the people of Blackstone Castle who sang and danced every time I set foot in the hall. All of these were imaginary spectators that evening as the Gypsies sang.

"So," said Raoule, as he leaned against a wagon wheel beside me. "You have given up on your legend?"

I cocked my head to one side. "What more can I do about it? There are no records that I have been able to find. Only some drawings that were preserved at the manor. Rosa spoke of love, fortune, evil, danger. It seems I have encountered only the last two."

He nodded, gazing into the fire. "Ah yes, the Blackstone fortune. We too have heard of it."

I looked at him sharply. "You have? Why have you never mentioned it?"

"No one has ever found it. It is one of many legends one hears."

I shook my head. "If it's been buried, I don't know where to look for it."

He chuckled. "Yes. A fortune in gold. But one never knows. Perhaps when the castle changed hands, so did the gold."

"And then was spent."

"Hmmm. It is easy to let gold slip through one's fingers."

"I suppose."

I decided to tell Raoule about my visions. If anyone would understand it would be he. As I described the clothing, the music and the banners hanging in the castle as I thought I had seen them, he listened attentively, giving me an encouraging nod now and then.

"You see," he teased, "you have the second sight, just like a Gypsy."

"You're teasing me," I said.

"Not at all. Making contact with the past is a very old ability, lost by most people now."

"Then you believe me?"

"Of course." He said it so matter-of-factly, I sighed

deeply. Perhaps I did have more in common with these Gypsies than I had thought.

"I wonder what it would have been like to live here then," I said. "Or even a hundred years ago. If I had been here a hundred years ago, perhaps I would have been able to find the Blackstone fortune. The parish fire wasn't until fifty years ago."

Raoule shrugged. "A hundred years ago things were much the same as they are now, so they say. Except that was before the stream was diverged."

It took a moment for his words to register in my mind. *That is what the Bible passages said.* "Who hath divided a watercourse . . ."

Suddenly I sat up straighter. The other passage said "Ye are as graves which appear not."

"Raoule," I said "Is this true? When was the stream diverged?"

He shrugged. "Before our time, but not before our grandparents' time."

"And when it was diverged, did it . . . cover up anything?"

"Most likely. Why?"

I clamped my jaws shut. Raoule was a friend. I was almost sure I could trust him. But as he had said, Gypsies take a special interest in gold. I was not yet ready to have the entire Gypsy camp swarming over Blackstone property looking for the fortune.

I forced myself to lean back again. But what was I even thinking? A hiding place under water—a grave of some kind. A family vault? The very idea gripped me. Could I at last have stumbled onto the answer suggested by the clues left by some long dead ancestor?

I saw and heard almost nothing of what went on in the little circle of Gypsies after that, so preoccupied was I with my own thoughts. I had not forgotten that someone else was most likely on the same trail I was. Did my rival know of any sort of tomb that now might

246

be covered with water? How could I find out?

Mia made room for me to sleep in her caravan, and when at last heads nodded and the fire was stamped down, I got under the thick down coverlets. I lay in the dark, listening to the even breathing of the woman beside me as I stared at the darkness. The graves at the cemetary in the village were all more recent than the time of the restoration. The idea of a family vault made sense. But if there was a vault or tomb under water, how would I get to it?

The next morning I got up early and helped gather more wood for the fire. Coffee boiled outdoors over an open fire tasted better than any I had ever had. Not wanting to be a burden to the Gypsies, I pitched in with the work.

The day was mild, and Raoule asked me if I would like to accompany him up to the flocks. I heartily agreed, for I thought I would find an excuse to slip off to the castle. I would follow the stream that flowed down the cut on the far side of the castle and eventually came to the village. Perhaps I would gain some clue as to where it had been diverged.

We set off from the camp, but just as we began to climb upward on the path at the edge of the moors, Raoule paused and shaded his eyes. I looked in the direction of the manor and saw horse and rider approaching.

My heart gave a lurch. I half-hoped, half-feared it would be Byron. Raoule seemed to know that it was.

"He'll be wanting to speak to you, no doubt," said Raoule. I thought I detected a trace of disappointment in his voice.

Anger colored my words. "I don't think I want to speak to him."

Raoule grinned. "Do you have a choice in the matter?"

He left me standing there and, swinging his shepherd's crook, he climbed the path to his sheep. I resigned myself to a confrontation with Byron and waited where I was, hands on hips.

I had forgotten my Gypsy garb, and when Byron approached, I could see the twinkle in his eye. He dismounted, hobbled his horse and then came to where I was standing.

"A most flattering costume," he said. "I am sorry I did not ask you to borrow Gypsy clothes before."

My exasperation made me snap at him. I had attempted to leave his household yesterday, had been anesthetized, abducted, and all he could talk about was how I looked in Gypsy clothing.

"You forget," I said. "I would have most likely come directly to the Gypsy camp when I first arrived in Hevingham all those weeks ago, except that Raoule was not able to meet me. Then you would have been saved the trouble of paying for new gowns to be made for me."

He raised a hand as if to defend himself. "Forgive me, Heather. I do not mean to offend you." A more serious look settled over his face. "You cannot know how shocked I was to learn that you had left yesterday. Luckily I found out in time to prevent you from leaving the area altogether."

My building frustration made me speak more directly than I might have, had we been in his house. "If you were so shocked, why did you not try to stop me yourself. Why did you send Raoule?"

"I did not think you would listen to me."

I pressed my lips together. I could not think of a reply, so I simply lifted my chin and took a step away from him, gazing up at the wooly sheep that dotted the moor. He followed me, placing his hands on my shoulders.

"Why did you leave, Heather?"

I turned in his hands, facing him. "Surely you can understand why. My life is not worth much in your house. Someone obviously wanted me to leave. I've given up trying to figure out who. Perhaps there is a curse on Worthington Manor. If so, I am not going to stay there and get in its way."

"I hope you do not think it is I who wants you to leave."

Guilt swept through me as I remembered all the times I had thought so. "I do not think you want me to leave, exactly."

He tilted my chin upward. "That is not a direct answer."

I lifted one shoulder and let it drop. How could I say that I did not feel right, living there as his mistress. The subject was too complicated. He would never understand my feelings.

"You must admit," I said. "Life at Worthington Manor could not exactly be considered normal, of late."

"I appreciate your irony," he said.

He dropped his hand and sighed. I thought despair colored his expression, and I fought the urge to reach out and comfort him. It seemed we had come to the end of a road. He turned to me, but he kept his hands to himself.

"I understand your hesitation to return to the manor. I cannot even offer you a roof over your head that would guarantee protection. Not until I've discovered where this strange menace comes from."

"Then you do not believe it is the curse?"

"Even if it is, someone must carry it out. I mean to find out who."

He was as interested as I in getting to the root of the matter. I gave him that. We walked a little way together, inhaling the damp air. The Roman Wall topped the ridge above us, and the heaviness of the air made it seem as if it had receded. I imagined Raoule walking among his herd, singing or playing music to them on his flute. Oh, happy flock to have no worries except to graze on scrub grass and listen to music in this expanse of sky, moor and distant valley.

"So," Byron said at last. "You are determined to stay among the Gypsies."

I was not a prisoner. I would eventually carry out my original plan to leave Hevingham altogether and seek employment.

"The Gypsy way of life suits me at present," was all I would say.

He lifted an eyebrow speculatively. "I have entrusted you to Raoule's care. I do not believe he would go against my wishes. But he is a strong, young man. Surely he is not blind to your allure, especially appearing as you do now."

He lifted a lock of hair off my shoulder and then traced his finger along my cheek. I blushed and lowered my eyelids.

"If you must know, Raoule has already spoken to me. He asked me once if I might like to stay with the Gypsies. He made his intentions clear."

"And?"

I was about to tell him that I had refused, but then feminine instinct made me think twice. What harm was there in seeing if Byron might be jealous? If he was not to tie me to him in matrimony, did he expect me to grant my favors only to him?

I cocked my head. "I told him I could not decide."

Byron dropped his finger. "I see. So you might marry a Gypsy, after all."

I shrugged. "I am like the Gypsies in many ways. I have no other home."

His features darkened, and I could tell he was not happy at the prospect, but he said nothing.

"Very well," he said, his tone formal now. "I will leave you here. At least I can be fairly well-assured of your safety among such a number. Take care not to wander off alone."

"I will."

We walked back to where his horse stood. There was one more question that pressed on me.

"How is Lady Liddicoat?" I asked.

"Hale and hearty," said Byron, swinging up into his saddle. "Distressed that you are gone, if you want to know the truth."

I could not help but be pleased that she had missed me.

"But she must be very busy entertaining guests and returning visits in the neighborhood."

My comment was a covert attempt to find out if Lady Liddicoat was presenting eligible young women for Byron to consider in marriage, but he seemed uninterested in the social affairs that had descended on his house since his mother had come for the holidays.

"She is keeping herself well-occupied. I will tell her you asked after her. I'm sure she'll be pleased."

His horse pranced about, and Byron kept a firm hold on the reins as he was not yet finished talking to me. "If you would consider calling on her at the manor, I believe she would enjoy that."

"Thank you," I said stiffly. "If I do call, I will come to the back door. I will not embarrass you by appearing on your doorstep in Gypsy dress."

He smiled rakishly. "On the contrary. Such a costume would grace our staid old home. Give the servants something to talk about, eh?"

I flushed again. His words had a way of conveying a meaning that I could not foil. Mercifully, he turned the horse and left me. I watched him along the path beside the trees for a while, and then I turned upward to join Raoule with the sheep.

I tried to sort out my thoughts as I walked. Truly, under the open sky on such a fine day, surrounded with people who I believed meant me well, my fears seemed foolish. But questions plagued me from every side, and though I had been ready to leave them behind yesterday, today they begged for answers.

I spent the day on the moors with Raoule. His sister brought us bread and cheese to eat at midday, then she took me with her to search in the ravines for plants the women used for medicine and in their cooking. Her knowledge was extensive, and she pointed out many plants that would bloom in a few months' time.

We were able to pick some chicory that would be useful

251

both in tonics and poultices. The dried, roasted and ground root would be blended with coffee, giving the brew a tangy taste, but reducing the stimulating effect. I marked where the plants were so that if I decided to go to the manor I could take some roots to Cook for her root cellar.

Mona pointed out to me the chickweed willow herb, dwarf cornel, bog whortleberry and other flora. I was impressed with the Gypsies' knowledge of the land. While I had been scrubbing floors, reading by candlelight and learning how to sew, these Gypsies had learned another kind of survival, skills that enabled them to make a life no matter where they found themselves.

Later I helped the entire camp, including the children, in cutting out blocks of peat and piling them to dry. Most of the peat bricks would be taken to the village and sold. The Gypsies themselves would use the rest.

My limbs were not used to such strenuous work, but the exercise was good for me, both physically and mentally. I appreciated the simple rhythm of the Gypsies' life, and thought that perhaps I could grow complacent living among them.

In the evening, the air turned colder. But I felt cozy wrapped in a woolen blanket, sitting with the others around the peat fire with its dense, black smoke, which rose to blend with the night sky. After not sleeping much the night before and after the brisk exertion of the day, I began to nod off and felt grateful when Mona led me off to bed.

The men stayed by the fire, strumming and singing soft music that lulled me to sleep. It wasn't until the next day that I persuaded Raoule to leave the sheep to his nephew and walk with me by the castle. However, it wasn't the castle I wanted to see.

I led Raoule down the slope to the west of the castle. We followed an overgrown path through the woods. We were making so much noise, stepping on branches and pushing through brush that I almost didn't hear it. But when we came to a place where the trees had thinned out, I stopped and held up a hand for Raoule to be silent.

Then the sound of horses' hooves and voices raised in conversation and laughter came to me. They passed some distance from us, but I could see the riders' bright velvets and the ruby and gold heraldry on the horse clothing.

"The hunt," I whispered.

"What?"

I turned to Raoule and blinked. Then I looked back through the trees where the riders were just passing out of sight.

"There," I said. "Didn't you see them?"

He looked in the direction I was pointing and then at me. "No," he said. "I did not see anyone."

Nineteen

Of course, it had been another of my visions. I sighed. Perhaps I was going mad. Certainly the number of strange occurrences I had experienced since coming to this county were enough to drive one mad. Raoule had not seen the hunting party.

Suddenly grief welled up in me. I put my hands to my face and sobbed. Was I fated to live on the moor forever, seeing things no one else saw? What kind of life was that.

"Come, come now, my pretty one. Tell me what is wrong."

Raoule cradled me against his chest, his chin resting on my head. He held me lightly, rocking me in a comforting motion as we stood together. In a few moments the grief passed, and I sniffled against his shirt.

"It's the visions again. I see them, but no one else does." I looked up at him. "What am I to do?"

His eyes took on the luminous quality I had seen so often in Rosa's eyes.

"Do? Why nothing. If you can see what others haven't the vision to see, it is our loss. It is a gift, you must not deny it."

"But these things, these visions, they do not help me."

"Ah, you do not know that. Perhaps your ancestors are trying to speak to you. Perhaps they only show you what once was. You must be patient. Nurture your ability, it will grow."

"Then you do not think me mad?"

His face took on a hard look. "Only those without imagination would call it mad. Those who deny the spirit and the mind and believe that we are nothing but meat bodies do so out of their own desire to control. Do not let them. Nurture your psyche."

I swallowed. Raoule often spoke lyrically, but this wisdom was new to me.

He took my hand and we pressed onward, coming to the stream at last.

"You said the stream was diverged a hundred years ago," I said. "Do you know where?"

He pointed. "The river divides somewhere in these woods."

We walked along an overgrown path for a while, ducking branches. Water tumbled over the rocks, and I could imagine the torrent that would flow along these banks in the spring rains. I was quite out of breath by the time we came to the place where the river divided in two. We stopped.

"Where does it go from here?"

"The right fork goes to the village. This fork flows into the lake."

I stared at the two forks. It made sense. "They must have diverged the stream to create the lake."

He nodded. "Yes, but why are you so curious?"

I decided I could trust him, or perhaps it was simply the desire to speak to someone about my secrets.

"I believe there must have been a family vault that was flooded over when the stream diverged. Do the legends say anything about that?"

He shook his head. "I have heard nothing of a family vault, but then the Faa Gypsies were not here then."

"Then I suppose you wouldn't know."

He looked at me curiously. "The Blackstone family vault, is that what you speak of?"

"Yes."

"Ah, a desire to see where your ancestors were buried."

"That's right."

I did not need to tell him that the family fortune might also have been buried there. Finished with our explorations for the moment, we went back to the castle. Hungry from our exertion we sat among the ruins and ate the bread and cheese we had brought with us.

After our lunch, Raoule had to return to his sheep. I declined the invitation to join him and remained by the castle. There was nothing more I could accomplish there, and I was not really waiting for another vision, but being in the shadow of Blackstone Castle brought me an odd sort of comfort.

Not that I didn't miss the manor house. I missed the company of the staff. I missed seeing what obstacles Lady Liddicoat was throwing in the way of Mrs. MacDougal. I wondered how the maids were coming along with their sewing and the lacemaking I had taught them. I sighed, sitting on broken masonry that once had been a mighty wall. There were many small comforts that could have made life at the manor most pleasant if it weren't for the constant menace that seemed to hang over that house.

I tried not to think about Byron. Of course I missed his firm embrace, the feeling of his lips on my hair. But I had to push such dangerous thoughts aside. I could see in his eyes that he missed me too, but he was not going to make me return. Perhaps he truly believed I was safer for the moment among the Gypsies.

I stayed in the vicinity of the castle until dusk, amusing myself by looking for some of the plants Mona had taught me to identify. When the sun finally lowered, casting the sky into a metallic sunset, I wandered slowly back to the camp.

Already, a peat fire was blazing in the pit, and Raoule stood just outside the camp waiting for me. As I came closer, I saw the distraught look on his face. At the same time I glanced past him and saw that the women all had their heads in their hands and were rocking back and forth, giving forth a sort of keening sound.

My heart constricted. "Raoule, what's happened?"

I saw now that his eyes were moist. When I approached him, he put a hand on my shoulder and looked deep into my eyes.

"I'm sorry, Heather. We just learned that Rosa," he swallowed and began again. "That Rosa passed away. She died in her sleep, without pain."

I stared blankly, not accepting the words. I looked at the grieving camp, then back at him. "No," I breathed. "Surely this can't be true. How do you know?"

I walked a few steps farther into the camp. I had an overpowering urge to go and see for myself, to look somewhere for Rosa to reassure me that she was not gone. I turned back on my heel to Raoule.

He nodded. "I know," he said. "I'm afraid it's true."

Grief surged through my chest, filling me like a wave. "How can this be? Was she ill?"

He shook his head. "She had a cough, nothing serious. Then one night she simply died."

I crumpled as if the support that had kept me erect had just been pulled out from under me. Raoule lifted me and supported me as I stumbled to the camp and sat on a blanket. Rosa dead! I could not believe it. I kept looking at the air around me as if expecting her to materialize.

Sobs heaved from me. Why? The question rang in my mind. She had died, and I had not been there. Guilt surmounted my grief. I had not been there to comfort her.

I babbled some of these thoughts to Raoule as I cried. He sat with me, his arm gently around my shoulder until I had spent my tears. Finally, I inhaled deep breaths.

"How did you find out? Was there a funeral?"

"Word was sent," he said. "And, oh yes, there was a funeral. She would have been pleased, do not fear that. We Gypsies have lavish funerals, and Rosa had many friends. Do not grieve for her on that account."

I pounded my knotted fist into my thigh. "But I was not there."

When I had calmed down enough to listen, Raoule said, "Perhaps she did not mean for you to be there."

I wiped my face with my hand. "What do you mean?"

"There was a message for you. The traveler who brought word said Rosa had said something the night before she died. It was meant for you."

"She said something for me?" As I said it, the eerie feeling came over me that perhaps Rosa had known she was about to die. The message she had sent seemed to confirm that notion.

"She said, 'Heather must know that I have seen her in the crystal ball. I have watched her, though she did not know it. Her destiny lies in Northumberland. Her strength comes from there. The prophecy will prove true'."

"She said that? Are you sure?"

How could such a message reach me all the way from Nottingham, carried by some traveler who didn't even know who I was?

He nodded. "Be assured, that is what she said."

I repeated the words over on my lips. She had watched me in the crystal ball? I did now know how that could be true, but I was beginning to accept the fact that some of the Gypsies did have psychic powers not known to the rest of us mortals.

The hollow in my chest began to fill with despair and anger.

"How can she be so sure? She is so insistent that I belong here? How am I to find my destiny?" Did she want me to stay among the Gypsies forever?

"Our loss is great," said Raoule. "Be comforted that she went in peace."

"You say she was not in pain?"

He shook his head, giving me a sad smile. "She simply went to sleep. Perhaps she chose the time of her going."

I choked out the words, "Yes, perhaps she did."

I crept into the caravan that night and cried myself to sleep.

I awoke with a leaden feeling in my chest, and then swiftly came the memory that Rosa had died. I sank back into the blankets, not wanting to rise. With Rosa's passing, my last tie to Nottingham was cut. Now there was truly no reason to leave Northumberland unless to start life over somewhere else. But that notion seemed less appealing every time I thought of it. I was so unhappy and confused I did not even know where to begin trying to sort out my thoughts. And entwined with my grief was the nagging, impossible thought that as Rosa died, she knew her death would be one more reason to keep me from returning to that city. Her words confirmed that she wanted me to remain here. Why?

Numbly I crawled out and went through the motions of my simple toilet over a barrel of water brought up from the stream. The rest of the camp was subdued, but the motions of work were carried out.

I hardly knew what to do with myself that day. I had a great urge to see Byron. But what would I tell him, that a dear friend had died? Would Lady Liddicoat be able to understand my grief? Did she even know any Gypsies?

Later that morning I found myself at the spot where I remembered the chicory root was, and when I found it, I dug up some, placing it in the basket I had brought with me. Then I started down the moor. I could see the manor ahead, and I began to worry about my reception.

Wouldn't they think it odd that I had left so suddenly and was now living among the Gypsies? It must have been the strength of my grief and the need to associate with people I had come to consider my own kind that made me go on. I would go to the back door in any case and avoid Byron or his mother. I also went directly into the garden, avoiding the stables, for I was still uncertain of the recep-

259

tion Robin would give me. And dressed as I was, I might come in for some ridicule from Lady Liddicoat's coach and driver, if only behind my back.

Effram stopped his work when he saw me coming and got up to nod to me. Then Sophie came out of the back door.

"Why if it isn't Miss Blackstone," she said. She took a step nearer and looked at my costume with some curiosity. "I hear ye been with the Gypsies."

"That's right, Sophie. But I've brought Cook some chicory. I wanted to see everyone."

She bobbed her head. "Maybe ye'll cure her evil temper. She's been in a fit lately."

"I know the extra work from having so many guests must be hard for her."

"All the high and mighty've left by now," said Sophie. "Just our master and his mother in the house now. And that lawyer fellow comin' and goin'."

"Lawyer?" I thought immediately of Stanley Symmes.

"Been meetin' with the master, though it ain't any of my business. Seems like master Byron's fixin' to sell some of his land."

"I see."

I knew that Stanley Symmes had wanted to do business with Byron for some time. It sounded like he had succeeded.

Sophie and I proceeded on to the kitchen. Cook and Louisa broke off midconversation and stared at me.

"Hello," I said, going into the kitchen. "I've come for a visit. I brought you some chicory from the moors."

"Well, if it ain't Miss Blackstone," said Cook. "Though I wouldn't a' recognized ye in that outfit. It's good to see ye nonetheless."

"It's good to see you too. I've missed everyone."

"Have ye now. Well, set down and I'll pour ye a cup o' tea. Come for a little gossip, now?"

Louisa smiled shyly. "It's not been the same since you

left, miss," said Sophie. "I do think Sir Byron has been in a black mood. Just barks his orders, never inquires after the time o' day."

"I'm sorry to hear that."

The tea Cook handed me was warm, and the luxury of resting in the wooden chair by the big fireplace gave me the comfort I had come for. I felt foolish to have run away like I did, but I reminded myself that my fears were real. I could not risk my life by living at the manor house where someone did not want me.

"And so, how is everyone?" I asked as the other two brought their work to sit in a circle with me.

"The same as ever," said Cook. "Lady Liddicoat has Mrs. MacDougal in a black mood as well. Stays in her room a great deal of the time, she does. Seems to think that if the great earl's wife wants to run things, let her have the job."

"And how is Lady Liddicoat?"

"She and her son been cooped up havin' long talks, though about what I cannot tell."

I hid a smile. From the amount of knowledge the servants gleaned about the doings of their masters, I had no doubt that the keyholes had been put to good use.

"And how is Hadrian?"

Cook frowned. "Come to think on it, I ain't seen him since you left. I'd come to think you might of taken him with ye."

"No, I didn't. Well, I'm sure he'll come around when he gets hungry."

We gossiped some more, and I was surprised at how quickly the time flew by. I confided about my loss, and they uttered sympathetic words. When Cook peered at the grandfather clock that sat in the passage, she uttered a few of her choice expletives. I knew I should get out of her way, for she would have to prepare dinner soon. Everyone made me promise to come back.

I put on my woolen cloak and tied the scarf around my

head, then, taking my basket, which was full now of bread, preserves and meat pies for our camp, I left the way I had come. I managed to avoid those I had not wished to see, and when I had put the lowlands behind me, I turned to look at the manor once more. I could see figures moving between the stables and the house, and I sighed.

The wind had turned bitter, and it whipped around me. I wished I had the second sight Raoule had told me to nurture. Which of the members of that household had been so anxious to be rid of me?

I still carried my loss, and I thought it would be some time before I got used to the idea that Rosa was gone. The thought that she still might be watching over me from wherever she was gave me some comfort.

The gifts I had brought from the manor house were greatly appreciated at the Gypsy camp. Raoule did not speak to me, but his eyes followed me around the camp. I knew he must be assessing me, wondering when I would give up my attachment to the great house and live like a simple Gypsy. Or perhaps he knew even then that that was not fated to be.

After supper, Raoule got out his flute and played soft, melancholy melodies, accompanied by his brother-in-law on the guitar. The music of the Gypsies had a mournful cadence that fit with my grief. I was glad, for it helped me express my emotion freely. The Gypsies can be both gay and sad, and the two emotions seem at times close kin, but that is because they are so much better at expressing themselves than we English, who put feelings second to getting on with life.

Later I crawled into my bed in the caravan and lay for some time, listening to the sounds of rustling trees and calling wildlife. Finally, I drowsed.

The clanking awoke me. The same banging of metal on stone or metal on metal that I had heard from a greater distance, when at the manor, floated to my ears. I sat up. Folks would claim that the Roman soldiers walked tonight.

But I pushed the covers from me, and stood on the wooden caravan floor. I wanted to see this night if ghosts were really about.

I did not fear the dead. If they were mere spirits, how could they harm me? If the clanging was coming from a more earthly source, I wanted to know that too.

I laced up my boots and slipped into my cloak, for the night was cold and damp. Then I climbed out of the caravan, the squeaking door surely waking Mia, though I did not wait to find out.

I crossed to Raoule's caravan and rapped on his canvas window covering.

"Raoule," I called in a low voice. I did not mean to wake up the entire camp, but I could not go out on the moors alone.

"Raoule," I said, louder. This time the canvas rolled up and Raoule's shadowed face peered out at me.

"Heather? What is it?"

"I want to go up on the moors. I need your help. Do you not hear the clanging noise?"

He shook his head sleepily. "What if I do? 'Tis only the Roman soldiers doing their duty eternally."

"Then let's go see them."

"Why?"

I reached in to shake his shoulder. "Oh please, Raoule. I must see if it's really ghosts or not."

Seeing that I was going to create a disturbance, he gestured for me to wait. In a few moments, he emerged from the caravan, turning up the collar of his jacket.

"Now why is it you want to see these ghosts? Can we not leave well enough alone?"

"The sound comes from the castle," I said, tugging at his arm. "I must see what is going on there."

He must have thought me mad, but he did not refuse me. Rather, he said we'd better have some more help and he knocked on his brother-in-law's caravan to rouse him. I heard grumblings from inside, but soon William emerged.

263

"She's crazy to want to go up on the moors at night," said William.

I noticed he carried his shotgun, and I thought wryly that he must expect to meet with more than ghosts.

"I don't care if you go or not," I said. "I'm going to find out what is going on up there."

I made for the path, and stumbled up it, knowing they would follow me. I had not gone very far when I began to regret not having any light. The moon was low and did not provide enough light for us to see where we were going. But as we got accustomed to the dark, I began to feel more confident. And soon the battlemented shape loomed before us.

"You see," I said to the two men who had caught up with me. "The sounds are coming from the castle, not from the Wall."

Indeed we could hear the sounds of chains rattling. The sound made the hairs on the back of my neck stand on end, and I had to fight the urge to turn and run. But I was determined to confront whatever specters were making such a clamor, frightening the entire countryside.

I would never have gone on had I been by myself, and I could feel the fear that emanated from Raoule and William, but neither one would show cowardice, now that I had brought them this far.

"There's the bridge," I said, pointing to the little footbridge I had crossed so many times. "Come."

We descended the slope and were just crossing the bridge, when Raoule put out a hand to stop me. "Look there," he said.

I held my breath. Something moved in the shadow of the castle, and I finally made out the shape of a horse.

"You see," I said, through chattering teeth. "Someone is there."

" 'Tis the horse of death," said William. " 'Tis black as the night."

"It is not," I said. "Someone rode him here. I intend to find out who. We'll go quietly."

Though my knees shook, and my heart hammered in my chest, I pressed forward. We ascended the rise and approached the gatehouse where we crouched. A footstep crunched on loose rubble, sending chills up my spine. I peered into the courtyard, then drew in my breath. A man in a dark cape crossed to an arched entryway.

I turned to Raoule, who had seen the figure over my shoulder. "We must follow him," I said.

Twenty

We waited for a moment in the shadows of the gatehouse. There was enough moonlight to see by, but I did not see how we could follow our quarry into the bowels of the castle without any light. The clanking sound was louder now, and whoever we had seen had entered the wing of the castle the sound was coming from. This clanging was not something in my own head, this sound was heard by everyone. We could not wait here forever. Finally I nudged Raoule.

"Come," I said.

We crossed the courtyard stealthily, avoiding rubble and fallen stones. When we came to the passageway the stranger had entered I saw that our way would be easy. A dim glow came from the other end of the passage.

But what awaited us there? Did whoever it was have a weapon? I glanced at William, making sure that his shotgun was at the ready. Now that I was certain we were not facing specters, the gun offered me some reassurance.

Creeping along the passage, we came to the kitchens. I remembered the room well. We were standing in the center of the large room, when the glow that seemed to have preceded us down another passage began to grow brighter. Raoule grabbed my arm.

"He's coming back," he said.

I swallowed. "Is the gun ready?" I whispered to William, to which he gave a grunt and raised it to shoulder level.

We stood our ground and waited tensely. Steadily, the light approached, until at last the man and the torch rounded the corner, then I gasped, for the flicker from the torch lit the side of Byron's face.

"Byron," I gasped.

He stopped, holding the torch up so that the room was lighted. Then he spoke calmly to William.

"I hope you're not going to blow me away with that thing. I can think of better things to do with it."

"Put the gun down," said Raoule. "It's Sir Byron."

I swallowed, my knees still knocking against each other. What was Byron doing up here in the middle of the night? A sudden anger flooded me. Had it been Byron all the time? Was he at the bottom of the ghostly sounds? Was he trying to frighten everyone away from his precious castle?

"What are you doing here?" I finally managed to ask.

He lowered the torch slightly and stepped closer to us. "I might ask the same of you."

For a moment we simply faced each other, still shocked at finding that neither party was alone in the castle at this hour. Gradually I became aware of the banging and clanging of chains that still had not ceased.

"It was the noise that brought us here," I said.

He nodded. "I think I can satisfy you as to that. Follow me."

I have to admit I had some trepidations about going with him. If Byron himself had been at the bottom of all the evildoings that had occurred these last weeks, then he might have been leading us to the dungeon to lock us up there. But I took the chance that this was not the case, and with Byron leading the way, proceeded down the passage to a set of stairs.

We gathered at the top of the stairs, and Byron held the light so that we could see down them. At the bottom, a door had been left ajar, and the draft was blowing the door back and forth so that it banged against chains suspended from above.

I had not seen these chains before, and I looked with wide eyes at Byron. "Someone has conveniently left this door ajar so that the sound of clanging drifts out to the moors. There is your ghost."

"Someone has hung up the chains then," I said. "They were not there when I came this way."

"Undoubtedly not. When it is convenient, they are lowered. During the day they must be kept in an alcove above."

"But why?" I said.

"I believe I can show you part of the answer to that as well."

We followed him down the stairs to the room where the chains hung. "At least let us shut the door, so we don't have to listen to that infernal noise," I said.

"We dare not," said Byron. "The noise may be a camouflage for something else more sinister. Look here."

He went to a recess in the wall and held the torch so we could see. An old shovel lay against the wall together with a rusted bucket.

"Digging tools?"

"Yes," he said. "Perhaps these are too old to be of use, but there are marks in the wall that show where others may have been kept very recently." He straightened.

"I began to see the pattern. Someone is looking for something." He looked directly at me. "Perhaps they are looking for the same thing you are. I do not doubt that this is why you have been in danger here. Someone besides yourself believes your story, and they wish to claim the Blackstone legacy for themselves."

At least he did not suspect that I was digging among the castle ruins at night.

"But who is it? And where are they now?"

"I was just beginning to search when I ran into the three of you." Then with a touch of sarcasm, "I am glad to see you brought protection."

"You do not think I would be foolish enough to go prowling about at night alone, do you?"

"My dear, nothing you do surprises me. But enough of that. We must make the most of our situation."

I pressed my lips together. Either Byron was on our side or he was doing a great job of bluffing. I decided to take a chance and confide in him what I suspected, for he was right: We had to make the most of our chance. If someone else were about tonight, we needed to find out who.

"I may have a clue," I said.

"What is it?"

I told him about the Bible verses and the revelation from Raoule that the stream that ran by the castle had been diverted some years ago.

"It could be," I said, "that there really is a fortune, or documents, or at least another clue, but that it has been covered by water."

He snapped his fingers. "Of course. I should have thought of it myself. The Blackstone family vault was flooded over, there being no descendents remaining in the area. I'm sorry."

I expelled a breath of air. "Then it's hopeless. We cannot go to the bottom of the lake."

"We will not need to."

All of our heads snapped to Byron. "What do you mean?"

"There is an underground passage that leads to it. I used to play there as a boy."

"Then why did you never tell me about it?"

"To tell you the truth, it slipped my mind. When I played there I was not aware of whose bones lay behind the great metal door. It was only later that I learned it was not our family. I had forgotten about it until now."

My nerves were on edge, and I felt even more irritated by this news of Byron's faulty memory. I snapped out, "Do you think you can find it now?"

He nodded slowly. "It has been a long time, but I believe

I can. Besides," he gestured to the rusty digging tools, "we may have a trail to follow."

My spine tingled with excitement to think that we might actually be on the trail of some culprit who was trying to rob my family vault. But I was not unaware of the danger. We had to be prepared. Byron handed the old shovel to Raoule.

"Take this, and do not hesitate to use it as a weapon if you have to." Then Byron picked up a long coil of rope and put his arm through it to carry it on his shoulder.

Thus armed, we made our way back across the courtyard to the south wing of the castle. After some hesitation, Byron found the passage he was looking for. He held the torch low, and we could see clearly that someone had disturbed the dust here. Byron turned to William.

"Go to the village, arouse the constable. Tell him we may need him to make an arrest. Tell him to bring help. I have a feeling this night will not end without some trouble. When you return, join us at the other end of this passage."

As William started to go, I glanced at Byron.

"What about the weapon? We'll be unprotected." I did not think a shovel was adequate protection for the three of us.

"I have thought of that." Byron patted his side pocket. He must have brought a firearm. The passage led gradually downward, but it twisted and turned so that I had no sense of direction.

As we approached a sharp turn, Byron stopped. "From here, we'd best do without the light. We'll have to feel our way along."

We all exchanged glances, then Byron extinguished the torch with a hiss in a puddle of water. We were left in complete darkness. Byron grasped my hand.

"Take my shoulder, and Raoule, you keep hold of Heather's. That way we'll not lose each other, but we'll have our hands to feel along the wall."

We did as he said, and, using one hand to guide us, we

270

made our way to where the passage turned to the right. We had gotten rid of our light none too soon, because as soon as we turned into this passage, I saw that from the other end came a dim light. My heart beat even faster, and every nerve in my body tingled with alertness. At that moment I knew I had never felt so alive and in the present, for I suspected that the next moment would prove everything one way or the other.

As we crept along slowly, I tried to feel ahead with my foot before I stepped so as not to dislodge anything that would make noise. I tried not to think about any scurrying rodents that might move of their own accord if I happened to stumble onto one. At last the passage jogged to the right and downward.

I put my hand to my mouth. Ahead, three figures were standing intently in front of a large metal door. Their torches were set into the passage walls, and we instinctively crouched against our wall. Byron moved his arm to remove his pistol. I hoped Raoule had his shovel ready, for I did not think the three would appreciate our presence. One of them wore a long skirt, but I could not see any of the faces.

"Stand back," said a familiar voice. The woman turned and I had to prevent myself from gasping once again as Annie came this way. I thought surely she would see us, but we had the darkness on our side. She stood a ways distant. Then the men turned to pick up tools so that the torches illuminated their faces.

"Oh Lord." The murmur escaped my lips, but it was no more than a whisper for I saw now that Stanley Symmes and Robin were attacking the handle on the vault door.

Their blows made so much noise that Byron gestured for us to move a little closer. Still I held my breath for fear that Annie, who was closer to us, would turn around any moment.

At last the vault handle seemed to give. The men dropped their tools and Stanley grasped the handle, applying his weight to it. All eyes were fastened on the vault door as he began to tug it open.

"Now that you have it open," said Byron, stepping into their midst. "You may desist from trespassing."

The other three stared at Byron almost as if he were a ghost. Then Annie saw me. She gave a shriek, her hands flying to her face. Robin bolted up the passage, but Raoule stopped him. Stanley started to reach into his pocket, but Byron pointed the pistol in his direction.

"I wouldn't do that. Bring it out slowly, and toss it to the ground."

Stanley's eyes bore into Byron's, and beads of sweat on his forehead glimmered in the torchlight.

"Heather," Byron said, "pick up the gun."

The hatred in Stanley's eyes turned from Byron to me as I moved forward, knelt and reached for the pistol. I tried to steady my hand as I picked it up. I did not know how to use it, but I could not show my incompetence.

Behind me, Annie started to cry. I cast a piteous glance in her direction as the pieces began to fall together. I did not know for sure what she was doing here with Robin and Stanley, but whatever it was, it bode no good.

I heard thuds and groans as Raoule and Robin had a round with their fists. By the time I turned in their direction, Raoule had Robin at his mercy. Byron slid the rope off his shoulder and handed it to me.

"Raoule, tie my erstwhile groom with this. Make it secure."

I handed Raoule the rope and then stood with the pistol pointed at Robin as if I could use it, should he choose to bolt again. I was not worried about Annie, for she had sunk in a heap on a piece of broken masonry.

"I didn't want to come," she blubbered, wiping her nose with her skirt. "They made me do it. I tried to warn you, miss. Truly I did."

Raoule got Robin tied up and Byron directed him to do the same with Stanley. With the two male offenders under guard I could turn my attention to Annie. I handed Raoule the pistol.

"I know you warned me, Annie. But what I'd like to know is how you got involved. In fact, I'd like to know just exactly what is going on here."

"If you know what's best for you, you won't be saying anything," Stanley said. Those were his last words before Raoule tied his scarf around Stanley's mouth.

Annie shook her head. "I didn't know what was going on, at least not all of it 'til now. What I said was true. I met Mr. Bailey in the village. It wasn't 'til two days ago that I found out he had another name."

I shook my head at my own stupidity. So Stanley Symmes had been her Mr. Bailey.

"I'm sure we'll have many questions for our friends here," Byron said, "but now we've other business to attend to."

"The vault," I said.

Byron held up a hand. "Wait here. It won't be a pretty sight."

I stayed where I was. I really did not have a great desire to see the caskets of my ancestors. And God forbid any of them might have been disturbed enough to reveal skeletons.

"If there is anything of interest, we'll soon see," said Byron. "Raoule, keep a gun handy. Even though the culprits are tied up, I don't trust them."

Raoule helped Byron shove the heavy door back. Then Byron took one of the torches and entered the dark tomb. Annie was still sniffling, and even though she'd been somehow in league with these other two, she looked truly repentant. What she said proved that she had been lured in by Stanley Symmes. As to his treachery, my skin crawled. I wanted very much to know how he had stumbled onto my plans. My mistake was in thinking that he became interested only after meeting me on the train. When I learned the truth, I was deeply shocked.

273

Annie wiped her nose and looked up. Anger and betrayal flashed in her eyes. "He promised me a new life. A house and servants of my own. But he lied." She shook her head. "Oh, I'm so sorry, miss."

I knelt and took her hands in mine. I believed her, but I couldn't be too careful.

"When he told me he wanted me to do certain things for him, I agreed. I know what most men want. I was used to that. But when he asked me to steal your Bible, I thought it was strange."

I stared, open-mouthed. "He asked you to steal my Bible?"

"Not the first time. Mrs. MacDougal took the Bible the first time it was missing. She'd been arguing with the vicar, who was trying to convert her, and when she unpacked your suitcase she decided just to read it while you were sleeping. I saw her in the kitchen with it, and she told me about arguin' with the vicar. She was goin' to prove him wrong. She didn't think you'd miss it while you was asleep. She said she was plannin' to take it back soon as she was finished."

Our discussion was interrupted as Byron reappeared, carrying a small chest.

"What is it?" I exclaimed, rising.

"We shall see," he said.

We gathered around the chest, and even through the blackened layers of grime and age, I could see the scrolls of flower and leaf on the engraved lid. An ancient lock held the lid shut. Our rivals must have expected to find something like this, for among the tools next to the vault were a large sledgehammer and a crowbar.

"Stand back," Byron said, and he picked up the sledge hammer.

Giving it a mighty swing, he broke the rusty lock. Then he knelt beside it, looking at me.

"I believe Heather should do the honors. After all, whatever is in it belongs to her."

My heart hammered as I dropped on my knees beside Byron. I placed my hands on the old lid and tried to open it. It stuck at first, but I eventually managed to lift it back. Then my eyes rounded in disbelief. A mound of gold coins filled the red velvet inner lining.

I stared at Byron, who gave me an encouraging nod. "Go ahead, take one out."

I picked up a coin and examined it. The engraved writing was not familiar. I showed it to Byron, who squinted at it in the torchlight.

"Seventeenth century French." He handed it back to me.

"Rosa was right," I breathed.

Byron gave me a curious look. "About the fortune?"

"French gold coins. She said the fortune would be in French gold coins."

Raoule, who had been hovering over us murmured something in Romany, the meaning of which I could almost guess. His eyes had never looked so large. I think if Byron hadn't had the sense to take care of business, we would have simply sat there staring. I perceived footsteps behind us, and Byron stood. William had returned, and with him were two sleepy-looking constables who came alert when they were confronted with the scene.

"Take these two," said Byron, pointing to Symmes and Robin.

One of the constables mustered himself. "What charges?"

"Attempted robbery, trespassing, attempted murder, and possibly fraud."

Stanley had been watching the proceedings with a dull resentment on his face. Now as the constable approached him to untie his feet and help him up, rage filled his eyes. I saw for a moment the look of a madman. A deep roar came from his throat and for a moment I thought he would break his bonds.

He lunged toward Byron, who raised his arms to fend off the attack. Stanley fell on top of him, and both men tumbled to the ground. The ropes around Stanley's arms had loosened, and I saw his hand reach for the pistol that Byron had dropped. The constable raised his billy club, but Byron rolled and kicked the pistol out of Stanley's hand, then came to his knees and shoved his fist into Stanley's jaw. Finally the lawyer went limp.

For a moment Byron bent over the fallen man, and I saw him clench his fists. He told me later that in that moment he might have killed Symmes, if it weren't for the fact that he wanted him to talk first. He wanted satisfaction that the man had been at the root of our troubles since he had arrived in Hevingham.

The second constable handcuffed Robin to himself, and then William and the first constable carried Stanley out. Then we turned our attention back to the gold. I dipped my hand into it. Finally, we turned the chest over, spilling out the contents onto the ground. Byron and I looked at each other.

"Was there," I hesitated, "anything else?"

He stood up. "See for yourself. I know you'll never be satisfied unless you do."

He put the coins back into the chest and stayed with it while Raoule and I went into the vault. Chills ran up my spine as Raoule held the torch so that I could read the inscriptions on each casket. Then we looked into every corner. There was nothing else."

"Let's get out of here," I said. "My ancestors deserve to rest in peace."

Back in the tunnel, we shut the chest and Byron and Raoule hoisted it up by the handles on each side. I went to Annie, who had been watching in bewilderment.

"We'll go back to the house," I said to her. "Then you can tell us what you know."

Twenty-one

My ancestors must have buried the gold when the Worthingtons took over the castle. Perhaps they meant to retrieve it, but never had the chance. And what of the deed, if there was one? Rosa had promised me a fortune, but not the castle itself. I am not sure which was greater, my amazement or the horror of the greed that had set so many people against me.

Back at the house, we got the rest of the story out of Annie as far as she knew it. Stanley wooed her and promised her a new life. But first he had some business to attend to in Hevingham. His work for the railroad company must have been a cover for his hunt for the Blackstone fortune. When Annie met him, he asked her many questions about the household where she was employed. I could see now why he was so anxious to buy the land on which the castle stood. Whether or not a railroad ever passed that way was a moot point. Ownership of the land would allow him free access to search.

Stanley had finally put the purchase proposal before Byron, but Byron turned him down.

"I did not like the man," said Byron, getting up to pour himself another glass of sherry as we talked in the informal parlor.

"His offer was attractive. But when I wired Nottingham to check out his company's credentials, I found holes in his story. He did represent the company he claimed to, but the company itself did not seem to have a reputable history. I do not do business with those I do not like."

"Then you suspected that Stanley Symmes was at the bottom of everything."

"I had no proof."

I turned back to Annie. "We saw you meeting someone in the garden one night. I should have guessed who it was, but I could not see him clearly."

She hung her head. "We'd had an argument. I tried to get your Bible again for him that night, but I saw you come out of your room, so I ran down the stairs and into the garden to tell him I hadn't got it. He told me I had to do what he asked, or there would be no new house for me."

"What about Robin? How did he get involved?"

She shrugged. "I don't know. When I started seein' Mr. Bailey, that is, Mr. Symmes, Robin was mad. He went to see him. I guess Mr. Symmes was persuasive enough. Robin came back talkin' about a fortune that we would all split. That we should cooperate with Mr. Symmes. I didn't know it was your fortune they was talkin' about, honest."

"I believe you, Annie. I suppose that for the rest of the answers, we shall have to ask Stanley Symmes himself."

Byron and Raoule had carried the chest of gold coins up to my room, and I sat before it for a long time that night. I believed more than ever in Rosa's psychic gifts. I could only wonder if she had known in some way that my destiny was about to be fulfilled. If so, then I could rest assured that she passed away in peace.

The next morning, after only a few hours of sleep, I donned the blue-gray grosgrain dress and my coat and met Byron downstairs. He was dressed in a dark gray suit. His mother's coachman had harnessed the brougham, and we trotted off to town. Constable Cairns met us, and I could see from the dark circles under his eyes, that he'd not slept much. But he handed Byron a written statement. Robin had signed it. Then he brought Stanley to talk to us.

Symmes looked rumpled and reticent after his night in

ail. The constable shoved him to the table and made him it down in front of a piece of paper, pen and ink.

"Would ye like to give us yer statement now?" asked the onstable.

"Certainly not," said Symmes. "I will save my statements for the courtroom."

"No, you will not," boomed Byron's voice in the small oom. He walked over to Stanley. "You will tell us now ow you conspired against Miss Blackstone for longer han she knows."

I looked questioningly at Byron, who continued to grill Stanley.

"When I wired for your credentials, I learned that you ad been established in Nottingham for twenty-two years. That your cases to begin with were small, but that you often specialized in family disputes and had much occasion to look up family histories."

Stanley jutted his chin out, running a hand over his unshaven face. "What is that to you?"

"I am just wondering if eleven or twelve years ago you might not have had a call from a Mr. and Mrs. Blackstone."

My jaw dropped, but I had seen the admission of guilt n Stanley's eyes. I stood, aghast. "You knew my parents."

Stanley's eyes flickered, but he would not meet my gaze. He said nothing. Byron reached into his pocket.

"You might as well tell us now as later in the courtroom you so look forward to. We have Annie's and Robin's evidence."

Byron extracted the folded papers and threw them on the table in front of Stanley, then he leaned down, his fist on the statements. "The game is over, Symmes. The fortune you have been so avidly seeking has been returned to its rightful owner."

We waited as Stanley thought it over. Finally, he leaned over, his head in his hands. I could see from the sagging shoulders that he was a beaten man.

"That's what I meant to do at first," he mumbled.

"Sit up, man, so we can hear you," said Byron, and the constable, pulled him upright in his chair.

Stanley talked in a monotone. "Your parents came to see me, they did, with some wild story about their heritage. Could I do anything about their claim? But they had no proof." He shook his head as if reliving it. "They went on about the family Bible, but after I had looked at the records kept therein, I found nothing that would substantiate their claim.

"But the thought wouldn't leave me alone. Intriguing it was, and of course entirely possible. But what we needed was proof. I thought maybe I should have the Bible back, that there might be a clue of another sort. But when I called on your parents, they had changed their minds. Your mother," he said to me, "decided it would be wrong to pin their hopes on such a fantasy. She made her husband give up the idea. Said it was foolish.

"I got angry. If the claim was true, and I could prove it, I'd earn a nice commission. But they were denying me the chance and I needed it."

"So you took matters into your own hands," said Byron.

Stanley shrugged.

"You!" I said, pointing to him. "You broke into the cottage that night." Hysteria mounted and I lunged for him. "You killed my parents."

Byron held me back, keeping me from scratching his eyes out, but the rage I felt was uncontrollable. Byron grasped me tightly. "Wait Heather, we must get the full confession."

When I had calmed down enough to listen, they told Stanley to go on. "I killed no one," Stanley said, brushing his rumpled jacket as if to assuage himself of the guilt. "It's true I did hire some incompetents to try to get the Bible back. Their timing was bad, your parents caught them, and there was a scuffle. Unfortunate."

My knees crumpled, and Byron handed me into a chair. "You," I gasped. "The night the cottage was broken into . . . your ruffians. Oh, my God."

280

My head went into my hands as the grief and fear of that night returned.

"I had the Bible," I cried. "My parents must have known that was what the men were after."

Great sobs wracked me, and again we waited until I had myself under control. Now Stanley told the story with glassy-eyed irony as he recounted it, almost as if he were reliving the obsession.

"I washed my hands of the entire affair. But I knew there was a little girl. I found out where she had gone, and I kept track of her, just in case she knew anything of the intriguing and possibly profitable claim."

"But that isn't all you did, was it?" Byron coaxed.

Stanley gave a laugh. "I checked many title claims over the years. Finally documents came to light verifying the names of those who had helped Charles the First's cause while posing as Roundheads after the Battle of Marston Moor gave the North to Parliament. Among them was Blackstone."

"So it was true," I gasped.

"It gave me more to go on." He shook his head. "If only your parents had listened to me. But now it was too late. But not too late for me to lay my hands on the claim, in the name of a little girl whose parents had left instructions to me."

"What instructions?" I asked.

"Forged ones, no doubt," said Byron.

Stanley continued his story. "I kept an eye on you, my girl. From the orphanage to the factory, I checked on you from time to time. I just happened to see you bolt from the factory that last night. Late it was, and I had seen Biggleston and his wife leave just before that. I was curious, so I followed you to that Gypsy fortune-teller's. I knew something was up. I returned to watch your tenement in the wee hours the next morning."

"Then you followed me to the train." I shook my head in disbelief. I had been so duped.

"You wanted me to lead you here. Then after you had

deciphered the clues, you wanted to be rid of me. You must have removed the sign from the lake, hoping I would fall in. But what about the loose stone that nearly killed me? Were you in the house that day?"

"That is where bribing your servants came in handy," he looked at Byron.

"Surely not Annie?" I said. "She would never do such a thing. That must be why you recruited Robin."

He shrugged. Byron intervened. "According to Robin's statement, he was trying to play two ends against the middle. He left a certain note, trying to warn Miss Blackstone."

"The note Annie found," I said.

"And he returned the battle-ax you'd asked him to borrow to make it look like the specters were at work in the graveyard."

I remembered how often I'd seen him emerge from the clerk's office and all his visits with the vicar.

"Your time with the parish registry and the land surveys must have been well-spent," I said. "You learned about the diverging of the stream, and you tore the pages from the Bible."

"I was mislead for some time. Thought that reference to the graves meant the churchyard. It was no problem to look there—the villagers already thought ghosts were about there."

"So you added a few of your own to keep intruders away," said Byron.

"Unfortunate that Worthington here would not simply sell me the land. It would have saved us all a lot of trouble."

He seemed almost to shrink as he sat there, his shoulders sagging. Gone was the solicitous manner he had manifested when I had thought him so satisfied with his business affairs. How stupid I had been not to know it was all bravado. Seeing him now, I could almost feel sorry for him. His greed had led him after a dream that was not even his to seek. His mind was twisted.

I realized how the rest had happened. "It must have been you in the garden that night, pushing the statue over in an attempt to frighten me away. You followed me to the castle that day and shut the door behind me. Of course, if anyone had seen you, you could claim you were just surveying the land for your speculations."

He did not deny it.

Byron placed his hand on my shoulder. "It is unfortunate that Heather's parents went to such an unscrupulous lawyer. I believe we've heard enough. There's pen and paper, Symmes. You'll have plenty of time to write your statement down."

He turned me toward him. "At least Miss Blackstone's fortune is in the right hands. Come, my dear. Let us leave Mr. Symmes to his thoughts."

We were silent in the carriage, but when we returned to the manor, Lady Liddicoat greeted us. "So," she said with a twinkle in her eye. "I hear you brought back a small chest from the moors."

Byron gave his mother a rueful glance. "There's no stopping the servants talking, I suppose."

"Never mind how I get my information. What was so heavy that it required two men to carry it upstairs?"

"Something belonging to Heather."

I had thought at first Byron might not let me keep the coins since they had been found on his property.

"Then it's really mine to keep?" I asked.

"But of course," he said. "Those weren't my ancestors in that tomb."

"Well let's not stand here talking about it. Do show it to me," said Lady Liddicoat, propelling me upstairs.

"Mother, this is not your affair."

"Oh nonsense."

I smiled. "It's all right. I'd love to show the chest to Lady Liddicoat."

I led her to my room where she admired the coins and the quaint chest. I told her the story about Stanley Symmes, and how he had had us fooled.

"My, my," she said at last. "You are a wealthy young woman now."

"I hardly know what to do with it. It all happened so fast." I frowned. "But I didn't find what I'd hoped to find."

"And what was that?"

"The deed to the castle and the document from Charles the First, expressing appreciation that my ancestors helped him. I have no proof that the legend is true."

"You do not think that this is proof enough?" she asked, lifting out a few coins.

I shook my head. "Perhaps this proves that there was wealth." I gave a little secret smile. "I believe I knew that was true. This proves it. But as for the rest."

"Do not concern yourself about it, my dear. There will be time to look further now that that scoundrel is behind bars. I have also located the drawings you wished to see. They had been stored away."

I sighed. "I shall look forward to seeing them."

"But I must let you rest. You have had much excitement." She squeezed my hand, her eyes twinkling. "Perhaps I will have the pleasure of hearing more of this story this evening at dinner."

"I would be happy to tell you all I know."

"Until this evening, then."

She bustled out, and I stared at the dull gold coins, finally shutting the lid. I was wealthy, but what did it mean? That I would not starve or ever have to worry about a roof over my head. But the thought was not enough to make me completely happy. I hardly knew what to do with myself now. I tried to do a little sewing, but I was greatly relieved when evening came and I could dress for dinner.

I took care with my appearance. Annie helped me into the red velvet gown. She was so downcast that I had to tell her to stop worrying. Eventually everything would be sorted out. I did not think she would be implicated.

Dinner was a curious affair. Lady Liddicoat was in high spirits, obviously enjoying my good fortune. Byron, on he other hand, seemed somber. We took our coffee in the formal parlor, and Lady Liddicoat made excuses to go up early, coming to kiss my cheek. As she did so, she whispered in my ear.

"My son is stubborn," she said. "Have patience."

Her words made me curious. I felt almost as if she were conspiring with me. But I was not conspiring at all. I simply did not know where my place was anymore.

Byron and I were left alone, he standing by the windows gazing out at the dense evening.

"So," he said. "I suppose you have a few choices before you."

"Choices?"

"You were about to leave the place as I recall, before I so forcefully made you stay. It was for your own good, of course." He turned. "And I have not congratulated you on your good fortune."

"But it was you who helped find it."

His speech was confusing to me, and I did not know what he meant by it. But he went on.

"Then you decided to stay with the Gypsies. Again, for your own good, I did not argue. But I did not fail to notice that you seemed to enjoy their company."

"They are good people. But I did not consider that a permanent arrangement."

"No?"

"Why do you ask?"

He did not answer. "Of course, there is your job here. But I will not hold you to that agreement in light of your new status."

"That is . . ." I hesitated. "Generous of you."

"So," he said, pouring himself a glass of sherry and offering me one.

The atmosphere was strained. He would not look into my eyes. Did my change in status change things between us so? I would have thought it otherwise. And yet he had said nothing more. Courage from the drink made me ask him the question that in the end made

Rosa's prophecy come true for me.

"Do I have no other choices?"

Finally, his dark eyes met mine. I saw in their depths the old humor, curiosity, and, yes, the desire that he hid so well when we were in polite company.

"Perhaps," he said slowly.

I moved closer to him, shedding the stiffness that had restricted me all evening. I moistened my lips, and his eyelids lowered then raised again. He set his glass down and took me in his arms. His kiss was casual at first, but I held nothing back, and soon he moved against me with the passion I recognized.

"You are not satisfied with the choices I have outlined?" he asked, as he nibbled my shoulder.

"No," I said. "I am not."

He raised his head and led me to the sofa, handing me into the seat. "Then," he said. "I have one last offer."

"What is that?"

"Marriage to a poor baronet."

I thought my heart would burst through my chest to hear the words I had so longed to hear. Then he was on the seat beside me, pulling me to him.

"I did not plan to ask you. Surely you might think I only wanted to marry you for the money."

Tears of happiness slid down my cheeks. "I thought I was not good enough for you," I murmured.

"No, no, not that. I simply had to find out who was threatening you. I wanted to catch the culprit. Then I realized I had waited too long. And I feared you might not want me."

"I have wanted no one but you."

The moment was tender, and when I think back on it, I realize that from that moment on, my life was almost nothing but joy. After a long kiss, Byron raised his head and gave me a teasing wink.

"I will not touch your fortune. It belongs to you."

"What do you suggest I do with it then?" I said.

"I have a moldering castle with a questionable

deed on some land of mine. Perhaps you will make me an offer for it."

Out of nowhere, Hadrian announced his presence with a meow. Then he jumped into my arms, licking our faces with his approval.

Twenty-two

Nottingham was gray and cold, and I was glad we would not be there long. Our luggage was checked through to London, where we would begin our honeymoon. But there was one thing I had to do here first.

The cab let us off at the gate to the cemetery located on a hill overlooking the town. We walked among the graves until we came to a modest one. From here, Sherwood Forest was visible in the distance. I could not stop the tears that came to my eyes as I read Rosa's name and the inscription. If only I could have been here for the funeral. Byron squeezed my waist.

"I wanted you to know her," I said.

He nodded. "I feel as if I did."

I knelt beside the grave, on which flowers had been scattered. Then I held out the coin from the treasure we had found at the castle. The ground was still soft, for it had only been turned a week ago. With my fingers I dug into the earth and laid the coin there, burying it deep enough so it wouldn't be disturbed.

"I promised to pay you back," I whispered, my voice breaking.

The wind rose as I stood, and Byron and I watched as the breeze bent the grasses around us. We both knew it was Rosa's spirit. Her prophecy had been carried out at last.